THE GEMINI CONNECTION

AN INTENSE SCI-FI THRILLER

TERI POLEN

Black Rose Writing | Texas

ISBN: 978-1-68433-034-8
PUBLISHED BY BLACK ROSE WRITING
www.blackrosewriting.com

Printed in the United States of America
Suggested Retail Price (SRP) $18.95

The Gemini Connection is printed in Cambria

To Tanner and Reese—Raising boys with even less in common than the brothers in this book has been a whirlwind of sports, art, music, dinosaurs, Pokémon, superheroes, Legos—and a wondrous adventure.

Acknowledgements

Thanks to my beta readers—Dad, Rachael Garza, and Jo Anna Young. Your invaluable advice and input helped shaped the course of this book.

C.J. Redwine - Your suggestion of making this story a dual POV was ingenious. It couldn't have been written any other way.

Chase Perkins – Thanks for the technical information on tattoos, your 'guy' perspective, and letting me bounce countless ideas off you. I didn't kill you off this time, but I reserve the right to do so in the future.

Staci Troilo - Believe me when I say her editing skills made significant improvements to this book. Any remaining errors are entirely my own. I'm still looking for a shock collar that will connect to unnecessary dialogue tags and –ing constructions.

Susan Thomison – My computer/marketing guru and biggest cheerleader. Without you I'd probably still be trying to figure out how to save a file.

Mike – Asking to borrow your finance class notes was undoubtedly the smartest decision I've ever made—both for my grade and the rest of my life.

THE GEMINI CONNECTION

AN INTENSE SCI-FI THRILLER

Ugly. That was the first word that came to mind. Deadly was next.

The twisted creation was courtesy of a new client, a scientist. The nightmare had been tormenting him for the past couple of weeks.

The monster stood roughly fifteen feet tall, walked on two legs, and stretched two muscled arms in front of it, but its elongated head was a grotesque combination of goat and demon. Treacherous horns protruded from either side of its skull, torso, and upper thighs, making it difficult for anyone to get close to the beast. Not that we especially wanted to, but it was part of a Bender's job requirement to eradicate nightmares. So, we took up battle positions—Syd to its right, me to its left—crouched in anticipation of this formidable creature's attack.

"I'll go high, you go low," I called to Syd. Besides a hideous appearance, the goat thing screeched like a deranged bird, and we strained to hear each other, even with the com units.

"Got it, Evan." She unsheathed a ten-inch dagger from her utility belt, the silver blade glinting in the eerie cast of yellow-green light in this nightmare-scape. Being somewhat vertically-challenged (she hated it when I said short), Syd might not look intimidating, but give the girl a knife and she was absolutely lethal. The creature's leg tendons would be sliced to ribbons in seconds.

Syd dived to the creature's right, spinning and coming up behind it, as she avoided an angry kick to her head. She carved into its left limb, and it let out an ear-piercing shriek.

I withdrew an iron mallet from my own belt and catapulted myself off the wall, soaring over the goat-demon and landing a blow to the left side of its skull. Its head jerked in my direction when I came down on its other side. The sharpened tip of the horn caught the left side of my rib cage, and a warm flow of blood seeped through my shirt. Wouldn't be the first time I'd walked away from a nightmare with a permanent scar.

Syd scrambled around its legs, careful not to be trampled. Her dagger was a silver blur as she slashed the gray-haired appendages, the goat-demon staggering in its efforts to avoid her blade.

The ground was wet—possibly blood. But with dream or nightmare creations, you couldn't be sure. Because this thing's creator was a scientist, they tended to more detail-oriented. Odds leaned in the blood direction.

The light around us took on a red hue. Did the ambient illumination correlate to the creature's anger level? If yellow-green meant annoyed, did red mean take no prisoners?

I sailed through the air again, keeping my distance from the sharp tips of the two horns, and managed a solid strike to the top of its head between them.

It floundered, the screeches growing weaker, and movements sluggish as liquid spilled down the beast's face. As the creature slowed, the surrounding light faded to more of a blush color.

Standing to the side, I kept the mallet raised in case Syd needed help. She'd sliced and diced so much that skin, muscles, and tendons hung in shreds around the creature's legs. It wouldn't last much longer. "Pull back!"

She nodded that she'd heard me, then somersaulted behind the goat-demon to get out of its path. At the same time, it lurched forward and slipped in the liquid gushing from its wounds, tilting precariously backwards. Toward Syd. Its razor-sharp horns on a direct collision course with her body.

There was no way the goat-demon would miss her.

"Eject, Syd! Now, now, now!"

Without question or hesitation, her hand immediately shot to the cuff strapped around her left wrist and pushed a red button, expelling her from the nightmare. The creature landed hard where Syd had been only seconds earlier. I exhaled in relief, but it was short-lived. I still had to deal with one seriously perturbed goat-demon. On my own, with no backup.

The beast struggled to rise, unsteady on what was left of its legs, determined not to be banished so quickly. It seemed to have gained a second wind, and now there was only one target.

I needed to move fast. My hand reached for the dagger strapped to my belt, and I groaned in annoyance at the empty sheath. It must have fallen out when I'd landed.

I'd stressed to trainees that a backup plan may save their life, and they should always keep other options in mind. Especially when finding themselves in situations such as this. Tightening my hand around the iron mallet, I propelled myself into the air once again. The beast had managed to stand, but instead of flying over him, this time I hovered just above his head.

His arms sliced through the air trying to reach me, but I was pretty agile when it came to the flying thing, and managed to roll and twist around his blows. I drew back the mallet and swung with everything I had, connecting with the goat-demon's right horn. It shrieked, but the impact with my mallet had nearly ripped the horn from its head, and I readied myself for another strike. I pummeled it once more, wrenched it off the creature's head, and maneuvered around to the other horn when the goat-demon tried to shish-kabob me.

I increased my speed, flying faster around its head in a random pattern, keeping my movements unpredictable. The com unit crackled in my ear as Charlie, who was still in the lab, checked my status.

"Evan, are you all right? You're bleeding from your upper torso."

"Affirmative."

No time to talk, if my plan was going to work. An attack wasn't as difficult now, as the monster only had a nonthreatening stump protruding from its head. With the detached horn still clutched in my hand, I faked a turn to the left, rolled to the creature's right side, and stabbed its eye with the finely-honed appendage, shoving it in until it would go no further. Then I dropped to the ground behind it.

Its wails pierced my ears and echoed off the walls, but I never let my guard down. Sometimes nightmares were surprisingly resilient and recovered quickly.

That didn't seem to be the case with goat-demon, as its gray, hairy body crumpled and folded in on itself, becoming smaller and smaller until it gradually disintegrated, extinguished with a final whimper.

Shoving the iron mallet back into my belt, I bent over and rested my hands on my knees, gulping in deep breaths. I felt like collapsing myself, but needed to begin my exit sequence.

God, I loved my job.

Ⅱ

When I came back to my body, a medbot was tending to the wound on my torso. It was a minor injury compared to others I'd received. Some of the more memorable ones were the talon marks on my back from some sort of gargoyle/human blend, a dislocated shoulder after being slammed into a wall by a hulking blob-type of thing, and broken ankle from being stepped on by a giant, one-eyed teddy bear. A couple of stitches on the torso hardly rated a second look.

I tried shoving the persistent medbot away, then ripped the vital sign lead wires off my body. "Where's Syd?" I was relatively sure she'd ejected before the goat-demon touched her, but that didn't stop me from swallowing anxiously. I needed confirmation.

"She's fine," Charlie confirmed, gently pushing my shoulder so I'd lie back in the Bender chair. "No injuries. She's in the download room right now. That must have been a pretty good one."

Giving in and resting my head against the chair, I closed my eyes and let the medbot do its job. "You have no idea."

Syd and I were Mindbenders at Scientific Innovations. With permission from our clients, we entered their minds for various reasons. Sometimes our mission was to locate important memories buried deeply in their subconscious, other times to assist in pulling their swirling thoughts or ideas into a cohesive concept that could help Tage, our dying planet. Occasionally, as was the case with this latest mission, it was to obstruct recurring nightmares that interfered with a client's health or well-being. Continuously disrupted sleep caused increased stress, irritability, lack of focus, and, depending on the client's job, could potentially affect millions of lives.

I rubbed the bandage covering the stitches, annoyed that it caught on the fabric of my shirt. Crossing the stark white hall, I entered the lab where Syd was downloading any residual fear, hers or the client's, left over from this nightmare or any other recent cases. We didn't need to download after every nightmare case, but were strongly encouraged to when the anxiety reached a certain level. Absorbing a client's fear and trauma came with our job, but carrying it around wasn't healthy, and Benders could potentially project that fear onto the client while in his mind. Not a good thing.

Syd had just finished, and the tech was removing the leads from her head. She smiled at me. "Well, that was something I haven't seen before, but what an adrenaline rush, right? Are you hurt?"

"Just a few stitches, nothing major. Ready for debriefing?"

"Sure." She followed me out the door and down the hallway to my office, where the rest of my team, Isaac, Zia, and Amelia, were already gathered around the conference table. As team leader, I doled out assignments at the beginning of every shift, then we debriefed at the end. Sharing data about how we handled situations, techniques we used, and unusual things we encountered, whether about simple cases or level five nightmares, could prevent injuries or save lives later on.

"Evan, do we have anyone lined up to replace Maya?" Zia asked. "That guy filling in from beta team is totally subpar and needs remedial training."

"I'm working on it. Gabriel has a line on a new grad from the Academy."

She grimaced. "Seriously? A new grad will probably be just as useless. Can't we get someone more experienced from another team?"

"Maya was experienced, but that didn't prevent her from being eviscerated," Isaac said.

"That wasn't her fault, and you shouldn't speak ill of the dead." Amelia stared him down. "It could have happened to any of us."

The biggest job hazard of a Bender? If we were killed while in a client's dream or nightmare, our physical body lying in the lab also expired. We'd all had close calls, but last month, our team had suffered the loss of Zia's work partner, Maya. Since we normally worked in pairs, unless the assignment was more complicated and required additional Benders, our group had been off balance and out of sorts while we each grieved in our own ways. Even though Maya wasn't my partner, as team leader, I still blamed myself and took responsibility for her death.

"Not another word, Isaac," I said. "Amelia's right. It could have been any of us in that situation. Zia, Gabriel's chosen all of us individually, and if he sees potential in this new grad, we'd be fortunate to have him or her join our team. Let's get started."

After the meeting came to an end, Isaac, Zia, and Amelia huddled together at the end of the long table, whispering and casting glances in my direction. Zia gave Amelia a light shove toward me, and she approached slowly.

"Evan? Um...we're all going out for breakfast and wondered if...um, you'd like to come? Maybe?"

I stared at her silently.

"So...that's a no?"

"I'm busy." My gaze flicked to Isaac and Zia, who looked relieved at my answer.

Amelia returned to her chair, and the three of them gathered their things, chatting and laughing with each other as they left.

Syd had hung back and waited, leaning against the table with her arms folded over her chest. "She was trying to be nice, you know. And politeness never killed anyone. You forget—I know you actually have a soft gooey center. Too bad it's buried deep down inside all that festering darkness."

"You're going with them?"

"Unless you have a better offer." She raised one eyebrow.

"I don't." Syd was the perfect team partner for me. She didn't take my crap, stood up to me, shot down my ego when it grew too big, was dependable and fierce in battles—and she'd been my best friend for the past ten years, since primary school. We'd met when Max Delacort tried to take her water ration card and I'd stood up for her. Turned out she didn't need my help. She shoved him against a wall, dared him to do it again, then invited me to sit with her at lunch.

She threw up her hands. "Fine. Go home and sit by yourself in that big empty house. I'm going out to socialize, you know, with friends. Which you don't have."

"Except you."

Her lips twitched in a smile. "For now, anyway. See you later."

I watched her walk out the door to meet the rest of the team. Once upon a time I would have joined them, but not anymore. Zia and Isaac would never have invited me if the choice was left to them, and that was fine, because I preferred they keep their distance, but in Amelia's world, everyone should want to be friends, and life was easy and fair.

But I knew better than anyone that life wasn't fair. It was cruel, heartless, and ripped away the things you loved most.

Then it left you alone to deal with it.

CHAPTER 2
EVAN
PRESENT DAY

I hadn't been lying to Amelia about being busy, but it wasn't anything I'd discuss with her. It wasn't her business, and was something deeply personal to me.

Chase's tattoo shop had a peculiar smell. Not bad, just a strange type of incense with a spicy/musky sort of blend. The familiar hum of the tattoo needle comforted me, and I rested my head back against the chair, my mind drifting as I began to doze. Because Benders worked primarily at night when people slept, I was tired after coming off a shift, and questioned scheduling this appointment so early in the morning. Maybe that wasn't such a bad thing since, other than the two of us, the shop was empty, and I was able to get some rest while Chase worked on my shoulder.

With so much dark ink on this new design, the pain level would be more intense, but I welcomed it with open arms. Today marked one year that my identical twin brother, Simon, had disappeared, and any discomfort I experienced was minor in comparison to what had happened to him. I deserved to suffer. After all—it was my fault he was gone.

Shuffling steps and the sound of someone dropping heavily onto the nearby chair let me know I had a visitor. "I don't know how you can sleep with a needle continuously stabbing you."

Sydney's comment shattered the tranquility of the moment. Opening my eyes, I rolled my head in her direction. "Breakfast over already?"

She shrugged. "The three of them together just aren't as compelling as a day in the life of Evan Resnik."

I smirked, but didn't believe her explanation for a second.

Her hazel eyes locked with mine. "I know what day it is, and knew you'd be here." I'd been in this same chair six months ago on my and Simon's seventeenth birthday when I'd gotten the first tattoo. Syd had also been here on that day.

I glanced to my left at Chase, who was intently focused on my left upper arm as he worked. Despite my limited ability to explain the kind of design I wanted, he seemed to instinctively understand exactly what I meant. Words and ideas had always come more easily to Simon. He'd disappeared from a locked room, and there had been no requests for ransom, no clues, and no leads...nothing. The lack of evidence was maddening. The investigators, our parents, and just about everyone assumed he was dead. But no matter what anyone said, I knew with certainty he was still alive, because if my twin brother had died, I would have felt his death as viscerally as if it were my own.

"What's that symbol? It kind of looks like the Roman numeral for two." Syd's curiosity had drawn her from the chair to get a closer look at Chase's work. As she leaned over his back, her long strands of sandy hair spilled over his shoulder, blending with his own shoulder-length dark brown.

"It's the universal symbol for twins," Chase replied, scrutinizing his design on my arm as he retracted the tattoo needle. "The dual vertical lines represent twins, the horizontal lines on the top and bottom indicate balance, and the rectangle formed in the middle signifies a strong foundation."

Syd tilted her head to the side. "Pretty impressive. Isn't that twin thing also your astrological sign? Some coincidence, huh."

"Syd, can you move back a little?" Chase asked. "You're blocking my light."

"Oh, yeah. Sorry." She stepped back and returned to her chair.

"You good, Evan?" He was still fixated on the design as his gloved hand swiped away dots of blood from my arm.

"Perfect."

"Then we're finished."

I rose, approached the mirror hanging over Syd's head, and examined the new tattoo. "Excellent as always. Nothing personal, but I hope this is our last visit." Because if I saw Chase for another tattoo, that meant my brother hadn't returned yet. This new twin design joined the white and black yin and yang symbol on my right upper arm. Simon and I were opposites in every way, but always a part of each other.

"Nah, I get it, man." He waved me off before applying a healing ointment and waterproof bandage, then went over the aftercare instructions. "Hope your brother turns up soon, Evan."

So did I. Now I was headed for my weekly appointment to see when that would be.

♊

"A year ago today my brother disappeared, and you're still no closer to finding him? Your primary job is to find people, Deckard, so maybe you should rethink your career choice."

Agent Ryan Deckard was the lead hunter on Simon's case. I'd gone straight to his office from the tattoo parlor. Syd had volunteered to come with me, probably to prevent me from creating too big of a scene, but it was a little late for that. For the past ten minutes, I'd badgered, accused, and belittled Deckard, and from his outward appearance, he remained calm in the face of my attack, but fury danced in his eyes.

"Look, Resnik, I understand your frustration. I'm frustrated myself over the lack of evidence in this case, but we're doing everything we can." His professionalism was actually kind of admirable. I would have thrown myself out of here long ago.

"Everything you can?" I paced in front of the agent's desk. "What does that include, exactly? Show me some shred of progress you've made over the past month. Six months, even. Any progress at all. I'll wait."

His jaw was locked so tightly, the tendons in his neck bulged. I'd bet his blood pressure was through the roof right now. "I've reviewed everything we…"

"You've reviewed, meaning you've sat in this chair and read files on your data pad." I buried my hands in my hair and pulled on the ends in annoyance. One year, and nothing. No sign of Simon. I stopped pacing, braced my hands on his desk, and loomed over him. "You're incompetent,

Deckard! Get someone on this case who knows what they're doing, someone who cares about finding my brother."

He leaped from his chair, planting his hands on the desk and meeting my stance. We were nearly nose to nose. "Enough, Resnik! Every week you come in here and harass me because I haven't found Simon. Do you honestly think your tactics increase the chances of locating him? I'm in here all hours of the night and day." He pounded a fist on the wooden surface. "I've located every person I've ever been assigned. Every. One. I don't give up. So just lay off and let me do what I do best."

Flecks of spittle hit my face, but his anger only fueled my own. I wouldn't back down.

"If this is what you do best, then maybe…"

"Enough, guys. This isn't helping anyone. How about everyone step back and take a breath." Syd stood, one hand pulling my upper arm, and the other pushing lightly on my chest to put some distance between Deckard and me. He shoved off the desk and slumped to his chair, and I fell back into mine, dropping my head forward and resting my elbows on my knees. The two of us took a moment to settle, each of us breathing deeply.

"I get it, all right, Evan? People don't disappear from a locked room. It just doesn't happen, and I've slammed my head repeatedly against the walls of this office at the lack of evidence. In my twenty-year career, I've never come across a case like this, and I'd sell my soul for a break."

My hair curtained most of my face, and I nodded at his statement. I knew he hadn't given up on Simon, but I liked to think my weekly rants in his office prevented anyone from forgetting about him. They needed to remember Simon was out there. Somewhere.

"I've twisted my mind sideways trying to come up with a theory, but so far, nothing holds water." He massaged his temples, then cracked his neck. "You work with all those geniuses at Scientific Innovations. Why don't you ask them if there's some magical way a person could break through four walls without detection? I've talked to a few people there, but you have the inside track. Maybe they'll be more candid with you than with me. Or maybe someone's come up with new technology or theories over the past year."

I rubbed my face and stood. "Yeah. Okay. Let's go, Syd." I threw open the door and strode into the hall.

She thanked Agent Deckard for his time, then followed me out.

Talk to the geniuses at SI, he'd said. Maybe that wasn't such a bad idea. And I knew exactly who to ask.

⚏

We took a ten-minute tram ride from the city to my house in the suburbs. While Syd sat, reading something on her data pad, I preferred to stand and look out the window, holding onto an overhead strap. Strips of blurred landscape whizzed by—varying shades of brown land on the bottom and blue sky overhead. Nothing ever changed. No vibrant seasonal flowers bloomed, no explosion of colors in the fall. Without rain, everything just shriveled up and died. I expected to see tumbleweed ambling through my yard any day now.

When Simon and I were much smaller, before Tage's condition had reached the critical stage, our mother had enjoyed keeping a small garden of vegetables, flowers, and herbs. Most of what she grew was related to her work, breeding new strains of food and edible flowers. At the time, I didn't understand the significance of her work. I wanted to please my mother and thought presenting her with a bouquet of flowers from her garden would put a smile on her face. Her shock and subsequent scolding ensured I never made that mistake again.

I sighed heavily. Nearly all the items she'd grown were now extinct. Not much grew in our water-starved landscape anymore.

Syd had to nudge me at our stop, and we exited the tram station to walk the couple of blocks to my house. Many of the houses we passed were empty now—several families had relocated in the hopes of more resources, others had decided to try their own luck at living off the land in more remote locations, and some of the occupants had simply died.

Dry leaves skittered across the sidewalk leading up to the front door. Other than the occasional chirping of birds and laughter of kids a few doors down, the usual neighborhood sounds were absent. The hum of lawnmowers had been nonexistent for years now.

The scanner placed at the side of the door approved my handprint, and the lock clicked open. I entered and tossed my jacket over to the chair in the corner. It fell short and slid to the floor, resting atop shoes and another heavier jacket.

Syd stepped around me and headed to the kitchen. I trudged in the opposite direction toward the couch and slumped down heavily, tilting my head back and raking my hands through my hair.

"Don't you have any food in the house, Evan?" she called from the kitchen. "Of course you don't. You didn't have anything to eat when I was here four days ago."

"I forgot to send in the order again last week."

"What have you been doing for meals?" She poked her head around the corner.

"Mostly eating at work," I shrugged. "I live there more than here, anyway."

She disappeared again, and I heard her rummaging around in the kitchen, probably still looking for food or cleaning up the few dishes left over on the rare occasions I'd eaten at home. After several minutes, she strode into the room carrying a plate. She kicked my legs to the floor, placed the food on the table in front of me, then sat next to me, one leg tucked underneath her.

"It takes pure talent to make a meal out of what you had in that kitchen. Now, give me your data pad." She snatched it from the space beside me. While holding it with one hand, the fingers of her other hand flew across the screen. "There. Next week's meal order is done and it only took, what, a minute? Hardly an inconvenience."

"Thanks, Syd." I sighed and reached for the snack she'd made. When I shoved a hummus-coated cracker into my mouth, I winced. My upper arm was still tender from the new tattoo.

"You know, opening a window wouldn't hurt. The place could use a good airing out. And you should drop off some clothes at the laundry center tonight on the way to work." She wrinkled her nose as she swept the room, taking in the discarded clothing that lay wherever I'd shed them.

My hands curled into fists as my nostrils flared. "If you don't like it, you're free to leave. I haven't needed a mother since mine walked out on me four years ago, and I don't need one now."

Her eyes narrowed as she turned her gaze on me. "I'm not trying to be your mother, and I'm certainly not your housekeeper. But it's time you took some responsibility around here."

"Household chores aren't exactly high on my list of priorities. More important things come first."

Syd inhaled deeply, held the breath, then exhaled slowly. She leaned toward me, rested one arm on the couch behind me, and placed her other hand on my thigh. "Yes, Simon is your priority, but you can't stop taking care of yourself, and your weekly tirades at Agent Deckard's office aren't helping anyone."

"Don't tell me what I need to do." I shoved her hand away, and she jerked it back as if it had been burned. My words had cut her, but I selfishly wanted her to hurt as much as I did.

She drew her leg out from under her to sit cross-legged. "I don't need your attitude, so quit taking your frustration out on me. I'm the friend who stayed around to help you, remember? So just suck it up, act like an adult, and quit blaming yourself for something you had no control over."

I crossed my arms over my chest and stared straight ahead, refusing to meet her gaze. "You weren't there. You have no idea what happened."

"You're right, I don't. But neither do you."

I turned and glared at her, my guilt threatening to overwhelm me again, but she never broke eye contact. It wasn't fair to Syd, dumping my anger on her. But she was here, convenient, and could handle it. How long would it be before she'd give up on me and leave, like all my other friends?

Like my parents.

Syd uncrossed her legs, twisted around, and slouched back against the couch, taking a deep breath and rubbing her hands over her face before looking over at me again. "I reserve the right to be straight with you, because that's the kind of person I am, and you wouldn't expect anything less. I know you'd do the same for me, so listen. You need to realize we may never know what happened to Simon.

"It's been a year, and I know your bond was incredibly strong, even more so because of that weird twin-thing. But you bark and snarl at people, you're always in a bad mood—you're like a drifting thunderstorm searching for a victim to strike with lightning. You've driven everyone away."

"Except you."

The corner of her mouth turned up, giving me a half smile. "Yeah. Except me. I know how much you miss him, how deep the pain is, and that it hasn't lessened. But it's time to start living again. Maybe we'll find him. But maybe we won't, and you need to accept that."

Syd might have been right, but that didn't make it any easier. Simon was my missing half, and since he'd been gone, it felt like I'd lost a limb. He'd been everything I'd never be. No matter what I told her, getting over his loss would never happen. But I'd tell her what she needed to hear. Reaching over, I took her hand and squeezed it lightly. "I'll try. I promise."

"That's all I can ask. You know that no matter what, I'm always here for you, right?"

I snorted. "It's a good thing, 'cause no one else wants the job."

She gripped my hand tighter. "You're tired. Why don't you get some rest? I'll see you at work later tonight."

As we stood and walked to the front door, I took note that she still hadn't let go of my hand. When I opened the door, she turned and slid her arms up around my neck and hugged me, her fingers tangling in my hair. Which was odd. Syd and I had hugged a thousand times over the years—when we'd been accepted into the Bender program, after Simon disappeared, or for no reason at all. She wasn't the type to hold back her emotions.

But this felt...different. Not bad, but like it meant something else. What had changed?

I wrapped my arms around her waist and returned the embrace.

She held on a few moments longer, then pulled back slightly and looked up at me, holding my gaze. I caught a flash of something in her eyes before she released me. Something like disappointment. In me?

"You'll be okay, Evan. Never exactly the same, but you'll find a new normal."

"Yeah. Maybe. Thanks, Syd. I mean it."

"I know you do." She slipped out the door.

I closed it behind her, then leaned my forehead against its cool, firm surface. Syd was right. With Simon gone, I'd pushed everyone away, built a wall around myself, and smothered nearly every emotion. Except anger. After a year, I should be coping better with my loss. That sounded good in theory, but the guilt still ate me alive, gnawing away a piece of me every day since the night Simon disappeared.

What Syd didn't know—what no one knew—was that I'd heard Simon calling for help that night and ignored him. When he'd called my name, instead of charging into his bedroom, I'd stayed in my own room beside his, and slung the pillow over my head to muffle the sounds of his screams. If I'd only done the right thing, been smarter and less insecure, he'd still be here with us, my parents wouldn't have left me, and remorse and misery wouldn't be my constant companions.

Keeping this information inside me was more difficult than splitting an atom. I'd won the opportunity to intern for the person I most admired in the science world—Dr. Lucas Sebastian, the founder and chief scientist of the research company, Scientific Innovations. SI was responsible for nearly every technological advance made in the past twenty years toward sustaining Tage.

The chances of winning the competition had been slim. More than one hundred people had applied. But I'd worked diligently on my project, going without sleep and food numerous times until my brother had brought me meals, forcing me to eat or threatening to carry me to bed if I didn't rest. Evan was the first person I most wanted to share this with.

Although anxious to tell him the news, my soul cried out for the welcome isolation of my lab in the basement of our home. This was valuable time that could be spent on my project, and I didn't care to be around all these people. But Evan came first, because he'd been just as invested and excited as I was.

I took a short cut through Central Square Park, and stopped beside a park bench. Various groups congregated around some kind of sport ball, an activity for which I had no time or interest. But if I wanted to locate Evan, my best bet was outside somewhere—anyplace without four walls to constrain him. When I didn't see him in the clearing, I expanded my search to the rock-climbing section. I found several of his friends scaling the face of a twenty-foot rock or belaying at the bottom, but my twin wasn't among them. A couple of them called out to me, thinking I was Evan. No point in correcting them. I waved and kept walking.

He was close. I felt the familiar swirling vortex of his emotions—dark and light, high and low—that was all Evan. Whatever he was feeling always rose easily to the surface. There were no hidden agendas with him. He'd laughed when I described the sensation, stating I was exactly the opposite—a river of calm, never slowing or speeding up. A constant he could always depend on. The ability to sense each other's presence had always been with us. We called it a twin connection, and had assumed it was common to all twins. But in speaking with others, we discovered that wasn't the case.

I turned in the other direction and spotted a familiar petite sandy blond sitting on a bench, her head lowered as she read something on her data pad. If I wanted to find Evan, she was my best shot. I headed over to her and blocked the late afternoon sun so I could see her face. "Sydney, where is he?"

"I'm not your brother's keeper, Simon. Use your Wonder Twin powers and find him yourself." She didn't even look up to acknowledge me.

"Syd, please. It's really important."

She sighed heavily, and reluctantly lifted her eyes from the data pad, glancing to my right. Spinning in that direction, I observed a group of guys playing football on an adjacent field. Evan carried the ball and sprinted for the end zone, the closest person trailing at least ten feet behind him. He crossed the goal line, and was soon surrounded by his teammates, laughing and high-fiving each other. Even though I found sports to be a waste of my time, I made an attempt to keep up with football because Evan was on the team. I hadn't missed a game.

The grin slipped from his face and he looked over the heads of the other guys, searching, probably for me. When his eyes locked on mine, he immediately left the field, despite the loud protests of his teammates as he ran in my direction.

"Hey," he said, not even breathing hard.

A run like that would have left me gasping for oxygen.

"What's got you so excited? It feels like you're about to burst into song or something."

I couldn't hold it in any longer. "I won. They awarded me the internship."

His smile could have lit up the center of a black hole. "You won? I knew it! I told you not to worry!" He gripped my shoulders and pulled me into a hug.

It was hard to squeeze out any words with his arms wrapped tightly around me, but I managed a few. "While I appreciate your excitement, I'd really rather not have your sweat seeping into my clothing."

"What? Oh, sorry." He released me.

I wiped the side of my neck, damp from his perspiration.

"Congrats, Simon. Pretty awesome news," Syd said, closing her data pad and smirking at my reaction over Evan's sweat.

"Simon, this is seriously amazing. At fifteen, you'll be the youngest research assistant at Scientific Innovations."

I smiled, savoring that information and letting it seep in before commenting. Evan was sincerely happy for me, but having no interest in science, he truly had no grasp of what an honor this was. "Working with Dr. Sebastian will be a privilege, something I never thought possible. At least, not before completing school. But he was very interested in my research on developing nutritional alternatives."

"I'm sure it's fascinating stuff. No time to discuss it right now, though." Syd fluttered her hand in the air. "You'll finish your schooling with tutors at SI, then?"

I chuckled. Any attempt to explain the details of my research would cause their eyes to glaze over due to their lack of interest and comprehension. "Yes. Six hours per day in the lab, two hours on school working at an accelerated rate."

"You mean more like twelve hours in the lab," Evan corrected.

I sighed happily. "One can only hope."

With Tage facing the crisis of an unidentified disease killing the animal population, daily activities had undergone dramatic changes—traditional schooling being one of them. SI had opened several of its programs to gifted students, especially in the area of science. Anyone able to contribute to the planet's survival was fast-tracked, allowing them to continue their education with private studies and finish much earlier than normal.

Evan snorted. "Simon, you and I have vastly different definitions of fun. I wouldn't mind leaving school, but not to work in some lab like Mom and Dad. Wait…we still have parents, right?"

I rolled my eyes. "Don't be so snide. Their project is one of the highest priorities at SI, and they can't be home every night."

"Once a week is more like it," Evan muttered, throwing his leg across the back of the bench and stretching. "Guess you know where we rank in the scheme of things."

"Eww, Evan! Pull your shorts down and quit flashing people." Syd turned sideways to avoid the view.

His response was to shrug and continue stretching.

"Dr. Sebastian just informed me today that our shortages aren't the only dire ones. Earth's situation is more extreme than we'd thought. Their fresh water supply is nearly depleted, the population in some areas has been cut by more than half, and we're in no position to help them. You should be proud of Mom and Dad. They've made great strides in their fields. The needs of the many need to come before the two of us. Besides, we're capable of taking care of ourselves."

Evan lowered his leg and dropped onto the bench, stretching out and laying his sweaty head in Syd's lap. She didn't seem to mind. "I get it, Simon, but you'd think they'd check in every now and then to see if we're still alive."

"Mom messaged me this morning, wished me luck with the internship results, and said they'd be looking forward to good news when they arrived home this evening. They'll be here working at the local offices of Scientific Innovations for a couple of days."

"Guess that tells you who the favored child is." Syd flicked Evan's head with her fingers.

"That can't be a surprise to you. We're the spawn of two gifted scientists—one of us born with the heightened intelligence and abilities of our parents, and the other good at….well, we're still waiting for confirmation on that."

"Your talents are in other areas, Evan." I was troubled by the way he always compared himself to me. "I could never deal with people the way you do. You're a keen judge of character and have dozens of friends. I prefer the solitude of my lab. Whether you realize it or not, you're a natural born leader, and have the ability to sort out the root of a problem and develop solutions faster than most people I've met."

Someone who didn't know Evan as well as I did might have missed the way the corner of his mouth turned up slightly, and mistaken the light crimson color that splashed across his face to be caused by his physical exertion. But I knew better.

Syd shoved Evan's shoulder. "See? I've been telling you almost the same thing. Even though you're identical twins, comparing you and Simon, other than looks, is like comparing river rocks to diamonds. And I'll give you a hint which one of you is the rock."

"Whatever." Evan rolled his eyes.

But I could sense his pride as if it were my own. In a way, it was, since we felt each other's emotions. At almost any given time, we knew what the other was experiencing. Distance hindered it somewhat, but when we were at home or school, it could be disconcerting, especially if one of us felt an especially strong emotion. Evan's temper had threatened to derail me numerous times.

"Mom and Dad should be home soon. Are you ready to leave?" I asked.

Evan tilted his head back and raked his hands through his hair. "I guess. But we both know it's not me they're anxious to see."

♊

We would have beaten our parents if a group of admiring girls hadn't distracted Evan for nearly a half hour. By the time we got home, I didn't have the opportunity to give Mom and Dad the news of the internship, because word had spread rapidly through the company. They grabbed me the second I walked through the door.

Mom drew me into a hug. "Simon, we couldn't be prouder! What an honor for someone your age to be working with Dr. Sebastian."

Dad pulled me away from her for a hug of his own.

"You can learn a lot from him, Simon. Having Sebastian as a mentor can mean great things for your career at SI. Your project on nutritional alternatives must have really impressed him. Excellent job, son." And he slapped me on the back.

"Evan scored two touchdowns in the game last night." I untangled myself from Dad's arms. Although my brother and I had walked in together, our parents had yet to acknowledge his presence, and he now reclined on the couch, arms stretched across the back, mere feet away from where they stood.

Mom's focus had been on Dad and me, her eyes shining with pride, and at the mention of Evan's name, a look of confusion clouded her face, almost as if having another son had slipped her mind. "What?"

Evan held up a hand and waggled his fingers in our direction. "Hi, Mom, Dad."

"Evan, that's... good news." Mom moved in his direction.

Evan narrowed his eyes as if gauging her reaction. Lowering herself beside him on the sofa, she placed a hand on his shoulder, but Evan hesitated before allowing himself to be hugged. From where I stood, it looked excruciatingly awkward.

"Well, yes, Evan." Dad cleared his throat, "That's good news. Physical activity is important, of course. But how are your classes going?" He advanced to the chair adjacent to the couch, while I took the opportunity to go in the kitchen and give them a moment alone.

Our parents had always given more attention to my classes and grades than Evan's. I'd explained to him it was because they and I spoke the same 'language'—science. They'd both received recognition in their fields, were highly driven, and were committed to developing ways to aid our planet until more long-term solutions could be found. When opportunities to advance their projects arose at a remote branch of SI, neither hesitated at accepting those assignments, believing it to be their ultimate responsibility to our people and planet. Keeping our family one cohesive unit was a distant second in their list of priorities.

I didn't doubt they loved each of us in their own way, but Evan had always struggled with their choice to leave, and there remained a rift between them. Especially since his grades were nowhere near my own, and his interests were so diverse from our parents' expectations. There had never been any doubt in my mind Evan was intelligent and gifted, but his talents were in areas that didn't parallel our parents' goals for us.

My thoughts were interrupted by rising, tension-filled voices coming from the living room, and I felt Evan's emotions churning between anger, sadness, and disappointment, anger rapidly gaining a lead. That hadn't taken long at all. I dropped what I was doing to back him up. Not that he really needed it. But I'd always supported him, nonetheless.

I rounded the corner to see that battle lines had been drawn, with Evan standing behind the couch, and my parents on the opposite side. I took my place beside my brother.

"Not everyone is born to be a scientist! There are other ways to help, you know. If you're both as intelligent as people say, why can't you expand your minds and see that?" Evan ranted, holding his arms out wide.

Mom stood beside Dad, her arms crossed as she spoke. "Evan, we certainly don't expect you to reach Simon's level, but if you'd only apply yourself, perhaps you could obtain some sort of support position at SI and contribute in that way."

He dropped his arms and leaned over, bracing his hands on the back of the sofa. "Did it ever occur to you that maybe I'm just not smart enough? That maybe Simon got all the brains and this is the best I'll ever be? Or is that too horrible a concept to imagine? A Resnik with only average intelligence—the shame would be too much to bear."

"Just stop. Your father and I know you've never given academics your best effort. Simon has spent hours upon hours studying and working in the lab, while you've played sports and traipsed around with your friends wasting your time. Maybe it's not too late to get on the right track and make something of yourself."

"Mom, Dad, you both need to quit." Between Evan's anger and my outrage at his treatment from our parents, I strained to maintain a civil tone. "How can you speak to Evan this way? It's as if you don't even know your own son. You've been so wrapped up in your own projects and my academics that you've never taken the time to learn about his interests."

Our parents stood motionless at my outburst, their eyes wide in shock, and Mom's mouth hung open. Evan's emotional surges were a fairly common occurrence, but any outpouring from me was unusual.

Evan huffed. "Maybe if you hadn't abandoned your children and had stayed around to raise us, you'd have figured out Simon and I are different people. We'll never be the same, and I'll never be like the two of you." He spun to leave the room, but stopped and looked over his shoulder. "But it was nice of the two of you to drop by." He escaped through the front door, probably going for a run.

I turned back to see Mom's eyes narrowed, and Dad's head shaking slowly, his lips pressed tightly together.

"You've almost lost him," I said, my voice low. "Is it really worth berating your own son and making him feel less just because he doesn't choose the same path as you?"

"Simon," Mom called.

But I ignored her as I went out into the night in search of Evan.

CHAPTER 4
EVAN
PRESENT DAY

The alarm on my data pad woke me. I squinted at the dim early evening light streaming in from the windows. Lifting my arms above my head, I stretched and remembered the dream I'd been having. Simon and I were about six years old when we figured out I could 'play' in his head. A smile slid across my face as I relived the memory.

Simon whispered from my bedroom door. "Evy, are you awake?"

I didn't answer, because he already knew I was.

He tiptoed over to my bed so he wouldn't disturb our parents down the hall. The bed jostled as he pulled back the covers and slipped in beside me.

I rolled toward him, my face only inches from his. The close proximity enabled us to keep our voices low. "Is it the stuff in your head again? Is that why you can't sleep?"

He nodded. "Yeah. Lots of ideas spinning around and my brain can't rest. I'm so tired." He yawned.

I rubbed my burning eyes. "It's hard for me to sleep when you can't sleep, so I'm tired, too."

"Is it like this in your head? Really busy?"

"Not when I want to sleep. When I'm awake, I think about fun things, like playing ball outside or swimming at the beach, but your brain is full of school stuff all the time. And none of that's fun. You were remembering that story we had to read yesterday about not having enough water."

Simon's brows drew together. "How do you know what I was thinking?"

I shrugged. "Guess it's that thing we do, when we know how the other one feels."

"But that's not the same as knowing what I think." His eyes widened. "Do you know what I'm thinking now?"

"No."

"Try, Evy. Like you did before."

I wasn't really sure how I'd done it, but I squeezed my eyes shut and thought about Simon and what was inside his head. For a minute, it felt like I floated, but then I was standing in the middle of a whirling cloud surrounded by Simon's voice. It sounded like he was talking to himself about stuff we'd learned at school, and numbers I didn't understand. But then I heard him say very clearly, 'Evy snores.'

I giggled. "No, I don't. You snore."

Simon gasped. "I didn't say that out loud. How did you do that?"

"I just thought about being in your head and I was there. Why do you like to talk about numbers so much?" I wrinkled my nose.

This time Simon shrugged. "I just like numbers and science stuff. Numbers make sense to me. My turn to try and get into your head." His face scrunched up like he was concentrating really hard, and he held his breath.

"Did it work?" I asked.

"No." He released the air from his lungs with a huff.

"Maybe you just have to practice." We lay quietly, staring at each other, and all I could hear was the sound of our breathing.

"Evy, I just had another idea."

"Maybe if you stopped thinking up so many ideas, we could both sleep," I mumbled.

"But this might help both of us sleep, I promise."

I sighed. "Okay, tell me your big idea."

"You said you can make it quiet in your head when it's time to sleep. Do you think you could go in my head again and make it quiet?"

"I don't know." I shrugged. "Guess I could try. Close your eyes."

Simon obeyed, and once again, I floated into his swirling thoughts, wondering how someone could have this many things going on inside his head at once. No wonder we couldn't sleep.

No more than a minute had passed when he opened his eyes. "How did you do that? It's not loud anymore."

"I just thought about having a big box, like where we put our toys, and I put all your ideas inside, then closed the lid."

His eyes widened. "Did you lose my ideas? What if I need them again?"

"When you want to think about them, just open the lid and take them out," I replied, like it was the simplest thing in the world.

Simon exhaled in relief, and then we both fell into a deep sleep, still facing each other, never moving until Mom woke us for school the next morning.

I hadn't thought about that memory in years, and it left a warm feeling inside me, almost like Simon was here. It had been a while since I'd last attempted to sense him. Maybe it was time to try again. I closed my eyes tightly and reached out, searching for a sign, some inkling that my twin was near.

Nothing.

The hole in my chest left by his disappearance ripped open a little wider, filling me with a deep, bone-chilling cold. Exactly as I'd expected.

Putting that thought out of my mind, I shoved off the covers, swung my legs over the side of the bed, and stood. It was time to go to work.

♊

After entering Scientific Innovations, I had to pass through the lofty, two story common area before reaching my office. Conversation and laughter echoed down the hallway as I approached, but when I entered the room, the laughter came to an abrupt halt, and people detached themselves from groups, either scurrying in the opposite direction, or trying to look busy as I strode past them.

Overhead were large monitors displaying the current and scheduled cases in each lab. Directly in front of me on the second story level was a long expanse of glass which made up one wall of our director's office. Through one of those windows, I saw Gabriel Minnick standing with his hands clasped behind his back. He looked down, nodding imperceptibly in greeting when our eyes met. When I'd been going through the assessment program to determine my suitability for the Mindbender Academy, Gabriel had all but singled me out and mentored me, saying he'd spotted my strengths immediately.

Stopping at my office first, I checked a few things, then headed to Gabriel's office for our daily briefing.

"Come in." The door muffled his reply.

I stepped inside and was thrust into the serenity and calm of his domain. Nearly everything was beige or white, and nothing was ever out of place. No leftover food containers or trash, just clean lines and sharp corners. His desk held only his data pad, a separate computer, and a picture of his wife. She was a beautiful woman, but something had happened and she wasn't in his life anymore; I wasn't sure why, and had never asked him about it. It was an unspoken rule that any information regarding her was off limits, never to be a topic of discussion.

Like his office, Gabriel's appearance was crisp and clean, his hair pulled back with a leather tie at the base of his neck. No strands escaped—ever. His clothes were always pressed and spotless, with no stray crumbs or stains. Syd had suggested I could learn a thing or two from Gabriel about laundry, but sometimes I wondered if he was really human. Seemed like someone that perfect would have to be a cyborg.

"Come in, Evan. Have a seat."

I approached the chair facing his desk and pulled out my data pad to receive this evening's list of cases.

"What's on the agenda tonight?"

"Nothing too heavy. A pretty textbook night for your team." He touched the screen of his data pad, then pointed to mine. Immediately, a list of the evening's scheduled clients and their information appeared on my own data pad. Scanning the cases, I noticed nothing out of the ordinary. Gabriel was right. Just some basic cases of misplaced items, and a couple of recurring level one nightmares.

"So, Doc is back again."

"Yes, he is," Gabriel chuckled. "Such a brilliant, accomplished scientist, but sometimes I have to wonder how he even remembers the location of his lab."

I smirked at his comment, because he was right. Dr. Paul Quill had made significant strides in Tage's food situation and water conservation. He'd created underwater biospheres anchored to the sea floor that grew produce. The sea water evaporated from the heat of the sun and condensed on the ceiling of the biospheres, then dripped back down as fresh water to feed the plants.

The problem was, if Doc didn't immediately enter his ideas into his data pad when epiphanies struck, they were lost in his subconscious. My team and I had helped him relocate those ideas numerous times. His mind was a fascinating place to be, constantly active with theories and concepts swirling around. It was very similar to Simon's, and while in Dr. Quill's mind, I'd thought about how much Simon would have loved to be with me and gain an insider's view of Doc's inner sanctum.

But even if Simon were here, that wouldn't be a possibility. Bender cases were classified, and we were required to sign rigid confidentiality agreements. We discussed nothing of what we saw or learned. Ever. Allowing someone to access your innermost thoughts and granting them permission to enter your mind was an act of the utmost trust. Betraying that trust was grounds for immediate dismissal and, depending on the severity of the breach, could potentially involve banishment to the Criminal Realm.

The Realm was a parallel world made up of citizens who broke the laws of Tage in the most atrocious ways. For minor offenses, a facility existed to house them for certain time periods, but those who committed the worst crimes were sent to a place from which they could never return. The Realm was made up entirely of criminals. Receiving no supplies or assistance from Tage, its inhabitants built their own society, and survived any way they could. Stories about life there could provide a lifetime supply of nightmares, and therefore job security for a Bender.

"I'll leave it up to you to distribute the caseload to the team." Gabriel slid his data pad to the side and leaned toward me, clasping his hands together on top of his desk. "I know yesterday marked a year since your brother disappeared. How are you doing?"

So, work talk was turning to a more personal agenda. "Fine." I looked down at the white rug while twisting the silver earring in my left ear. My eyes flicked upward and took in Gabriel's concerned face.

"Did you talk to your parents?"

Leaning back in the chair, I crossed my arms over my chest, and diverted my gaze to the wall of glass behind Gabriel. "It's been a few months. I knew I wouldn't hear from them on the anniversary, because they don't want a painful reminder that I'm the one who's left. They might as well have lost us both, because they act like I don't exist—not that they paid much attention to me before he was gone. I thought family were supposed to be supportive when things went off the rails, but I was stupid to think anything would change."

It didn't used to be that way. When Simon and I were younger, before our parents had left us, our home had life and laughter—the way a family should be. Things I'd taken for granted at the time. It had never occurred to me our parents wouldn't be there one day, but they'd chosen to leave us when we were barely teenagers. They'd said we were mature and responsible—they probably meant Simon—and were sure we'd understand the importance of their work and their decision. Promises were made about everyday communications over the data pad. It would be almost like they were here.

And then promises were broken. They'd skipped a day here or there or were too busy to talk when we'd contacted them. Soon enough, communication had all but stopped between us. Until Simon had gone missing and they'd blamed me for not taking care of him. After efforts to locate Simon had failed, they'd returned to their work and all but forgotten me.

Like both of us had disappeared.

Syd had stayed with me the following three nights, never leaving my side, as I'd alternated among sobbing over my brother's absence, raging about my parents' abandonment yet again, and withdrawing into myself from grief and blame. On the fourth day, Gabriel came, and the two of them cleaned me up, forced me to eat, and then got me to SI to start bending, all against my will. But it had been the best thing for me, exactly what I'd needed. My job offered the stability I'd lacked at home, purpose, and a reason to get out of bed. It also gave me a physical outlet for my emotions. I threw myself into it, and my hard work paid off when I became the youngest team leader at SI.

The sympathetic expression on his face never wavered. "You're right to be angry. Your parents have failed you. Anything you need—someone to talk to, a place to get away, whatever—I'm here for you. Remember that."

The burden of guilt and pain I'd carried for the past year was exhausting. I'd blamed myself for so long, and I'd allowed my parents to do the same. But not anymore. I was going to bring Simon home. Me. Not my parents. Not Agent Deckard. Me.

He shifted in his chair. "But I'm telling you as your supervisor, I hope you'll listen to what I'm about to say. This anger you've been harboring has resulted in you alienating most of your friends and sequestering yourself in your office or at home. I've also checked the logs. It's been quite some time since you've downloaded any residual fear, and combined with your anger and grief, it makes for an unstable mixture.

"I'm concerned about you, Evan. Our relationship has always been more than just supervisor and employee. That being said," he leveled his gaze at me, "get yourself to a lab and download." Gabriel's stern tone left no room for argument.

I slunk down, exhaling and rubbing my hands over my face. "I'll try to make time. I didn't mean to take it out on you. You're the last person I should be dumping on."

His lips curved into a smile. "I didn't take it personally, Evan. You're not the first person to sit in that chair and take out some misplaced aggression on me. It's part of being a boss. And a friend."

♊

Prior to Dr. Quill being escorted to the lab and prepped for his case that evening, I was able to catch a few moments with him in the client lounge. When Deckard had mentioned geniuses at SI, Doc was the first person who came to mind. I'd worked with him for several months, and felt I could speak freely with him.

The lounge was decorated in muted, calming colors with reclining seats and plush pillows designed to provide a relaxing atmosphere for clients before they were prepped. Upon entering, I inhaled the pleasant smell of eucalyptus and heard the soft sounds of ocean waves from speakers hidden within the walls. Doc was lying in a recliner staring at the ceiling.

"Doc?"

At the sound of my voice, he brought the seat back to its original position. "I know I'm supposed to be meditating or letting my mind wander, but I can't sit here and do nothing, Evan. It's unnatural. Without anything to record my ideas, I'm probably creating concepts you'll have to locate in future cases."

I grinned and lowered myself to the seat opposite him. "Don't worry, I'm not here about that. I have a question. Can you think of any way a person could disappear from a room, with a locked door and windows, and leave no trace of how he got out or where he was taken?"

"Is this a riddle?"

I tilted my head. "No, it's a serious question, I promise."

He stroked his chin and stared at the wall behind me, his eyes somewhat unfocused. "Well, I wish I had a solution to offer, but the technology hasn't been discovered yet."

Air whooshed from my lungs in disappointment. I'd allowed myself a sliver of hope, only to see it crushed. "I didn't think so, but thanks anyway."

"That's not to say it won't be, Evan."

I stood and clapped him on the shoulder.

"See you in the lab, Doc."

Chapter 5
Simon
Two Years Ago

Evan wouldn't take no for an answer when I'd said I didn't have time to take off work for dinner.

"If you don't meet me, I'll drag you forcibly from your lab on the grounds that you deserve a break. Just because our parents deserted us doesn't mean we can't have a meal together like a normal family."

So, as dinnertime neared, I left the lab. Glancing at the time on my data pad, I noted I was ahead of schedule, and decided to take advantage of the extra time. Evan was somewhere in the park and said he'd meet me by the rock climbing section. A weathered park bench ahead of me on the left was empty, so I ambled in that direction and took a seat, enjoying just being still. Closing my eyes, I tilted my head back, basking in the warmth of late afternoon sunshine on my face and inhaling the musky smell of wet leaves from a recent rain shower.

My work day at Scientific Innovations began in the early morning, and I often never left until nine at night, sometimes later. Balancing on-site tutoring with my project work was challenging—not that I was complaining, because I truly believed this was my life's calling. Working at SI had exceeded my expectations, but I couldn't say when I'd last seen the sun or taken a few moments to myself to just...be still. To sit there and do nothing felt wrong somehow, against my genetic makeup—an act of selfishness when Tage's situation was so precarious.

But Evan always stressed the importance of downtime and rest, saying I wouldn't be of use to anyone if I was exhausted. In theory, he was correct, but slowing down my mind was the equivalent of preventing ocean waves from crashing ashore.

The brisk chill in the air reminded me winter was right around the corner, and I was glad I'd grabbed a jacket on my way out the door this morning. Only after putting my hands in the pockets and finding Evan's football gloves did I discover I'd taken his by mistake. He'd probably never miss it anyway.

It was time to get moving, and after inhaling deeply once more, I pulled the collar of Evan's jacket up around my neck and rose from the park bench. I'd only gone a few feet when I heard running footsteps behind me, and assumed it was someone jogging or kids playing around—until I was grabbed by the back of my jacket and spun in the opposite direction. Before I could catch a glimpse of the person responsible, his fist connected with my face. I staggered backwards. A warm gush of blood spurted from my nose and flowed over my mouth.

Another blow glanced off my cheek bone and struck my ear, but the next one caught me squarely under the chin, gnashing my teeth together. I dropped to the ground, curling into a fetal position and covering my face. When my attacker paused, I hoped he'd finished, but it was only to roll me to my back and sit astride my chest. Through my fingers, I saw Max Delacort, who had clearly mistaken me for Evan. "Resnik, I told you what would happen the next time I saw you!"

"Delacort! What the hell are you doing?" Evan. He must have witnessed the attack. Not a good thing.

Max's head spun toward Evan's voice, then whipped back to me, his forehead creased. "Simon?" he asked in a coarse whisper. I nodded, holding my hand over my nose in an attempt to stop the flow of blood. "I should have known when you didn't fight back."

To the right of Max's shoulder, I saw Evan sprinting toward us. I didn't need to see his face to know he was furious. I felt the rage surging through every vein in his body.

Max's eyes were wide in apology. "Simon, I'm so sorry, I would never intentionally hurt...." He touched my face softly and shook his head. "Evan's going to kill me."

"A definite possibility," I said in a distinct nasal tone.

Before Max could climb off me, Evan leaped over the park bench, grabbed him by the back of his collar, yanked him up, and spun him around.

If I didn't intervene, Evan might actually kill him. I wiped my nose with the sleeve of Evan's jacket, pushed myself from the ground, and staggered between the two of them, facing Evan. His breathing was heavy, eyes bulging, and nostrils flared. If he wasn't my brother, I'd have turned and run in the opposite direction, but instead, I brought my hands up and pushed lightly against him.

"Move, Simon!" Evan tried to dodge past me and get his hands on Max, but I moved with him. He looked over my shoulder and yelled, "Do you have a death wish, Delacort? You don't ever touch my brother!"

I shoved harder, but me trying to hold Evan back when he was this worked up was about as effective as butterfly wings keeping a storm at bay. "Stop it, Evan! It was an honest mistake. I'm wearing your jacket and Max thought I was you."

"He's right, Resnik. I swear I thought Simon was you. I only saw him from the back, and it's getting darker outside. You know I'd never go after him." Max's voice was pitched higher than normal, and his hands were up in a defensive stance.

"Look at his face! He's bleeding and you're hiding behind him like a coward."

"Just hit me if it makes you feel better. I deserve it." Max dropped his hands to his side and closed his eyes, as if resigned to accepting his punishment.

"Hitting you is a good place to start." Evan lunged again.

"No one else is getting hit, so both of you just calm down!" I never raised my voice, and it caught them both by surprise. Max's eyes popped open, and Evan backed away in shock. But he didn't drop his steely gaze from Max's face. I breathed in through my mouth and exhaled. My nose was throbbing and filled with coagulating blood. "He already apologized, Evan. It was just a misunderstanding."

"It might have been a mistake thinking Simon was me, but assuming it had been me, what was your problem, Delacort? What's got your panties in a wad this time?"

Max squared his jaw and narrowed his eyes. "That crap you pulled on the field yesterday. You knew I wouldn't let that slide."

Evan's mouth twisted into a smirk. "Seriously?"

The two of them hurled insults back and forth, and no doubt fists would fly again without my intervention. I sighed heavily. The clash-of-the-alpha-males drama had been playing out since Evan and Max met in primary school, and had grown very tiresome for me. What had started this enmity was a mystery. It seemed to be hatred at first sight. "Can we call a time out?" I stepped between them once more, my hands gently pushing against their shoulders to separate them. This wasn't the first time I'd acted as mediator during one of their confrontations. "Let's go to dinner, Evan. I need to get cleaned up anyway."

"Fine." Evan pointed at Max as he backed away. "Don't think this is over."

Max eyed Evan, his mouth set in a hard line.

"Excellent, because I'm famished," I sighed.

Evan turned to walk away, and as I fell in behind him, Max tugged on my sleeve to stop me, speaking too low for Evan to hear. "Simon, again, I'm so sorry. You have to know that I'd never hurt you." He held out his other hand.

I shook it, noting my hand seemed to be perspiring all of a sudden, and my pulse quickened. "No hard feelings. I know it was an accident and, given your history with my brother, I'm surprised it hasn't happened before," I chuckled.

Max smiled, and while I was occupied with the unusual amber color of his eyes, he moved his other hand to my shoulder and gently squeezed it.

"Are we leaving or what? We're going, we're staying. I thought you wanted food?"

"I'm coming," I called over my shoulder. Looking back at Max, I met his eyes and smiled again, ducking my head slightly. "Guess I'd better go."

"Oh…yeah. Sorry again." Max dropped my hand, then rubbed the back of his neck. "See you, Simon."

I nodded in reply and turned to follow Evan, but hoped I'd see Max sooner rather than later.

II

I huffed out a breath and shut down my lab equipment for the evening, syncing my data pad with what little I'd accomplished today. Distraction had never been a problem for me, not in school or work. Evan joked that my mind was like a laser—program a goal, activate the invisible blinders, and it became my sole focus in life until completion. He compared it to giving a scent to a hunting dog. Canine attribute or not, it was an ability I prided myself on, considering it one of my greatest strengths.

However, that ability had lain dormant for the past few days. Ever since I'd had my run in with Max, my thoughts had drifted to his strong jawline and the way his tousled, flaxen hair fell over his forehead when he'd apologized for hitting me. Or the stunning amber shade of his anxious eyes when the setting sun filtered through the trees and lit up his face. All very unscientific thoughts, and completely unrelated to my current projects. I found myself in foreign territory.

Evan and I had always confided in each other about things of this nature. Or, more accurately, Evan confided in me, since I had no time for such dalliances. He was rarely without a wide-eyed, adoring girl attached to his arm, but his interest in the opposite sex changed as often as colors in a kaleidoscope, and I'd ceased my attempts to remember their names. Until Abbi.

Abbi was a new transfer to our school, and when Evan saw her the first time she walked into class, I felt something in him change, like the shifting of tectonic plates. Even I could see how attractive she was, something that undoubtedly caught his attention initially, but over time, I came to know her as a friendly and intelligent person who had a keen interest in quantum physics. For Evan, she became his sole purpose for existence. The problem was, Abbi was the first girl he'd met, other than Syd, who wasn't waiting in line to be with him. She never looked in his direction. Only I knew how deeply this affected him, because underneath that undeniable charisma and self-confident flashing smile, Evan still questioned whether he was enough. It was a deep-seated doubt planted by our parents that had grown and flourished over the years.

Being inexperienced in relationships, I wasn't much help, but encouraged him to take a more subtle approach instead of his current borderline stalking method. And he did. Evan got to know her as a friend, discovering that he genuinely liked her. Confident that the interest was mutual, he planned the perfect first date, Abbi accepted his invitation, and things went as he'd anticipated. He returned home that evening a taut bundle of smiles and excitement, and I felt the stirrings of confidence and hope building inside him.

Those budding euphoric feelings stuttered and came to a grinding halt when Evan learned Abbi also had a first date with Max. And the competition began, each trying to outdo the other, with Abbi completely unaware she was now the prize in a years old rivalry. She had to make a decision, and she did. It was Max.

Maybe he'd genuinely cared for her, or perhaps Abbi was just another challenge to be won over my brother, but I felt Evan's growing self-confidence shatter. In his mind, her choice had confirmed that our parents were right, and he'd never be good enough. It took him weeks to emerge from his blanket of depression, once again slapping on his mask of indifference and attaching a new girl to his arm. But I caught the flash of pain in his eyes every time he saw Max and Abbi together.

All of this drama and suffering reaffirmed my belief that relationships were a waste of time, and would only divert attention from my studies. Besides, no one had ever given me reason to look twice.

Until now. And that could cause problems not only with my work, but also with my twin. Abbi had been one tangle among many others in the adversarial relationship between Evan and Max that apparently was spawned over nothing more than each other's existence. Losing Abbi had left a permanent gouge in Evan's psyche, and another tick was added to the ever growing list of reasons he'd loathed Max. Especially since he'd broken up with Abbi a few weeks after she'd dumped Evan.

Evan had tried to influence my feeling towards Max, but I'd refused to let my brother's views color my perception of him. As a scientist, I preferred to gather facts and form my own opinions. I supported my brother, but he wasn't infallible and sometimes created more conflict than originally existed.

I'd interacted with Max occasionally at school, and since he also played sports, had seen him at Evan's games. The times we'd interacted, I'd found him quite engaging. We'd once had a long, enjoyable conversation regarding string theory. The discussion had gone late into the evening and continued over a quick dinner. With a sudden start, I realized how unusual that was. Max hadn't been in any advanced classes, but he seemed very knowledgeable about the subject, and had even caught up with me a few times after that for further discussions.

Had he spent grueling hours studying string theory purely for the sake of spending time with me? Was that dinner a date? My heart rate quickened at the thought, and my face warmed. With my 'blinders' on, getting to know Max hadn't been a priority, but after he'd nearly knocked me unconscious, the anger and contempt I'd seen in his amber eyes had abruptly transformed to pain and regret upon the realization it was my blood he'd spilled instead of Evan's.

If I mentioned having these sorts of thoughts about Max to my twin, I could confidently predict the outcome of that discussion. When Max was around, Evan's thoughts were dark and temperamental, a vortex of antagonism without a hint of respect or admiration. Not even as a competitor.

No. Best to keep my thoughts to myself on that topic.

I walked through the dimly lit front lobby, and pushed open the towering glass doors at the entrance of Scientific Innovations. The evening air was crisp, with the brightness of the full moon lighting a path along the sidewalk. Movement in my peripheral vision startled me, and I turned to see someone step from the cluster of trees lining the walkway.

"Simon?"

I stopped abruptly, knowing the source of that voice. He'd been the primary reason for my diversion over the past few days.

Max walked hesitantly toward me, as if afraid I might bolt. His shoes crunched the dry leaves littering the ground beneath the trees.

"Max? It's late, what are you doing here?" I seemed to be slightly short of breath. Odd.

His hands were shoved deep in his pockets, and the slight evening breeze ruffled his hair. "Um, I wanted to apologize again for the other day, I—"

I shook my head, lifting my hand up to interrupt him. "No need. It was a misunderstanding." Then a thought occurred to me. "You came all the way here just to apologize? How did you know I'd still be here at this hour?"

He dropped his head and looked up sideways at me. "Well, I kind of overheard Evan complaining about your late hours and how you lived here more than you did at home."

I laughed. "He's mentioned that a couple of times. Or twenty." Max smiled, then all was silent except for the sound of dry leaves scraping against the sidewalk. He held my gaze and chewed on his lip. I tried to speak, but my mouth was too dry.

"Do you have to go home right now?" he asked, in a jumbled rush.

Tilting my head to the side, I managed to form words. "Not really."

"Would you, uh, maybe want to grab some dinner with me?"

And there it was. Evan's self-proclaimed nemesis, the one person who knew how to push his buttons with just a look, his primary cause of anguish over the past several years, had asked me out. I'd always been loyal to my brother—he was like an extension of myself, and I knew his heart as well as my own. I also understood the conflict and anger my spending time with Max would cause. So it was quite surprising when I heard myself answer, "Yes."

His radiant smile was brighter than the full moon.

Chapter 6
Evan
Present Day

Gabriel and I stood in the back of the ceremony hall away from the friends and family gathered for the event. Instead of our usual meeting at the beginning of my shift, he'd asked me to join him at the Mindbender Academy to meet the person he had in mind to replace Maya.

"The new trainee graduates are promising," he said. "Some of them possess natural talent, but there's one in particular I have my eye on. He seems to have an aptitude for the work and his test scores are high, but he possesses a bit of an ego. Not unlike someone else I know." His eyes twinkled as he glanced in my direction. "I think you would be the best equipped TL to reign in the ego and develop his talents."

"Sure, Gabriel. I'll break him down and have him begging for mercy before I build him back up."

His face was stern. "Evan, I don't think—"

"Kidding." I held up my hands in a placating gesture. "I trust your judgement. If you think he'd be a good fit for my team, I believe you. I'll train the guy and tame the attitude."

Gabriel pinched the bridge of his nose, shaking his head slightly, then resumed his study of the thinning crowd. "I've asked him to meet with me after graduation and—Ah, here he comes."

I followed Gabriel's line of sight, but several people were still milling about, congratulating one another, hugging and laughing. There was a break in the crowd, and one person dodged a few well-wishers, then headed in our direction. My eyes narrowed and a heaviness settled in the pit of my stomach. It couldn't be. Not him.

His face was bright with excitement, but he stopped abruptly upon noticing me standing at Gabriel's side.

Gabriel held out his hand, and the new grad hesitantly shook it, his eyes never leaving my own. "Evan, I'd like you to meet…"

"Max Delacort." My voice was flat, and I folded my arms across my chest. No way was I shaking his hand.

"Resnik." He dropped Gabriel's hand and jutted out his chin as he regarded me with contempt.

Gabriel's look of surprise was genuine, because I'd never told him about my history with Max. Or Simon's. "I didn't realize you two knew each other. How fortuitous."

"That's not the word I'd use."

"Why is he here?" Max's voice was gruff.

Gabriel paused. "I'm sensing the relationship between the two of you isn't exactly amicable. How about we go to the lounge for some privacy and discuss this situation?" Without waiting for an answer, he pivoted and strode down the hallway. He never looked back for confirmation that we'd follow.

The last time I'd seen Max was the day after Simon's disappearance, and saying we hadn't parted on good terms was putting it kindly. We'd always considered each other adversaries, and after what happened the night Simon disappeared, I didn't see that dynamic changing. I'd been accepted to the academy and eventually worked my way up to being a team leader. I had no idea what Max had done since then, nor had I cared, and he'd made no attempt to contact me. Not that I was surprised. That's the kind of guy he was—only worried about himself.

I fell in behind Gabriel, not caring if Max chose to accompany us or not. Upon reaching the lounge, Gabriel entered and held the heavy wooden door open. I stormed inside, and Max, unfortunately, followed. Gabriel closed the door behind us. "Gentleman, take a seat." He gestured to the grouping of four cushioned chairs and a couch by a floor to ceiling window overlooking the grounds. Max took the seat adjacent to the couch, and I claimed the chair furthest away, while he chose to avoid my eyes, staring at the floor instead.

Gabriel strolled to the couch, which sat between us, eased himself down, and cleared his throat. "Would one of you like to share with me how you know each other?" We both remained quiet, Max apparently as reluctant as I was to explain our combative history. After a few moments of silence, Gabriel grew tired of waiting. "Fine. Evan, begin."

I gripped the arms of the chair, and inhaled deeply, releasing a long, slow breath. "Max and I have known each other since primary school. We played sports together."

"Being teammates, I'd assume you were friends, but that's not the impression I'm getting. Max?" Gabriel turned in his direction.

"Friends? No. We definitely weren't friends."

Gabriel sighed, steepled his index fingers together, and brought them to his chin. "Gentleman, I don't have the time or patience to be a mediator. Society considers you adults, and each of you has a responsibility to perform your duties to the best of your ability. As you're no longer in school, I'd expect both of you to leave any petty, childish issues in the past where they belong. Evan, as I mentioned, Max has been assigned to your team because you have an opening, and he's shown a keen aptitude for Bender duties."

Exactly the words I'd been dreading. Accepting Max on my team, assuming I even had a choice, meant interacting with him daily and training him personally. I'd managed to avoid him for the past year, but it seemed he was about to become a regular part of my life.

"Why his team? Why Evan?" Max asked, his voice tight and brusque.

"Quite frankly, he's the best team leader at Scientific Innovations, and the best person to continue your training. You should consider yourself fortunate there's a vacancy," Gabriel replied. "What I need to know is if the two of you can work together. Considering the upgraded urgency of Tage's situation, I'd expect both of you to put your civic responsibilities above your personal issues with each other."

As much as I hated to admit it, when Gabriel phrased it that way, my problems with Max paled in comparison to the big picture. Priorities shifted, and things fell into proper perspective. I should be the bigger—and better—person. "Yes, I can work with Max, but I have to know that he'll respect my position as his TL."

Gabriel gave a satisfied smile, and I might have detected a glint of pride in his eyes. "Excellent. Max?"

He cast me a dark scowl, but the second Gabriel's attention shifted in his direction, Max plastered a smile on his face and sat taller. "Of course. I'll have no problem setting aside our differences."

I rolled my eyes. What a scam artist. Max didn't want to work with me anymore than I wanted to work with him, but Gabriel had spoken the truth. My team had the highest success rate at SI, and I was the best TL there. If Max couldn't handle the pressure, I'd just get rid of him. The correct way, of course, but that didn't mean I couldn't add a little extra pressure.

"Wonderful," Gabriel said, clapping his hands together once, then rising from the couch. "I'll expect to see you on tomorrow night's shift, Max. Perhaps you and Evan should take some time now to discuss your differences and make a fresh start."

"A great suggestion, Gabriel. I completely agree." Max's eyes tracked him as he left the room, closing the door behind him. He then turned to me as the compliant mask slipped from his face, revealing the real Max who'd hurt Simon. The Max who had then lied to get what he wanted.

"Don't think for a second you can fool Gabriel with this game you're playing, Delacort. He has a knack for seeing through people and he's probably already on to you."

Max huffed out a breath. "Of all the people at SI, they put me on your team. It's like a cruel joke. Did you have something to do with this? Figured it was a way to get back at me for what happened that night? I wouldn't put it past you to use your position to do something like that."

"If that's what you think, then you're an even bigger idiot than I thought." I shook my head. "The last thing I want is to see you every day. I had no idea you'd even gotten into the Bender program. Keeping up with your life has never been a concern of mine."

Both of us considered the other, staring intently, neither wanting to be the first to look away. It was a stupid, alpha-male kind of thing, but a still a challenge.

Max broke first, closing his eyes and lowering his head. "Do you have any news about him?" he asked in a small voice. Surprising. I had no idea he could sound that way. Almost like he genuinely cared, which shot my anger level from medium to maxed-out in the span of a second.

I sprang out of my chair. "Don't pretend you feel anything for him,

Max. If you did, you would have tried to contact me. In a year, I haven't heard a word from you, which tells me I was right about you all along. You were just using Simon as a way to get back at me."

His head jerked up at my words, and he leaped to his feet. "I've *never* stopped caring about Simon. Just because I didn't talk to you doesn't mean I haven't kept up with his case. I've checked with the investigators at least weekly since he disappeared."

"You expect me to believe that?" I asked, leaning on the back of the chair. "That's easy enough to say, but actually doing it would require some effort on your part. You probably forgot about Simon the second I told you he was gone."

Max's eyes burned with anger, and from the subtle way he crouched I knew he was coming for me a second before he lunged. But I was ready for him. I charged forward, grabbed his wrist and pivoted behind him, twisting his arm toward the center of his back with one hand, and pushing him to the floor with the other. He was breathing hard, and I could only imagine the various ways to separate me from my extremities running through his head. That's what I'd be thinking about if our positions were reversed. He struggled against me, his whole body taut, trying to loosen my grip or get his feet in a position to kick me. I admired his perseverance, but there was no way he was getting loose until I freed him.

"Stop, Delacort. Calm down and I'll let you go." He gave it one last shot, then collapsed. "Are you done?" He nodded, and I tentatively released my hold, then stood.

Max rolled to a sitting position, leaned against a chair as he drew in his legs, and lowered his head between his knees. When he looked up at me, his eyes were red-rimmed and glassy. "I don't care what you think about me, Evan. Simon's opinion was all that ever mattered. For him, I'll work with you and take instructions, orders, whatever you want me to do." His face hardened, and his next words were said through gritted teeth. "But don't ever, for one second, believe I used Simon or never cared about him. I loved him, and I miss him every day."

His heated words stunned me, and the force of emotion behind them gave me a flicker of doubt. Could I have been wrong about him all this time? He rose from the floor and walked toward me, stopping only inches from my face. We were the same height, and his steeled eyes were level with mine as he glowered at me.

"I know you miss Simon, too. But I will always believe within the depths of my soul that you could have done something to save him from whatever happened. That's something you have to live with, and I hope you suffer. Every. Single. Day." He punctuated his last three words with a stabbing finger to my chest, then backed away and strode out the door, slamming it behind him.

Max's accusation left me speechless and wide-eyed, because he was absolutely correct. I could have done something and had chosen not to. I'd bitterly regret that choice every day of my life. It was a parasite that gnawed at my insides, chewing its way to the surface.

I'm sure Max would be thrilled to know that I did suffer. More than he could imagine.

♊

After an exhausting shift that night, I arrived home and climbed the stairs, my footsteps echoing through the stillness of my empty house. I yearned for rest. Besides having to deal with three level four nightmares, my thoughts kept returning to Max joining the team. I feared my haven away from an isolated existence at home would become a place of animosity and accusations, and I dreaded the change.

Out of habit, I stepped over the creaky spot on the sixth step, and smiled wistfully. I'd always avoided that step when sneaking in or out of the house when our parents still lived here and we were a family. Simon, too, had dodged it when coming up the stairs after hours, but his late nights were spent in his basement laboratory.

When I reached the top of the stairs, I turned left down the hallway, and stopped in front of his closed bedroom door.

For months after his disappearance, I'd left it open. Some days I'd pass by and look in, expecting to see him bent over his data pad or studying graphs and charts strewn about from his latest project. He'd ask if I wanted to hear about what he was working on, and even though it was usually incomprehensible, I'd still throw myself on his bed and listen to him talk, the excitement of discovery evident in his voice.

But then reality reared its ugly head, and I remembered how that couldn't happen anymore. Not since I hadn't gone to him when he'd called for me that night. Soon it became too painful of a reminder, so I'd closed the door.

Now, I stood outside of it, my forehead pressed against the rough surface, silently pleading to anyone who was listening to let Simon be behind the door, let this have been a cruel, tortured nightmare I'd wake from. Please.

My hand reached for the doorknob. I turned it slowly and pushed, my tightly closed eyes tearing up, aching for him to be there. The hinges groaned from months of disuse as the door opened inch by inch. For those few moments, I clung tightly to my fragile hope. Then I opened my eyes to view what was sure to be an empty room.

The door hit the stop behind it, and I gasped. The room still smelled of him, a chemical kind of essence from so many hours spent in the lab, blended with the spicy body wash he'd preferred. I squinted from the brightness of the early morning sun streaming through the windows, dust motes dancing in the light. Simon wasn't here. Even though I'd known he wouldn't be waiting for me, it didn't lessen the sensation of a gut punch.

I wiped my eyes with the sleeve of my shirt, then turned to close the door. A movement in the corner by the window caught my attention. As I turned in that direction, a thin, silver splinter of light flashed, nearly blinding me. Icy tendrils trailed down my back, and my eyes widened in shock. No. It couldn't be. It wasn't possible. Simon's energy shot up my spine and fanned out into my brain, my body twitching as if I'd been electrocuted. I clung to the door frame for support and let out a sob. My brother was here.

The shimmer of light in the corner faded just as quickly as it had appeared. At the same time, the feeling of warmth, comfort, and all that was Simon was wrenched away, leaving a deeper gash than had previously existed.

I knew this anguish intimately, and closed my eyes. Please, please....not again. Simon was just here. The belief that I'd felt his presence was unshakable.

Please bring him back. Please.

CHAPTER 7
SIMON
ONE YEAR EIGHT MONTHS AGO

"Simon, my boy, are you expecting me to believe these calculations are correct?" Dr. Sebastian sat behind his desk, my data pad in hand, reviewing my findings.

"I'm certain, sir. I've worked and reworked it from every angle. The numbers are accurate." My voice held strong and steady, but my pulse galloped. This was a huge discovery. Massive. It could quite possibly change the course of life on two planets. *Save* billions of lives on two planets.

While in school, I'd been restrained by rules, financial limitations, and lack of state-of-the-art equipment, all of which hindered any advances in my research. Not that I blamed the school—they did what they could for students, and I'd been fortunate to have some highly qualified and supportive instructors. Upon accepting the internship at Scientific Innovations, I'd been encouraged to research, investigate, and hypothesize. The opportunities had been limitless, the only barriers self-imposed. Once my mind was given creative leeway, I developed projects that seemed a distant dream while in school.

"But this is....I wouldn't have....," Dr. Sebastian was rarely flustered. His eyes tracked the information as he double checked my research, swiping pages back and forth, comparing and calculating numbers in his head. Skepticism and disbelief gradually transformed into acceptance and awe, and he nodded his head at the concrete proof I'd presented. "When you first began investigating ways of traveling to Posarius, I was quite certain you were headed down an unproductive path, yet I kept my promise not to interfere with your research. But this....Simon, do you understand what you've done? You're on the brink of the single most important discovery in the history of our science. This may very well save not only our people, but those on Posarius as well. I couldn't be prouder if you were my own son."

We'd discovered and made contact with Posarius nearly four years ago, shortly before Earth had fallen. Like Tage, Posarius was struggling for survival. While our planet's protein sources were dying off and water levels were critical, Posarius suffered no shortages whatsoever in those areas. Their problem was overcrowding. They'd simply run out of habitable land. Tage had an abundance of land to offer. The problem? Posarius was light years away, and with our current technology, it would take thousands of years to reach them.

At Dr. Sebastian's words of praise, a warm sensation fluttered in my chest and expanded, spreading into every fiber of my being. Despite all my accomplishments, awards, and recognition, despite the way I'd excelled at school and been placed on an accelerated career track, knowing Dr. Sebastian was proud of me was far more gratifying. "Thank you, sir. That really means a lot."

"After meeting you a few years ago, I knew you had the capacity to make great strides in science, but you've more than surpassed my expectations. Are all the calculations complete then?" He continued to scrutinize my data pad.

"Nearly. I have some sequencing to follow up on, and should be ready to run initial testing within a few weeks."

He rose from his chair and came around the desk where I stood before him. "Excellent." He handed back my data pad while resting his arm across my shoulders. "I'm beginning to think offering you that highly-coveted internship position might just be the smartest decision I've ever made. And considering all I've done, that's a bold statement to make." He winked. "Send me your follow up reports by the end of next week, and we'll schedule the beta testing."

⚏

Several hours later, I was still in the lab. The rumbling in my empty stomach signaled I'd forgotten to eat dinner again. When I worked at home, Evan usually forced me to break for meals, but at SI, I tended to immerse myself in work and lose all track of time.

"I heard that, Simon," Alyssa said. "You forget you're a mere human who requires sustenance to live? Again? Come downstairs with me and grab something to eat before you pass out. Your brother would kill me if I let that happen."

Alyssa and I shared a lab, and she'd become a friend, something that was a rarity in my life. Working alongside each other for so long had allowed us to learn each other's habits, while still maintaining a semblance of distance and privacy. Ethics were of the highest importance in our field because, although working on different projects, those who shared labs were privy to each other's research and had ample opportunity to take advantage of that fact.

But I trusted Alyssa implicitly, and she assured me the feeling was mutual. We'd bounced ideas around and openly discussed our research, developing a healthy respect for each other. "I guess it's been a while since I ate." I glanced at the time and calculated it had been nearly twelve hours since my last meal. No wonder my body was protesting.

There was no such thing as regular hours at SI—everyone was free to set their own schedule and come and go as they pleased, as long as their work produced results. If a scientist's projects or research produced nothing useful over a period of time, they were released from SI. Of those who had been asked to leave, it was as if they'd vanished from the planet or ceased to exist. They were never heard from again, their careers destroyed. Subsequently, the pressure to produce was an oppressive weight all of us felt every minute of every day. SI was the pinnacle, the top of the food chain. Everyone in the scientific community aspired to be a part of it.

Our footsteps echoed through the sterile white hallways that were largely void of people at this late hour. Each wing of the facility required security clearance to enter. Employees scanned the identification badge hanging around their necks, then personal codes were typed into keypads. Most of us only had clearance for the wing where our labs were located, but the common areas, like the food court we were heading toward, were open to everyone.

"What do you think is down this wing?" she asked. "It's not the typical scanner, and I've never seen anyone enter or exit. Don't you think that's kind of odd?"

I'd passed that way hundreds of times, but had never given much thought to it. SI was massive, spanning dozens of acres of land, and housing numerous departments and areas I'd never seen.

I shrugged. "Perhaps some top secret project, or a storeroom for controlled chemicals." My voice trailed as my mind and body focused on the enticing smells snaking down the hallway from the food court.

Once there, we browsed our options, considering each of the late evening/early morning offerings. To the chefs' credit, they'd developed creative and appetizing dishes with limited amounts of protein. The selections were always heavy on fruits and vegetables, with smaller portions of legumes and soy products, and we were fortunate to have those. After making my selection, I joined Alyssa, placing my tray and data pad on the table.

"What I wouldn't give to have a big, juicy steak." Alyssa stared wistfully at her vegetable stir fry with soba noodles.

"You remember steak? I've only seen pictures."

"Technically I've never actually tasted it, but I've dreamed of eating it. The taste was blissful, divine—it was almost a religious experience."

I laughed at the idea of a teenage girl's dreams consisting of steak instead of boys—or whatever usually paraded through their nocturnal thoughts.

Alyssa focused on something over my head, and her posture stiffened. Only one person could cause a reaction like that. "Look alive. Here comes Dr. Sebastian."

"Keeping some late hours tonight, I see?" Dr. Sebastian placed his data pad on the table, then he ripped open a protein packet and dumped the contents into a cup.

Alyssa quickly wiped her mouth with a napkin. "Good evening, sir."

"Ms. Conley. Am I correct in assuming you'll have some good news for me at our progress meeting tomorrow morning?" He stirred the protein mixture.

"Oh, absolutely, sir. I've made significant advances since our last meeting." Alyssa's voice was unusually high-pitched, and the table vibrated as her leg bounced against it.

Finished mixing his drink, Dr. Sebastian tapped the spoon against the side of his cup, placed it on the table, then clasped my shoulder. "I trust you're aware of Simon's most recent ground-breaking achievement. Perhaps you could seek his advice with your own stalled research."

A crimson flush rose from Alyssa's neck up to the roots of her hair, and she swallowed heavily. "Yes, sir. Th—that's probably a good idea."

"Probably?" His icy gaze forced her to break eye contact and stare down at her plate.

"I'm calling it an evening, turning off my data pad for the night, and getting some much needed rest. Excellent work today, Simon." He squeezed my shoulder before retrieving his data pad from the table. "Ms. Conley? Make sure you're on time tomorrow."

Alyssa nodded, not even raising her head to acknowledge Dr. Sebastian as he turned to leave.

When he exited the food court, I reached under the table for her hand. It was icy and limp as I squeezed it. "Alyssa, I'm so sorry. He shouldn't have spoken to you like that. I know your project has slowed somewhat, but you've made some real progress over the past week."

She shook her head, continuing to look down. "No, he's right. He hinted at our last meeting that my time here may be coming to an end if I didn't produce results soon."

My eyes widened. "Why didn't you tell me? You know I'm always here for you, whether it's just support, brainstorming ideas, or getting a second pair of eyes on your research. We're friends, aren't we?"

She tipped her head up, unshed tears brimming her eyes, and attempted a smile that more closely resembled a grimace. "Yeah. We're friends, Simon, but I was too embarrassed to ask for help. You're working so much already, and I didn't want to bother you."

I really was overwhelmed, and had no idea how I'd find time to help Alyssa, but my friends were few and far between, and for her, I'd make time. "Helping you work on something that benefits Tage isn't bothering me, Alyssa. Send me an outline on my data pad tonight, and we'll sit down tomorrow and look over things before your meeting, alright?"

She sniffled, grabbed a napkin to wipe her nose, and then nodded. "Thanks, Simon."

I smiled and squeezed her hand again, then wondered where I'd find the energy to stay awake tonight and read through her notes.

♊

Exhausted, but with more work ahead of me, I caught the tram home after our late dinner. Or early breakfast. Toeing my shoes off after entering the house, I padded quietly up the stairs to my room, hoping not to wake Evan as I tiptoed down the hallway. Maybe a hot shower would give me the added boost I needed to work through Alyssa's project updates. On second thought, make that a cold shower. My eyes drooped, my neck and shoulders were taut, and I felt completely drained. A hot shower might relax me too much.

After drying off and putting on sweatpants and a t-shirt, I curled up on my bed and opened my data pad. It took only seconds for me to realize it wasn't mine, and I cursed myself for grabbing Alyssa's by mistake. In less than half that time, I concluded it wasn't Alyssa's data pad, but Dr. Sebastian's.

I froze.

Looking at another person's data pad was the ultimate invasion of privacy, the equivalent of peeking inside their heads and being privy to their innermost thoughts and secrets. Each pad required a ten-digit personalized code to gain access, but in our most base desire for instant gratification, many people kept theirs on standby to avoid reentering their code every time. And that's what Dr. Sebastian had done. Immediately, I shut the pad, horrified at the breach of trust I'd committed just by opening it. Surely he'd recognized the data pad he had wasn't his own. But then I recalled he'd planned on turning it off for the night.

Lying on my bed, literally at my fingertips, was a wealth of information I had no clearance for. Information some would give anything to possess.

I would never steal or sabotage another scientist's research—my strong ethical beliefs prevented me from even considering such a heinous violation. All of us were committed to the common goal of saving our planet and people, not to attaining individual glory. So in the overall scheme of things, would it hurt if I had a peek at other projects? Logic dictated that different perspectives could offer alternative solutions. I warred with myself a bit longer, weighing the pros and cons but, in the end, curiosity conquered all.

I squared my jaw, and for the first time in my life, trespassed into another person's boundaries, opening the data pad of my mentor and personal hero. The home screen displayed the usual options—daily calendar, contacts, communications, and music. Dr. Sebastian preferred to work with classical music playing in the background, claiming it was soothing for the soul and mind, as well as efficient at clearing out the clutter. Alyssa and I had played it in our lab, and she found it relaxing. I found I focused so deeply while working that I blocked out the music entirely.

My finger hovered over the icon for projects, knowing if I crossed this threshold, there was no coming back or undoing it. Again, I reminded myself we all worked for a common goal, and no one ever had to know what I'd done, so I tapped the screen.

It looked as if the files were organized by building wings, then the various projects and research teams listed below that. Selecting the wing where my lab was located, I skimmed through the names, noting my own, then Alyssa's. Maybe I could gain some insight if I studied the information in her file, something that would give me a hint in dealing with the obstacles she faced. That's how I justified it, anyway. A quieter, more subtle voice in the back of my head told me I could also learn if she really was close to being forced out of SI.

My eyes darted through Dr. Sebastian's notes and Alyssa's progress reports, and I rapidly came to the conclusion that she hadn't been exaggerating. In fact, it looked as if the situation was more critical than she knew, and the meeting with Dr. Sebastian tomorrow was her final opportunity to demonstrate advances since their prior session. I continued reading to the end of the report, then noticed a curious notation. 'Possibly transfer to Project Sacrifice.'

Project Sacrifice? The name wasn't familiar. Whatever the case, transferring Alyssa to another project instead of releasing her from SI was a positive action. I'd miss her as a lab partner, but having the space to myself for a while wouldn't cause any regret on my part. We'd also be able to maintain our friendship. If I didn't see Alyssa at work, it would be difficult to fit her into an already crowded schedule between my research, Evan, and Max.

But what was this program? I flipped back to the main file page and perused the project titles in each wing. Perhaps it was a new venture Dr. Sebastian thought would be right for Alyssa? Searching through the wing projects and main file page revealed nothing, so I returned to the home page.

A sword icon in the lower right hand corner was the only unexplored area, and I was pleased to see the heading label of Sacrifice when it opened. As I read, my pulse quickened, and my breathing became labored. The horror of its contents jolted me to my core, and something ugly twisted in my stomach. My mind refused to accept the evidence displayed before me, despite the meticulous updates documented and approved by Dr. Sebastian.

I didn't want to believe any of it, because if true, Dr. Lucas Sebastian was the most heartless and callous human being to ever walk the face of Tage.

"Evan, wake up." As deeply as he slept, I questioned why I'd been so quiet upon entering the house a couple of hours earlier. "Please, I need to talk to you."

Jostling his shoulder only brought out a groan. I shook the mattress, and he rolled to the other side. As a last resort, I ripped the covers from his warm body.

"What's your problem, Simon? What did I ever do to you?" He stretched across the mattress and reached to the floor, pulling one of the blankets back over him.

"I need to talk to you. It's important."

He rubbed his eyes. "Now? What could—Whoa. That's a heavy load you're carrying."

I knew once he was awake he'd feel my outrage and distress.

Evan dragged himself to an upright cross-legged position, giving me room to stretch out on my stomach, my head propped on my crossed arms. "What happened to make you feel this way?"

I explained how I'd come to have Dr. Sebastian's data pad in my possession, and the horrifying information I'd unearthed. "He's experimenting on humans."

Evan's brow furrowed. "But that's not forbidden. People volunteer to be lab subjects all the time, right?"

"Yes, but these subjects aren't consenting adults. Some of them were scientists released from SI due to lack of progress, and this explains why no one has heard from them. These former employees are in a locked, secluded wing, and very few employees have access. Subjects are strapped down against their will, and he's torturing them by withholding nourishment, testing food substitutes, and introducing foreign matter into their bodies. Some of them have had windows surgically installed over their abdomens to observe the effects of genetically altered foods on their digestion system. Pesticides have been applied to their skin, injected into their bloodstream, and forced down their throats. They've even been injected with the disease killing off our live protein sources so the effectiveness of new vaccines can be determined. Evan, what he's doing to them is barbaric and inhumane." I still found it nearly impossible to believe. Maybe I'd just been overcome with exhaustion, fallen asleep on my bed after the shower, and was caught up in a nightmare, my own data pad lying beside me.

"But that can't be possible." He shook his head. "Dr. Sebastian is a renowned scientist, the most important in his field. Why would he do something like this? He's the guy everyone wants to work with, and hopefully the savior of Tage, right?"

I rolled to my back, the enormity of the situation crushing every ounce of admiration and respect I'd had for my mentor. "That's the popular opinion. But the evidence is there. It's all documented on his data pad. This is something I'd have never thought him capable of." Twisting to my side, I faced Evan and propped my head on my hand. "I guess you can never truly know another person."

Evan picked at a loose thread on the blanket. "So, what happens now? What are you going to do with this information?"

"Well, he can't be allowed to continue hurting and killing innocent people." Just thinking about it roiled my stomach. Yes, we were scientists and our planet was dying sooner rather than later. Our situation was dire, but there were other paths to take, more humane ways to help us. Experimenting on humans wasn't an option.

"How do you know those scientists didn't volunteer for the program? And maybe the other subjects aren't so innocent. Maybe they were used to experiment on instead of being sent to The Realm. Do you think that's a possibility?"

Evan's questions gave me pause. Scientists who volunteered, knowing their career was over. Criminals used as test subjects instead of being sent away. Those were indeed possibilities. Perhaps they were given the choice of the experiment or The Realm, and what Dr. Sebastian was doing wasn't illegal after all, a prospect that allowed a sliver of hope to float in a sea of overwhelming doubt. "Those are excellent points, Evan. We have no way of knowing if that's the case. I don't remember seeing it mentioned in the file, but it's possible I missed it. Even probable, given how disturbing the information was."

Evan leaned against the headboard of the bed and stretched out his legs. "Maybe it's all legit and everything's above board. I hope that's the case, Simon, I really do, because I know what Sebastian means to you." He leveled his gaze at me. "But maybe that's not the case, and he's actually torturing people. You need to have a contingency plan. Would you confront him?"

My need for him to be innocent was deep-seated and nearly palpable, but Evan was right. A contingency plan was necessary in the event my mentor was guilty. "I don't know if I could do that. Before any accusations are made, I have to go over the files again, and if that's not conclusive, I'll have to see the lab for myself." I rolled to my back again and rubbed my eyes. "But that's a separate problem, because I have no clue where it could be."

Evan was silent, and I swiveled my head in his direction to see the line between his brows, indicating he was concentrating deeply. I wondered if his expression mirrored my own when I was focused on my projects. Just because we were identical twins didn't mean our mannerisms were the same.

I'd just begun mentally walking through the halls of SI in hopes of finding the hidden wing, when Evan interrupted me. "I don't think confronting Sebastian alone would be a good idea. If the guy is crazy and demented enough to experiment on people against their will, who knows what else he's capable of doing. Especially if he thought his career and reputation would be ruined, and faced spending the rest of his life in The Realm. You can't trust him anymore, and should report him anonymously if it turns out all of this is illegal. It's the safest option." I couldn't imagine Dr. Sebastian hurting me, or anyone else for that matter, but considering my recent discoveries, I was beginning to understand he wasn't the person I thought he was.

♊

After a few hours of restless sleep, I gave up and arrived at the lab earlier than usual the next day, because I knew Dr. Sebastian would soon discover the data pad in his possession wasn't his own. Evan had a friend who had instructed me in covering my tracks indicating which files I'd accessed. Why he'd have that particular skill set unleashed a flood of questions in my mind, but in the end, I was grateful my activities would go undetected.

I'd waited outside his office only minutes before he stepped off the tube and rushed down the hallway toward me. Upon meeting my eyes, he practically jogged to close the remaining distance between us. "Simon, I've just been looking for you at your lab. I'm afraid there's been some kind of mix-up."

"Yes sir, I came directly to your office this morning to return your data pad. They must have gotten switched at the food court last night." I held it out to him, and he wrenched it from my hands in his eagerness to possess it again. "I realized it wasn't mine when my own code failed to open it."

He examined the pad, then typed in his code, regarding me with suspicion. "And you weren't able to access any files?"

I shook my head. "After discovering the pad wasn't mine, I retraced my steps, concluding it could only be yours, and immediately closed it." I held his gaze, knowing if I looked away, he might interpret the gesture as dishonesty. Lying wasn't something I'd done often in my life, and Evan had coached me on what not to do before leaving home earlier this morning. It was a skill he'd perfected over the years in situations where he hadn't technically lied to our parents, but wasn't exactly forthcoming with all the details, either. And he'd told countless white lies to various girlfriends and gotten away with nearly everything.

Dr. Sebastian studied my face intently, and was apparently satisfied with what he saw. "Occasionally I'm lax about locking it, and wondered if I'd forgotten."

"No, sir. It was definitely locked last night. I entered my code several times before it occurred to me the pad wasn't mine." I smiled, hoping he thought I found the mix-up to be a humorous situation, and not an opportunity to discover the allegedly illicit experiments he'd been conducting.

"I'd be lying if didn't say I'd attempted the same thing this morning." He flashed a confident smile as he opened his leather case and retrieved my pad. I took it, relieved this deception was coming to an end. "Thank you, Dr. Sebastian. I'll be on my way to the lab now, and I'm sorry for the confusion."

"Think nothing of it, Simon. It was as much my fault as anyone's."

CHAPTER 9
EVAN
PRESENT DAY

Simon was alive. I knew what I'd felt. The question was—where?

I'd contacted Agent Deckard and he'd brought a team to scour the house, yard, and neighborhood, but they'd turned up nothing. Once again, no sign of him. All they'd had to go on was my word that I'd 'felt' my brother. Deckard had ever so gently implied that with the sunlight streaming through the window, my deep-seated need to find my brother, stirred and shaken with my clearly evident exhaustion, maybe I'd imagined the whole thing.

He'd even not so gently asked if I believed in ghosts. Which triggered a whole new rant on my part, and Deckard straining to maintain his professionalism. He'd asked me to contact him if I experienced any other 'episodes'.

I'd spent the day dozing on and off in Simon's room hoping for a sign of him, but all was quiet. A very small voice in the back of my mind wondered if Deckard might have been right, but that doubt was quickly extinguished.

Syd was shocked, but she understood our connection and believed me. She wanted to help, but we had no idea where to go from here.

I wasn't giving up. One way or another, I'd figure this out, but for now, I had to try and maintain my own professionalism and introduce Max to the team.

"Welcome our new team member, Max Delacort, a recent graduate of the Mindbender Academy, top of his class and handpicked by Gabriel." My team was gathered around the oblong table in my office, the hologram in the center displaying the night's assignments. I managed to say those words without cringing, but my jaw was clenched so tightly I feared my teeth might crack. I shot a quick glance toward Syd, and her expression was neutral. Isaac, Zia, and Amelia were unaware of my history with Max, and gave welcoming nods in his direction.

"It's a standard night, guys. Nothing requiring more than the usual two team members on each case. Isaac and Amelia, you're in lab A, Zia and Syd, lab B, and Max and I will be with Dr. Quill in lab C." Until Max was fully trained, Syd would have to work with Zia. Besides not wanting to train him, I'd be dealing with someone inexperienced and unaccustomed to the way I worked. After being friends and coworkers with Syd for so long, we could almost read each other's minds—nothing on the level I had with Simon, but similar. The familiarity made things smoother and seamless, for the most part. To say I was agitated was an understatement, but training was my responsibility, and something I took seriously. Especially after what happened to Maya. "Take some time to go over the specifics while the techs are prepping the clients."

While the team reviewed their assignments, I hung around in case there were questions—which also allowed me to delay my first session with Max. Glancing around the table, I observed the interactions among them. Isaac nodded at Amelia, then turned to Syd on his left. He pushed back his shoulder length dreads, draped his arm casually across the back of her chair, then leaned in and whispered something in her ear. Syd gave a tight smile that didn't reach her eyes, then moved away from him and shifted back in her chair, leaving no room for his arm. I brought my hand to my mouth to cover a smirk. I'd long suspected Isaac had a thing for Syd, and had even mentioned it to her a couple of times. She insisted he was permanently in the friend zone. He was a good guy and hard worker, with a great sense of humor and strong competitive streak. He also deserved a chance, but she refused to listen. Whatever.

I studied Zia, who was tapping away on her data pad. She was highly efficient, had no patience for anyone who wasted her time, and had a low tolerance for incompetence. A satisfied smile tugged at the corner of my mouth when I thought about the significant hurdles ahead of Max. He'd have to prove himself worthy of being her partner.

Beside her, Max's face was plastered with the scowl he'd always reserved just for me, but upon meeting my gaze, his features morphed into a neutral expression. At least he was trying.

"Questions, Max?"

"No. Just anxious to get started." He fidgeted in his chair, tapping his right index finger against the table.

"Max," Syd said, "you've only been in a simulator for training so far, right?"

His head shot in her direction.

"Yeah, but I logged more hours in the simulator than any other trainee. I know it's not exactly the same, but figured it can't be all that different from the real thing, right?" At Max's reply, there were giggles and snickers from around the table, and the anticipation and excitement in his eyes were replaced by tentative doubt. "Um...what's wrong? I mean, obviously working with a real person is different."

"Did they warn you about the side effects of the sedative?" Isaac asked, struggling to keep the smile from his face.

"Well, yeah, I know there's some disorientation the first few times."

Isaac snorted. "Disorientation? Evan, you'd better put the extra-large bucket beside Max's chair. I get the feeling he'll need it when he comes down."

Lines appeared between his eyebrows. "Bucket? No one mentioned anything about buckets in training."

"Come on guys, go easy on him." Amelia placed her hand on Max's forearm and squeezed it reassuringly. "The first several times Benders travel, we get nauseated and...well, it's a good idea to have a bucket beside your chair when you come back to your body. It's a natural reaction. It generally doesn't happen in sims, only with live clients."

Max stared at Amelia, wide-eyed. Surely he wasn't that clueless.

Isaac leaned forward, resting his crossed arms on the table. "We hurl, Max. Sometimes it's a lot, sometimes not so much, but we've all done it."

"Not all of us," Syd replied. "Evan never got sick. The first time he came down to his body, he stretched and sat up like he'd woken from a nap. While my head was in the bucket, he laughed his ass off. Didn't even offer to hold back my hair."

I snickered at the memory of Syd cursing me between her bouts of sickness. She'd been furious over my immunity to the sedative and traveling side effects.

Max's face was pale and his hands trembled slightly as he ran them through his hair. Amelia rubbed his back gently. "Don't worry, Max, it'll pass. It always does."

I rose from my chair and cleared my throat, signaling it was time to get serious before heading to the labs. "I'll see everyone at the end-of-shift debrief. Contact me if there are problems." Syd, Zia, and Isaac chatted as they trailed out of the room, while Amelia cast a sympathetic glance back in Max's direction. I couldn't help noticing again how Isaac stayed as close to Syd as she'd let him. He was probably disappointed I hadn't partnered them, but he and Amelia had worked together almost as long as Syd and I.

And then I was left alone with Max. Might as well get started.

♊

Max followed me into lab C, a nearly blinding white, round room with lofty twenty foot ceilings. In the middle were four reclined Bender chairs that enabled us to operate with double the usual number of team members for more complicated cases. The client stayed in a partitioned section designed to resemble an average bedroom, an aspect meant to make them feel relaxed and more comfortable. This setup also prevented the client from knowing the identity of the Benders assigned to his or her case. Seeing us in public, knowing we'd been inside their heads and privy to their innermost thoughts, could potentially make for awkward and uncomfortable situations on both sides. Some people weren't able to compartmentalize images and ideas, and we'd witnessed some pretty embarrassing memories.

Ky, the prep/monitor technician, stood over by the partition, observing the screen displaying Dr. Quill's vitals and REM cycles. "Is he out yet?" I asked, peeking around the partition. Doc was stretched out in bed with a blindfold covering his eyes, his chest rising and falling at regular intervals. He was a brilliant scientist, but the classic stereotype of a frazzled professor, with his graying hair usually splayed out in various directions, and eyes magnified several times over by his glasses. In mid conversation, his mind sometimes wandered and he'd suddenly change topics. It wasn't because of declining mental acuity. It was just that Doc's mind worked on more than one level concurrently, but sometimes the levels merged and what came out of his mouth seemed nonsensical to those around him.

"Almost." Ky smiled. "Doc is in here so often, he could probably do my job. New trainee?" He gestured over my left shoulder with his chin. "He looks a little intimidated."

I followed Ky's line of sight to see Max standing in the middle of the room, head tilted up toward the ceiling, turning in a slow circle, his mouth hanging open. Closing my eyes, I took a deep, calming breath. Really? He acted like a toddler seeing balloons for the first time. This was going to be a long night. "Max!"

His head snapped toward me, and he grinned sheepishly as he approached, looking embarrassed at being caught gawking.

I clenched my jaw, reminding myself I'd probably had the same reaction upon seeing the lab for the first time.

"Max, this is Ky, our tech for the case."

They nodded at each other, but Ky did a poor job at trying to hide his grin. "Our client is Dr. Paul Quill, a frequent flier. Syd and I usually handle his cases, but this is a simple locate and connect assignment to get you started."

While Max scanned Doc's file again, I turned to Ky. "Is Gabriel ready?" During cases, Gabriel stayed in a control room where he could audit each team. He had no way of observing what we saw inside the clients' minds, but with screens displaying the labs, and Bender vital signs lining the wall of the control room, he could oversee each assignment.

"Gabriel's a go." Ky sat at his station where he also monitored our vitals, as well as Dr. Quill's.

I quickly scanned Doc's file again to make sure there was nothing I'd missed. "Max, if you're ready, get in your chair so Ky can strap you in and attach your body temperature, heart, blood pressure, and respiration leads." Completing the final case checklist, I sent a copy to Gabriel.

While I was locking my data pad, Ky came up behind me and whispered low enough that Max couldn't hear. "I know it's the guy's first case, but his heart rate's through the roof. I'm afraid he's going to stroke out before he even gets the sedative."

I smiled to myself, enjoying the idea of Max being nervous and on edge. "I've got my doubts about him even making it through training. He might have been top of his class at the academy, but it wouldn't be the first time a trainee couldn't make the leap from simulations to real cases."

Ky chuckled. "Good luck in there."

After strapping myself in and attaching my leads, I glanced over at Max. Beads of perspiration peppered his forehead, and his left foot twitched nervously. I huffed out a breath. "This is a routine case, Max. Doc's a little eccentric and still prefers using paper over his data pad. Ideas hit him suddenly, and he has a habit of writing them on scraps, then misplacing them in lab coats, his home, offices of colleagues, and any place he does errands. I'm pretty accustomed to the workings of his thought center, so just follow my lead and ask questions when you have them. This is as standard a case as you'll come across. Got it?"

"S—sure, Evan. No problem." This was shaping up to be a fun evening for me, seeing Max without his usual overconfident attitude. Working with Doc so often, I honestly didn't expect this to take long, but then again, we'd had cases where the client's mind was in such disarray that it took us hours to make connections.

"Ky, we're ready to inject." In addition to being sedated, Benders were also trained in transcendental meditation to quiet our minds and focus our thoughts. In a way, traveling to the mind of the client was a form of astral projection. The sedative contained a drop of the client's blood, and having that miniscule amount of DNA in our system enabled us to target them after detaching from our bodies. After injection, we could be inside Dr. Quill's subconscious in a matter of minutes.

After injecting Max, Ky moved to my chair. "The usual half dose, Evan?"

"Yeah." After Ky withdrew the needle, I lay back in the chair, closed my eyes, and began relaxation techniques. Before long, I enjoyed the euphoric feeling of lightness and the surreal ability to move up-and-down and side-to-side in my mind. Pushing at the boundaries enclosing my head space, I felt them give and surrender me to the lab. From this point, I could look down at my body and Max strapped in our chairs, while Ky monitored us and Dr. Quill.

In my peripheral vision, I caught a flicker of something moving. Max had just detached from his body. Once Benders were in this floating, aimless kind of state, we only needed to focus on the client, and we'd instantly be taken to him because of the trace of blood in our system. The second I pictured Doc's face, I was hovering over his sleeping form, and gradually descended toward his supine body, slipping inside his mind.

Max wasn't there yet, but I made the decision to wait a couple of minutes before searching for him. Before being trained as a Bender, I couldn't have imagined what it would be like to invade someone's head and witness the inner workings of their mind. We entered the information center of the brain, which sounded pretty standard, but everyone was different.

In some clients, it resembled a welcoming foyer or vestibule, similar to an entryway into a building or home. Sometimes it was an industrial warehouse, with row after row of stocked shelves. Whatever the case, this room contained the ideas and memories of the client, but they could be organized—or disorganized—in very peculiar ways. Some people stored them on shelves like books, with each book representing something different, such as days, years, people, topics, etc. Others had file cabinets or drawers. I'd even seen decades old cookie jars used as a sorting system. It always helped to know a little bit about the client to understand how their mind worked.

Max appeared before me, and I begrudgingly gave him credit for making the transition this soon. A previous trainee had floundered about the lab, floating aimlessly before I'd dragged him forcibly inside the client's information center. Luckily, there was no way his subconscious could have drifted away into space. An invisible tether connected the Bender's subconscious to the body, so there was no chance of permanent separation.

Too bad—that might not have been such an awful thing in Max's case. "Feeling alright?" I asked.

Max nodded while regarding our surroundings. Dr. Quill's mind was similar to being in my bedroom at home—a lot of things going on, but randomly tossed in piles. In Doc's case, there were an abundance of papers in different sizes, shapes, and colors—everything from full-sized pages to corners torn from what looked like receipts attached to old fashioned bulletin boards, stuck in folders and notebooks, and leaking out of desk drawers. Experience had taught me most of his hiding places, and I had a general idea of where we should start our search. Doc was unorganized, but fairly predictable and nonthreatening. The best kind of client to work with.

"It's so different from the simulation, seeing what they're actually dreaming." Max stared in awe at the domed ceiling where Doc's subconscious thoughts and dreams were on display.

"Yeah, well even though his subconscious is pretty tame, just remember to keep an eye out for threats. During a case, you watch your partner's back no matter what. Simple retrieval cases can quickly turn into nightmares, got it?" Sometimes, even though the client gave permission to enter their minds, the brain sensed invasion by a foreign object—us—and made an attempt to protect itself, occasionally taking the form of a nightmare. It could be something as simple as trying to delay us by moving things around in the information center, or as dangerous as causing a disturbance such as an earthquake or storm.

The more threatening nightmares were a level four or level five, and Gabriel required us to undergo even more extensive defense training than the academy provided. Fortunately, Dr. Quill never felt endangered while we were in his mind—I think he was just relieved someone was there to make the connections.

"Sure, Evan. Let's get started." Max rifled through papers on the bulletin board.

Maybe I wouldn't have to hold his hand through the case after all, I thought, turning to the desk and beginning my search.

Chapter 10
Evan
Present Day

After Doc's case, as predicted, Max hung his head in the bucket. Being such a nice guy, I gave him adequate time to recover, but then I moved him onto another client. Diving into the next case was the best way to get acclimated in transporting between your own mind and another. He didn't need quite as much bucket time after the second client, so I told him we'd break for dinner.

"Hey, guys. Easy night?" Syd asked.

I slid into the seat beside her, while Max took the chair across from me.

"Max, you're looking a little paler than usual."

Isaac and Zia both snickered, knowing the cause of his condition.

I had no sympathy for him. They'd all gone through a sort of hazing ritual from other Benders, and it was their turn to dish it out to Max.

"Not bad," he replied, fidgeting in his seat and keeping his head down as he moved food around on his plate. I doubted he'd actually be able to eat anything.

Syd leaned forward, reached across the table and placed her hand on Max's forearm. "Hey, look at me."

He slowly lifted his gaze.

"We've all been through this, but I promise by the fifth case or so, it gets easier. You'll get this." She smiled reassuringly and squeezed his arm.

A flash of annoyance sliced through me, and I wondered whose side Syd was on. After all I'd been through with Max, how could she be so nice to him? As if sensing my thoughts, she cast a disappointed glance in my direction. I'd let down too many people in my life, so I reminded myself this was business, and she was only supporting a team member who was feeling defeated—something I'd do myself, but knew it would require reaching deep, deep inside to find encouragement for Max.

Talk turned to clients and other activities, but inevitably back to updates of Tage.

"Any news from your dad, Isaac?" Syd asked. Isaac's father worked in the SI department concerned with preserving our live protein sources. Because of the virus that had run rampant through our cattle, deer, and poultry populations for more than a decade, most people on Tage had forgotten what meat tasted like—if they'd even had the opportunity to sample it in their lifetimes. The supply had been cut from scarce to almost none for years. Our two oceans were overfished, and most seafood was considered a delicacy only the very wealthy could afford.

Isaac shook his head. "Things aren't good. The newest vaccine tanked, just like all the others. That's what makes it so discouraging. Every time a new vaccine is developed and seems effective, the virus mutates, making the vaccine useless. Even worse, some of the soybean crops aren't looking too healthy. What happens when we lose those?"

"What about the new study that guy was working on?" Zia asked. "Everyone got excited and said it looked promising. What was his name? You remember, that scientist sent to The Realm over a year ago."

"Dr. Sebastian. Lucas Sebastian," Max replied, staring directly at me from across the table. Syd's leg pressed up against mine, either from warning or support, I couldn't be sure.

"Yeah, that was his name. Did you know him, Max?"

"No, but my boyfriend was very familiar with him."

"Who was—" Isaac started.

"He was Simon's mentor," I interrupted. "Dr. Sebastian was the scientist who hand-picked my brother to work with him." With that statement, it seemed as if Isaac, Zia, and Amelia entered a cone of silence while making the connections between Max, Simon, and me. The rest of the team knew next to nothing about my twin, and I certainly hadn't told them about his relationship with Max. My private life was none of their business—off limits—but Max being part of the team could make that more difficult and too tempting to ignore.

Even Syd didn't know about Max and Simon, and her hand clutched my thigh under the table as she glared at me questioningly. I gave a slight nod, letting her know we'd discuss it later.

Isaac leaned forward, nearly whispering. "But wasn't Dr. Sebastian sent away for experimenting on humans?"

I nodded once, then looked down at my plate, wishing this whole conversation was over.

"But, if Simon was working with him, wouldn't he have known about the illegal experiments?"

My whole body tensed at Isaac's words, while Max's fist struck the table, sounding like the crack of a baseball against a bat, and dinner trays slid sideways. "Absolutely not! Simon knew nothing about the experiments, and was horrified when he found out what Sebastian was doing. Don't ever think he could be involved with any activity that caused those people to die. One of his best friends was a victim," Max growled through clenched teeth.

Isaac couldn't have looked more surprised if Max had physically slapped him. His eyes slid over to mine in question.

"Never." I scowled at him, my voice low and even.

Isaac held up his hands in surrender. "Hey, I'm sorry, guys. I didn't mean to imply anything. I swear it was just curiosity." Zia and Amelia looked simultaneously shocked at Max's outburst, and relieved they weren't on the receiving end.

"They know you weren't accusing Simon. We're all good here, right boys?" Sydney asked.

I mumbled something that sounded more like a grunt, and after a few moments, Max nodded, but that didn't stop him from staring down Isaac every few minutes.

Amelia cleared her throat and shifted uneasily in her chair. "So, um, Evan, can I ask what Simon was working on with Dr. Sebastian?"

Not that I wanted to talk about my brother, but I'd never let anyone think he'd been involved with Sebastian's inhumane experiments. "He was working on a way to travel between here and Posarius."

Amelia's eyebrows shot up in surprise. "But Posarius is in the next galaxy, more than five billion miles away, and he was what, only sixteen years old?"

Sitting back in my chair, I folded my arms over my chest and smirked. "He might have been young, but Simon's a genius, and that's why Sebastian chose him when he was only fourteen."

"Seriously?" Isaac asked. "That's amazing, Evan, I had no idea. So, Simon got all the brains, huh?"

I gave him a dark look, kicked at his leg under the table, and smiled in pleasure when he yelped.

Zia leaned forward. "What happened to his work after he disappeared? That's a crucial project, and if he was making progress, wouldn't someone have taken over where he left off?"

I shrugged my shoulders, because I honestly didn't know. I'd been plunged into a world of loss and unbearable guilt after Simon went missing, and my focus was on who had taken him and where. With us being identical twins, there had even been speculation that I'd been the target, and whoever had taken Simon took the wrong twin, but all things considered, there was no reason anyone would have wanted me. Then again, investigators never found a motive for taking Simon, either.

"Someone took a lot of his research," Max said.

My eyes shot over to him in surprise. "What?"

"His research. All of his files from the Posarius project were missing, both from his data pad and backups. He was frantic and in a tailspin, thinking about everything that had been lost, and was trying to sort it all out and recover the data."

"When did this happen?"

"A few months before he disappeared."

"Simon never mentioned any of this to me."

"He'd planned to tell you about it when you got home that evening, but you never gave him a chance. Maybe things would have been different if you'd thought about Simon instead of yourself." Max's words dripped contempt.

Syd stared at me in question, brows raised, while Isaac, Amelia, and Zia looked uncomfortable, probably wishing they were anywhere else. His revelation shocked me, and another piece of my heart chipped away, because I knew what that catastrophe would have done to Simon. The loss would have been staggering, and must have required a tremendous effort to keep those feelings from overflowing to me. Or maybe they had, and I'd been too wrapped up in what was going on in my own life.

Just something else Simon had hidden from me.

Syd clamped onto my leg under the table and whispered so no one could hear. "What does he mean about that night, Evan?"

It felt like all the air had been sucked from the room, slowly smothering me. She wouldn't let this go, and everyone at the table could feel the animosity between Max and me. Syd had known about it for years, of course, but was intuitive enough to sense she wasn't privy to the whole story. I cringed inwardly, knowing it was time to reveal the truth about what happened that night, but dreading having to relive it and see her reaction at my behavior. Faced with the knowledge that I was a horrible, selfish person and could have saved my brother might push her away from me permanently.

Chapter 11
Simon
One Year Ago

I'd taken Evan's advice and turned in Dr. Sebastian anonymously. Without proof, my accusations wouldn't have been taken seriously— especially considering they were against the brilliant scientist who'd created the ground-breaking SI. He was also a maniacal, narcissistic psychopath who held no regard for other human beings, unable to comprehend the basic concepts of right and wrong, humane and inhumane.

As expected, I'd never seen Alyssa again after returning Dr. Sebastian's data pad. She'd never arrived in the lab that morning at our appointed review time. With my newfound knowledge of Project Sacrifice, I was certain she'd been sent there against her will. Just the thought of her becoming an experiment victim, knowing the horrible atrocities committed against them, sent me into a tailspin, and I was desperate to locate her, knowing her life was in danger.

Once I was aware of Project Sacrifice, determining the secret lab location was nearly effortless. After intense review of SI's layout, I'd come to the conclusion the locked wing Alyssa had asked me about, a door I'd passed every day for nearly two years, was the logical location of the secret lab. Getting in that clandestine lab was the challenge.

Having someone working with me would have been advantageous, but there was no one I trusted enough to confide in. If word spread of my actions, the outcome could be me lying in the lab bed next to Alyssa. I'd begun traveling past that wing more often, at various hours throughout the day and night, hoping to see someone enter or exit. Time wasn't on Alyssa's side, and after seeing no activity for several days, I'd asked Evan to contact his friend who'd assisted me in erasing my tracks in Dr.

Sebastian's data pad.

With his help, I'd gotten past the doors and, beyond all hopes and expectations, other than the experiment subjects, no one was there. What I'd discovered would visit me in nightmares for the rest of my days—unspeakable acts and cruelties committed against people who'd never done anything to deserve what happened to them. Recognition of several people I'd worked with, or what was left of them, left me shaken to my core.

My indisputable evidence had initially resulted in shock, disbelief, and outrage. Sebastian and those who'd assisted with Project Sacrifice were forcibly removed from SI, then sentenced to the Criminal Realm. Other than Sebastian, the names of those who'd worked on the project had been kept private in order to avoid harassment of their innocent families. Thousands had gathered to see him transported, his victims having been their sons, daughters, husbands, and wives. Curses and insults rang out as guards pushed and dragged him toward the gate. I'd arrived early and gotten a front row seat, needing to see this through for the loss of my friend.

Upon recognizing me in the crowd, Sebastian managed to stop in front of Evan and me, struggling against the guards' attempts to move him forward. His usual rigid posture and air of importance had been replaced by desperation and a disheveled appearance. "I know it was you, Simon."

My attempts at anonymity had failed.

"Don't you realize what you've done? Eliminating me means certain death for Tage and its citizens. Without my guidance, you'll never find a solution!"

His arrogance astounded me. Despite his fall from grace, the suffering and death, he still thought our survival was hopeless without him. "How could you subject all those people to such torture against their will? Who put their fates into your hands?"

He laughed bitterly. "The rest of you lack imagination. You need someone like me to make the hard decisions, to separate the contributors from the dead weight." Sebastian's head gestured toward Evan, and my body stiffened in response. He didn't even know Evan and, like our parents, assumed because he wasn't a scientist, he held no value in society. "None of those people were ever going to benefit SI. Their loss is inconsequential, leaving more resources for those who work for them."

"You're a sick man, Sebastian. Somewhere along the way, your inflated ego and narcissistic tendencies edged out common sense and humanity." I leaned in closer, speaking only so he could hear. "Besides, we both know I'm quite capable of finding a solution without you, and already accomplished something you never could." When I pulled back, his eyes burned with rage, and the guards tightened their hold as he strained at his bonds. This may have been the first time anyone dared to insult his intelligence.

His voice was low and laced with venom. "Know this, Simon. The Realm can't hold me. This isn't the last time you'll see me." Spittle flew from his mouth, and Evan lunged in his direction. I jerked his arm back, anticipating his reaction after feeling the spike in his temper over the dead weight remark.

As the guards fought to drag him to the gate, Sebastian kept his smug, hate-filled gaze on me as long as possible, and despite the fact no one had ever escaped the Realm, a quake of doubt snaked through my body. There was always a first time for everything.

Months later, the details of that threatening conversation were still crisp in my mind. When my files had vanished, I'd suffered almost a temporary paralysis. My thought processes were skewed and faulty, and my actions toward the recovery team had been closer to Evan's behavior than my own. I'd berated them, questioned their intellect, and cursed their worthless processes, all while rampaging through their offices and generally making an ass of myself. They reassured me the files would be located, stating this was the first time in history anything like this had disappeared without leaving a trail.

The first time. With that incantation running through my head, I calmed myself, snapped back into Simon mode, and reengaged my highly logical brain. Both Dr. Sebastian and my project files departing Tage around the same time couldn't be coincidental. Despite his actions, there were some who supported what he'd done and, if asked, would probably have assisted him in stealing my work and somehow getting it to him.

Once I'd learned about Project Sacrifice, I'd made excuses to cancel our weekly progress meetings, determined not to give him access to my final calculations. I was convinced he'd somehow use my discovery for nefarious reasons, instead of the purpose for which it was intended. Although I'd most likely never be able to prove he was responsible for the loss, only a person of his brilliance and familiarity with internal systems could have managed it.

I'd also experienced some unusual phenomena the past few weeks. Sometimes while working in my lab, I had the distinct impression I wasn't alone. No one was with me in the lab physically—the presence was closer to an energy, but nothing tangible. With a nearly eidetic memory, I'd been recreating my files in a journal, no longer trusting the internal SI systems or my data pad. Considering the strange occurrences I'd experienced lately, it was crucial the information be transferred where someone could find it, and some instinct was urging me to increase the pace.

This morning, everything changed. My peripheral vision detected a flash of light and, already on edge, I spun in that direction. A low rumbling sound filled my ears and vibrated deep in my chest. The energy I'd felt had become almost tangible and heavy, and my scalp prickled as my hair raised, nearly standing on end. In the corner of my lab, the mysterious white light blazed once more, then sputtered as if searching for something to feed on.

With the brilliant flares, I had to squint, but during one longer flash, I was able to identify a face before the light snapped out of existence, the vibrations halted, and my hair fell back into place. As he'd promised, Dr. Lucas Sebastian had nearly found a way out of the Realm. He was coming for me, and I needed to make contingency plans.

♊

The door swished open silently, the sound barely detectable. I paused a moment before stepping over the threshold, allowing my eyes time to adjust to the low lit room before me. Panic and nausea came in waves. Knowing the horrible discoveries awaiting me in the darkened lab, my body resisted forward movement, but I pushed on. My mind understood this was a recurring nightmare, but I had no way of controlling the outcome. It was the same every time.

I shivered involuntarily from the blanket of coldness that wrapped itself around me, seeping through my skin and penetrating my bloodstream. My hand trembled as I lifted it to the control panel and turned up the lights. Rows of beds lined the walls to the right and left of me, their occupants unmoving and corpse-like. I shuffled silently down the aisle separating them, and avoided looking at the lifeless bodies on either side of me, knowing the bed I sought was halfway down. Swallowing past the growing lump in my throat, I concentrated on my destination and continued moving. And then I was there, standing at the bedside and staring down at the occupant, tubes leading from her stomach and throat to machines and an IV bag attached to her hand. I looked at the atrophied arm muscles, and knew the legs beneath the sheet would have a similar condition after being confined to this bed for so long.

Tears rimmed my eyes, and again I silently begged forgiveness for not finding her sooner. My body collapsed in sobs at Alyssa's fixed and unresponsive pupils. I knew my friend was gone forever. Wiping my face with the sleeve of my lab coat, I forced myself to witness the heinous experiments my mentor had been conducting. Alyssa's hands clawed at me as she tried to scream around the tube in her throat, her widened, scared eyes pleading for help.

Jolting awake, I gasped for breath, searching for her, uncertain where I was. The bed dipped, and a concerned face came into my field of vision, his voice speaking in soothing tones as he wrapped his arms around me, and my body crumpled against his chest.

"Was it Alyssa again?" Max asked softly.

I nodded, still unable to speak as my heart thundered in my ears. Once I'd broken into the lab housing Project Sacrifice, I'd realized I was too late to help Alyssa or anyone else. The guilt still hung like a permanent weight dragging me down. I wondered if I'd ever be rid of it.

Max hugged me tighter, waiting patiently for me to talk.

When my pulse returned to normal, I eased back. "Why did you let me fall asleep? You know how behind I am on my project."

"Simon," he said, his thumb lightly tracing what I'm sure were dark circles under my eyes, "you were dead on your feet. Lost files or not, you can't keep going at this pace or you really will be dead. And I prefer my boyfriend to be alive." Max's teasing smile made my own mouth turn up at the corners, then he leaned forward and kissed me gently. "Alyssa would never blame you for what happened to her. I know deep down on some level you understand that." I nodded, but remained unconvinced.

Max squeezed my shoulder, then stood and moved back to his desk.

I reached across the bed for my journal. "I do, but I'll never forgive myself for not being quicker in getting to them. Maybe I could have saved her and some of the others."

"You'll never know what might have happened. You did the right thing, Simon. As much as I hate to agree with your brother, Evan was right when he advised you to turn in Sebastian anonymously."

I frowned at Max's comment. After the first time he'd asked me out, I warred with myself about continuing the relationship, knowing Evan wouldn't approve. Conflict between us was nonexistent, and the thought of anything affecting our bond unsettled me. But Max refused to give up on me. After weeks of trying to set aside my feelings for him, I knew it was pointless. We'd been together for a little over six months, and I still hadn't told Evan. Keeping this secret from him was crushing me. Being unable to share this important part of my life felt disloyal, and he'd sensed it. He'd questioned me, but I'd assured him my fluctuating emotions were a result of the fiasco with Dr. Sebastian.

"Simon? Are you with me?"

My head snapped back to Max, and I realized he'd been talking to me, when my mind had been elsewhere. "Yes, sorry." I swiveled on the bed to face him. "You have my undivided attention."

He snorted. "I know better than that. Your brain is incapable of focusing on only one thing at a time." His amber eyes sparkled as he teased me. "Any updates on your project files?"

"No." Anger and frustration clouded my mind, replacing the anguish over Evan and Alyssa. "Data Recovery has been unable to locate anything, and I refuse to believe no footprints or remnants were left behind. The file was far too large to disappear into cyberspace without leaving a trail. I was told even the backups of the backups were nonexistent."

"I'm sorry, babe." Max's eyes were full of sympathy. "I can't imagine losing years of work in the span of a second. You know I'll help you any way I can. I just don't know what to do."

I reclined against the pillows and opened my journal to where I'd left off before passing out from exhaustion. "Just being able to talk to someone about it helps more than you know."

He frowned. "You still haven't told Evan about the files?"

Max's words clenched my heart. Yet another thing I'd been keeping from my twin. Evan had been completely wrapped up in applying for the Mindbender Academy. He'd finally found something he wanted badly, a way to contribute that would make our parents proud of him, and he'd thrown his heart and soul into it. The last thing I wanted was to distract him with my own problems. Becoming a Bender was everything to him. Even Max had shown some interest in the program.

Max released a breath. "Simon, you know I try to stay out of your twin thing with Evan. That relationship is amazing, complicated, and strange all by itself without me getting in the middle, but what's going to happen if he finds out about both us and your files? Like you said, the two of you have never kept secrets, and now you're hiding two mighty big ones."

I sighed and slumped lower against the pillows. Make that three secrets from Evan, and one from Max. I hadn't told either of them about the strange occurrences and the haste to record my files in a journal. If something did happen to me, I'd handle it, but I couldn't bear the thought that either of them might be harmed as a result. Somehow, I'd leave a trail for them. "I know. We can't keep having these clandestine meetings at your dad's place forever, especially since he's returning in a few weeks." I rolled to my side, bent my arm, and rested my head on my hand. "I've been thinking about it, and decided Friday after Bender training might be the appropriate time to tell him. I'm confident Evan will be accepted into the program, which will make him ecstatic, and possibly more accepting of us."

Max tilted his head, looking skeptical. "Years of animosity between him and me, months of you keeping us a secret, and then the project files? I don't see Evan opening his arms and welcoming me to the family."

"That's not quite how I imagine it unfolding either, given his stormy emotions when you're around. But it's time Evan met the Max I know, not the nemesis he claims you to be." I rose from the bed and padded over to where Max sat at his desk. Leaning over, I placed my hands on the desk, trapping him between my arms, and gazed into those amber eyes that first caught my attention. "People are multifaceted, and you've taught me not all things can be explained by science, such as the fact that I love you." He couldn't contain his smile as I bent down to kiss him.

Chapter 12
Evan
One Year Ago

As far as memorable days in my life went, this one was the pinnacle. I'd done it. I'd been accepted to the Mindbender Academy at Scientific Innovations. After a strenuous and challenging six-week evaluation course, learning the ins and outs of what a Bender actually did, trying to impress the evaluators, and worrying every day if I'd even make the cut, I'd finished at the top of my class. The sun streamed through the leaves of the soaring trees overhead, creating disjointed shapes resembling puzzle pieces on the sidewalk. I tilted my head up towards the warmth, a smile sliding across my face. This would show my parents I didn't have to be a scientific genius like Simon to help Tage. Maybe Bender duties weren't as critical as a scientist's, but I'd be providing crucial support, and doing something that would make them look at me the same way they did my brother.

With the unprecedented increase in staff stress and sleep disturbances last year, SI announced the Mindbender program would be opening its doors to students and allowing them to complete their education with on-site tutoring. I'd felt pieces lock into place, and an overwhelming sense of finding where I belonged. The idea of being in someone else's head intrigued me like nothing else, and knowing I had a chance to escape the walls of this school and be a part of such an adventurous program had me ramped up so high, I doubted I'd survive not being accepted. Simon had been right all along when he'd told me I was a natural for the position.

"People like you, Evan, and they follow you," he said, the day I'd *submitted my application. For the past half hour, Simon had been giving me a pep talk while I sat on his bed, legs crossed, rocking back and forth,*

too worked up to sit still.

"You're a natural leader who makes sound team decisions without shining the spotlight on himself. I've observed it on the field and in group projects at school. Because of that, people respect and trust you. It's an inherent trait, something that can't necessarily be taught, and will give you a distinct advantage over other applicants."

It sounded logical coming from Simon's mouth—everything he said was logical, but it did nothing to curb my nervousness.

"Now, will you please take a few deep breaths and calm down so I can get some work done? I've felt your excitement and apprehension all day. It's been quite a distraction and difficult to block. Go for a run. Do something, anything, to work off your energy."

All those nights I'd stared wide-eyed at the ceiling, unable to sleep, worried about not making the cut. Then, when Syd and I had both been accepted into the evaluation program, I'd worried about what would happen if she was accepted to the academy and I wasn't—or the other way around. But Syd was also going to be a Bender, scoring not far behind me, and I'd be training with my best friend.

A perfect day. I couldn't wait to get home and tell Simon, but with the anticipation running rampant through my veins and making my skin tingle, he'd probably already figured it out on his own. Still, I was anxious to share the news, and increased my pace to a jog.

The closer I got to home, the stranger the vibes were. My own happiness flooded the surface of our shared kettle of emotions, but underneath that, I felt another kind of excitement. It was coming from Simon, but it was different, a feeling that hadn't crossed over to me before. Butterflies flitted in my stomach, sweat coated my palms, and my heart thudded against my chest. This wasn't a foreign reaction for me, but coming from Simon? Definitely unusual.

I threw open the front door and tossed my bag over the back of the couch. "Simon, you here?" Normally he was at SI this time of day, but he'd mentioned he'd be working at home today. The kitchen and living room were empty, other than the mound of dishes in the sink and clothes strewn about—I'd take care of all that later. I charged up the stairs and turned left down the hallway toward our bedrooms. His door was closed—nothing new since it was always shut when he was busy—but I heard the murmur of voices.

Wait...sweaty palms, swirling stomach, pounding heart. More than one voice. Either he was sick and talking to himself, or Simon had a girl in his room. A grin split my face. My perfect day just reached new heights.

Creeping to the door, I put my ear against it. Wouldn't want to walk in on anything too embarrassing, but there was no way I'd let this momentous occasion pass without some kind of recognition from me. I couldn't quite make out the low murmuring, but if there was talking, they couldn't be in too much of a compromising situation. Gently turning the door knob, I pushed open the door.

And my gaze fell upon Simon pinned against his dresser, held in place by Max Delacort.

Simon's hands rested on Max's chest and his eyes widened as they locked with mine, while Max's head jerked in my direction. And my earlier excitement and anticipation were trampled into shreds by the rage racing through my veins.

I closed the gap between us in the span of a breath, launching myself in their direction. Max moved to back away, hands raised in surrender. He'd only made it a half step before I shoved him against the wall, seized his shirt collar and drew my fist back.

"Evan, no! Don't hurt him!" Simon clutched my shoulders, attempting to pull me away, but I held my ground.

"Back away, Simon," I growled. The satisfaction I'd feel from pulverizing Max's face was within reach and I wanted it desperately. He held my gaze, jaw set and chin tilted up, challenging me. Which made me want to hurt him even more. I drove my fist into his jaw, whipping his head sideways. Max's knees buckled, and he slid down the wall, but I wasn't about to let him off that easily. He must have bitten his lip, and I grinned in pleasure at the blood trickling from his mouth.

Still gripping his collar, I slammed him against the wall again, and heard a satisfying crack when his head smacked against it. As if I were in a tunnel, I heard Simon screaming at me in the distance, but the blood thudding through my ears drowned out his words. I felt a dull ache in my fist from the first punch, but that pain was nothing compared to what Max would feel, and I readied myself for another blow.

Max's eyes widened in horror, but he wasn't looking at me. "Simon, no...don't," he choked out.

My twin ducked under my arm and stood between us, facing me, blocking my view of Max, while Max...tried to push him away?

"What are you doing, Simon? Are you *trying* to get hurt?" I asked.

This time he shoved my chest hard, putting his whole body into it—which still didn't have much of an effect, but I released Max and dropped my fist, backing away a few steps.

"Don't touch him again, Evan. Max wasn't hurting me. We're together." Simon's chest rose and fell rapidly as he slid his hand back to grasp Max's, tugging him forward.

His words crashed into me, sucking the air from my lungs, and I staggered backwards, as if I'd been the one hit. "Together?"

Simon turned to Max and examined his mouth, wiping away the blood, then rubbing it on his pants. "Yes, we're together. He's my boyfriend." He cast me an icy sideways glance as he continued to inspect Max's jaw.

Max was Simon's boyfriend? Max, the idiot who'd mistaken Simon for me and beaten him, not even stopping when Simon didn't fight back, holding his hands up in resignation. Max, who had been a thorn in my side since the day we'd met, competing against me for everything, no matter how small. Competing with me for *Abbi*! And now Simon was defending *him*? "I don't know what lies Max has been telling you, but do I need to remind you what happened that night in the park? And with Abbi? You can't trust anything he says. Let me take care of him, and I promise he'll never touch you again."

Max narrowed his eyes and scowled at me, which only confirmed what I'd said. He was upset I'd discovered what he was up to.

"I'm not lying," he said, gently pulling Simon's hand away from his mouth, but not releasing it. "I understand where your head's at right now, Evan, I get it. But it was an honest mistake that day. Even then, I wanted to be with Simon. Months before that actually, but didn't know how to tell him." He turned his head toward my brother, who smiled at him in a way I'd never seen—Simon, who rarely smiled unless he'd made a breakthrough in the lab, and almost never at people. The way Max looked at him almost convinced me he really cared, but for Simon to believe it, he had to be a good actor. "I was a moron, and there's no excuse for what I did. It's caused me regret every minute since it happened, and I've apologized."

He'd apologized. Right. Max had clearly fooled Simon, but I wasn't that gullible, and there was no way I'd let him take advantage of my brother and hurt him again. By the way Simon was looking at him, this kind of pain would be worse than the physical blows he'd gotten from Max that day. I couldn't let that happen. "Simon, no one doubts your intelligence, but when it comes to dealing with people, you put your trust in the wrong ones. I'm trying to help you, to keep him from hurting you again."

Simon closed his eyes, took a deep breath and released it, then gazed evenly at me. "I understand your need to protect me, but Max and I have been together for six months. He's had countless opportunities to injure me, but he hasn't. And we've discussed Abbi. Something else you should consider is the last time the two of you had an altercation was when Max mistook me for you. We're hoping you'll agree to lay your adversarial history to rest and make a new start."

His words were like a punch in the gut. Simon and Max had been together for six months? And I was just now hearing about it? Surely I'd misunderstood. We shared everything, knew all there was to know about each other, our emotions intertwined. Simon would never keep something like this from me, not something this important and life-changing. "Six months? You've been together for six months....and you never told me?"

The smile on Simon's face faded when he felt the weight my words carried.

"I was going to tell you." He dropped Max's hand and took a step forward, reaching for me. "We'd planned to talk to you today. That's why Max is here. I wasn't sure how to tell you, and I asked for his help."

I shook my head in disbelief. It felt like there was a knife in my stomach, twisting and slicing. "You asked Max for his advice on how to talk to your brother, your *twin* brother. Someone he's hated from the day we met. You asked *him* for help telling me you're dating. You asked someone who struck you and drew blood, then continued hitting you when you didn't fight back, for help talking to me. To *me*, Simon? Help me here, because I'm not understanding the logic."

Simon licked his lips, and his right eye twitched—his nervous tells. But I didn't need to see those tells to know how he felt. "I'd anticipated you wouldn't have a positive response at learning about our relationship."

"Good guess." Max moved even with Simon and opened his mouth as if to say something.

I held up my hand to stop him. "Not a word, Max. If you need help keeping your mouth shut, I'll gladly give it."

That made him think twice, and he snapped it closed.

"Stop being so belligerent and listen!" Simon said. "You're drawing conclusions before you have all the information. Take a breath and feel, don't talk." He placed his hand on my forearm. We'd always felt each other's emotions, but physical contact amplified it, making it bigger and unmistakable. "Please, for me." His eyes pleaded for my understanding and acceptance.

But I couldn't give it, not yet. The wound was too fresh and raw. I was bleeding out. But I'd try, for Simon.

I closed my eyes, moving the focus away from my spinning, escalating cloud of shock, hurt, and disappointment, and into Simon. Since we were children, Simon's inner space had usually been more quiet and orderly, especially since I'd shown him how to compartmentalize his ideas. His space wasn't exactly peaceful, but definitely not as frenzied as mine. The best way to describe it was to compare the noise of an all-night party, music blaring, people laughing, an air of excitement and uncertainty about what would happen next, versus a room lined with walls and walls of drawers, everything organized and cataloged, with no end and no beginning, just infinite possibilities. Instead of music, there was always the sound of Simon speaking to himself, his subconscious continually working, theorizing, fitting the puzzle pieces together.

It was different this time. Structure and calm predominated, but colors were brighter, the air not as heavy from the stress of his work. I'd never experienced anything like this from Simon, this lightness of being, the feelings circulating through him. He was happy—ecstatic, even. Logical, rational, everything-can-be-explained-by-science Simon...was in love.

And he'd betrayed our bond by lying to me, keeping this relationship a secret. He'd deserted me, just like our parents had abandoned both of us. Simon was replacing me with Max.

My eyes shot open and I dropped his hand, unable to stand the touch of his skin any longer. Simon staggered back in shock at my rejection. "You love him. Something that's completely altered your life and the way you feel, and you've been lying to me about it for so long, Simon, keeping secrets..."

"Evan, no." His expression softened. "You're so wrong. You're drawing incorrect conclusions. I'd never lie to you, you know that." He rubbed his hands over his face then through his hair, pulling on the ends in frustration. "I should have listened to Mom and Dad and taken a different approach," he muttered to himself, pacing in his frustration.

I froze, my breath stuttering to a halt, certain I'd misunderstood him. Simon had informed me of his infrequent communication with our parents about his work or theirs, and I'd asked that he give them no information about me. If they wanted to know how I was doing, they could contact me themselves. It came as no surprise when they didn't.

But to hear he'd been discussing me with them against my wishes? That our parents knew about his relationship with Max and I was the outsider? I swayed slightly, feeling like I was freefalling into a black void, untethered. "What did you say?" Despite my feeling of disconnect, my voice was quiet and even, but the anger was right under the surface, threatening to erupt at any second.

Simon stopped his pacing and raised his panicked eyes to mine, realizing I knew exactly what he'd said. "Evan, I..."

Shaking my head slowly, I held my hand out, as if able to halt the flow of excuses he'd offer, but it didn't matter what he said. The damage was done. "How long have you been talking to them about me, Simon? Longer than you've been with Max? Since the day they walked out on us? I can just hear the conversations, the three of you discussing your important discoveries, how you're going to save Tage.

"And then there's Evan, such a disappointment to the family, never quite good enough or smart enough." Tears brimmed my eyes, and I brushed them away angrily. "You're all I have, Simon, and to know you don't trust me...." My voice caught. It hurt to say those words, like I'd ripped out a vital organ. I didn't want Max to see me like this, but there was nothing I could do about it. Simon's face was twisted in anguish, and I was glad. I wanted him to suffer, to know the pain he'd caused.

He reached for me, but I jerked away. "Of course I trust you, more than anyone in the world."

I glanced in Max's direction and saw him wince at Simon's words, but at least he wasn't trying to interfere again.

"Evan, please believe me, I didn't want to keep this from you, but knew you wouldn't approve of him. If I'd told you about Max when he first asked me out, there would never have been a first date. I'd have missed the opportunity to see if he really cared about me, or if I was just another challenge involving the two of you. When I spoke to Mom and Dad, I unintentionally let it slip about Max, and then was relieved at being able to tell someone about us. They knew how you felt about him and the tension it could cause between us. I never mentioned anything else about you." He ducked his head in apology for what he'd done and what he was about to say, confirming my suspicions. "And they never asked."

His tortured eyes met mine again, seeking the forgiveness I wasn't ready to give. "I was unable to keep it a secret any longer. Not sharing this with you has been painful and unfair to both you and Max, but I'm fully aware of your instinctive reaction anytime his name is mentioned, and I wanted to avoid that. Please, please believe me."

I studied both of them, looking for any signs of deception. Simon's brows were drawn, his eyes pleading for my understanding. And I *wanted* to understand, to be happy for him. But not with Max. Before our parents left for their assignment, Dad had taken me aside and made me promise to take care of Simon, figuring I could at least handle that duty. And I'd kept that promise, forcing him to take breaks from work, making him eat—and keeping scum like Max from hurting him.

I considered Max as he stood slightly behind Simon, blood smeared across his mouth. I studied his face, his posture, looking for a subtle tell that he was lying. He drew himself up under my scrutiny, knowing this was a silent test. Could I truly accept him as Simon's boyfriend? He didn't come close to deserving him, but if he made him happy, wasn't that what was important?

My expression softened as I concluded I needed to try for Simon's sake. His shoulders relaxed, and he closed his eyes in relief. I looked at Max. From Simon's reaction, he must have understood my decision. While holding my gaze, he reached for Simon's hand, raised his chin...and smirked at me. Like I'd bought his lies, and he'd claimed his prize.

I narrowed my eyes and slowly shook my head, blackness clouding my vision. I'd been right all along. The weight of it was too much to bear—Simon keeping this from me, being with Max, talking to our parents. I couldn't breathe, like the oxygen had been sucked from the room. Fight or flight. And I chose flight. "No...just no. I'll never understand why you did this, betraying my trust, lying. You're choosing Max over me, abandoning me, just like them." Spittle flew from my mouth and my hands clenched, leaving fingernail crescent marks on my palms. "You have Max now, I get it. You don't need me anymore. But when he proves me right and hurts you again, I won't be here."

Simon paled. The agony he felt was like a bullet to my chest, and I'm sure my anger had a similar effect on him. Fight or flight. Leave or stay. I had to get away from here, away from Simon. And I never wanted to lay eyes on Max again.

"Evan, please...." Simon started towards me.

"Stop right there." I held out my hand to keep him from getting any closer. "I'm done. Leave me alone." I swung around and sped out the door, through the hallway, and down the stairs, taking them two at a time. I threw open the front door and ran down the darkened street, not caring where I went, just as long as I put some distance between us. The burden of our shared emotions threatened to bring me to my knees. It was too much to carry, nearly crushing in its intensity. I kept running, trying to block the last image I had of Simon, broken and destroyed, his eyes flooded with tears. A perfect mirror image of myself.

Chapter 13
Evan
One Year Ago

I'm not sure how long I ran, but inky darkness had descended, telling me several hours had passed. My body was limp, exhausted, and demanded rest. Climbing the steps to the front porch, I noted someone had closed the front door I'd left hanging open. Simon, I assumed. Walking inside, I closed it gently behind me, not wanting to alert him to my presence. The physical activity had helped somewhat, maybe even cleared my head a little, but I wasn't ready to deal with him yet. The gaping, jagged wound still oozed.

I crept up the stairs, careful to avoid the spot on the sixth step that always creaked, and had made it nearly halfway down the hallway, just steps from my room, when Simon called out to me. "Evan?" I sprinted the last few feet, slipped into my room, and slammed the door, locking it behind me.

"Please come out and talk to me." Simon rapped on the door. "We can't leave things like this. I know what you're thinking, and things aren't what they seem. Max could never replace you." He tried the knob and huffed out a breath. "Was it really necessary to lock the door?"

I threw myself on the bed. "Go away and leave me alone." I covered my head with a pillow, attempting to drown out the sound of his voice and ferocity of emotions.

Simon had always been better at erecting a barricade between us—probably because of his intense focus—so what I was feeling didn't overwhelm him unless he allowed it. He'd said it was necessary in order to concentrate. It had never been quite that easy for me, because my own emotions had always been so much bigger, taking up more space than Simon's. He'd agreed with my assessment. I lacked that same focus.

Simon continued knocking, begging me to let him in or to come out and talk, but I ignored his pleas, choosing instead to wallow in my own anger and misery. No matter how hard I tried, his pain and my rage never lessened, instead intertwining and expanding. In frustration, I grabbed my data pad and swiped over to my music, increasing the volume so that it overrode Simon's voice and stamped down my inner thoughts a few notches. I closed my eyes tightly and tried to block everything, just needing a break from the pressing heaviness that hung between us. Soon enough, my thoughts drifted, exhaustion swept through me, and I slept.

♊

My eyes snapped open. With music still playing, I couldn't hear much else, other than the thundering beat of my heart, so I shut it off and pulled out my ear buds. Something was wrong, very wrong, but I had no idea what. Just that a threat existed.

I bolted upright in bed and scanned the room, the bedside lamp providing dim light, but saw nothing out of the ordinary. Had I been dreaming?

"Evan!" Simon called for me.

I huffed. Couldn't he get it through that genius brain of his that I didn't want to talk to him? I glanced at the time, calculating several hours had passed, and it was the middle of the night. Normally my instinct would be to reach out to Simon or go into his room and check on him, but sleep had done nothing to alter my mood, and anger and betrayal still overshadowed everything else. Rolling to my side, I again slammed the pillow over my head.

"Evan, please! Help me!" Our bedrooms shared a wall, and the head of my bed rested against it. This time, something big enough to vibrate my bed crashed into the wall. My heart still pounded, and I figured it was due to Simon having a nightmare. Sometimes I wished we could sever this connection between us—now more than ever. Since Max was apparently going to be the biggest part of Simon's life, I didn't want to experience his feelings in their more...private moments.

"Stop! You can't take me!" Simon's voice was coarse from yelling, and he was only getting louder.

I reached above the headboard and beat my fist on the wall. "Simon, would you shut up and let me sleep!" Hopefully that would wake him. I punched the pillow and rolled to my side again.

"Evan, plea—" Simon's shrill voice cut off abruptly, and I'd swear the foundation of the house shifted. At the same time, my body jerked violently, and I felt as if something vital, deep down was wrenched from inside me. I gasped from the pain, beads of sweat covering my face, and curled into a fetal position. Had Simon felt this? I reached out to him to check, but felt...nothing?

The pain subsided as quickly as it began, and I leaped from the bed, racing the few steps that separated our rooms. I silently prayed he'd be in his bed, my earlier anger and betrayal all but forgotten. His door was locked. "Simon!" I yelled, pounding. After no response or noise from inside, I kicked at the door knob. When I rammed my shoulder against the door, there was a splintering sound, and I stumbled into Simon's room.

The lamp on his nightstand lay on its side, the light casting misshapen shadows on the wall. His bed covers were twisted and hanging half on the floor, which wasn't like Simon at all. I'd once asked him if he ever slept, because his bed was always perfect, even when he was lying in it. But he wasn't lying in it now. He was nowhere in the room.

Even when he'd been in his basement lab, I'd always known he was home. Sensing his presence was as natural as breathing. But now, nothing. The part nestled inside me that was Simon had been with me even before birth, and now it was gone. Again I reached out to him, only to find emptiness. A void. Like he didn't exist. I doubled over and fell back against the wall, sliding to the floor. A dark fear pierced my heart, because I knew for certain something was very, very wrong.

♊

Ideas churned through my head as I sought a plausible explanation for the emptiness. Maybe Simon had found a way to disconnect from me.

We'd never tried, or ever wanted, to sever our tether to each other. Had he changed his mind?

I leaned my head against the wall and scanned my surroundings, the bed the only object of disarray in an otherwise immaculate room. Simon always said a cluttered room led to a disorganized mind. My eyes fell on the closet and closed door to the adjoining bathroom, and I cursed myself for not thinking of it sooner. Maybe he was still here, just not in his bed. "Simon!" Leaping to my feet, I lunged toward the closet door and ripped it open, pushing the clothes aside and tossing things onto the floor. He wasn't there.

That left only one place—the bathroom. Maybe he was sick, and that's why he couldn't answer. What if he was unconscious? My heart thudded loudly as I pounded on the door, knowing deep down he wouldn't answer. "Simon?" The door was unlocked and I swung it open, only to find another empty room. In a last ditch effort, I checked the shower. Nothing.

I slumped against the wall and ran my hands through my hair in frustration, trying not to panic. Think logically. Think like Simon. Where could he be? His bedroom door had been locked, and there was no other way he could have gotten out. Our rooms were on the second floor, and it wasn't like he was adventurous enough to jump or rappel down the side of the house. Besides, his windows were closed and locked.

Maybe he'd locked and pulled the bedroom door shut accidentally, and was somewhere else in the house. I raced down the stairs, calling his name as I searched every room and closet. After finding his lab empty, I even went outside and scoured our yard. No sign, or feel, of Simon.

I hadn't tried his data pad. That should have been my first step.

I'd left mine behind in my bedroom and dashed back up the stairs to retrieve it. I messaged Simon and waited for his face to appear, laughing at me for falling for his prank. Even though he'd never pulled a prank in his life. The screen remained blank, but in the distance, I heard the familiar chime of his message notification. I sighed in relief—so he was here somewhere after all, hiding, or maybe injured. Simon was never more than a few feet from his data pad. It was his most prized possession, loaded with most of his life's work. All I had to do was find it, and I'd find my brother.

Following the sound of the chime into his room, I wondered how I'd missed him earlier, but maybe he'd been moving around the house to avoid me. No way would I let him get away with this. I was still angry, and he'd scared the life out of me. The chiming was louder, but slightly muffled, and I traced its source to somewhere around his bed. Of course Simon slept with his data pad. Why wouldn't he? Shoving the covers around, I felt for it, but came up empty.

The chiming continued, and I realized where the sound was emanating from. Dropping to my hands and knees, I looked under the bed and discovered it lying on the floor, partially wedged between two boxes. And unattached to Simon.

This wasn't a prank.

Seeing that data pad crushed the nugget of hope I'd clung to, and the empty void in my chest expanded and ached, like a part of me was missing. Never, in all the years we'd been aware of our connection, had I felt this way. It was like Simon didn't even exist anymore, and with every cell in my body, I regretted my earlier wish for our connection to be severed.

Chapter 14
Evan
One Year Ago

I notified the authorities and then made the call I dreaded for a couple of reasons. First, I hadn't spoken to my parents in months. Second, having to deliver the news that their favored child was missing wouldn't go well.

And it didn't.

I explained what had happened, but left out the part about our argument. Didn't mention Max, either.

They immediately set out for home, and arrived around dawn.

"You had one job to do, Evan." Dad held up his right index finger, blood engorging his face as his voice rose with every word. "The only thing I asked of you before your mother and I left was to take care of Simon. One job, and you failed. How can you not know where your brother is? From the day both of you were born, you've always known each other's whereabouts, and now you've failed at that, too. You've finally met my expectations." Dad stormed out of the kitchen and into the living room, where the investigators were waiting to speak to him.

Mom leaned against the kitchen counter, her head tilted slightly, scrutinizing me as if trying to read my internal thoughts or detect a lie. I wasn't worried. She wasn't a mindreader and, as an accomplished liar, I had no tells. Over the years, I'd lied to my parents several times about where I was going, who I'd been with. Stupid teenager stuff that seemed so unimportant now. They probably wouldn't have cared what I'd been doing, anyway.

"If you're not telling us the whole story, Evan, the truth will come out eventually," Mom said, her eyes narrowed and accusing. "Is there anything else you'd like to say?"

"Nothing," I answered flatly, shouldering past her and exiting out the back door. The early morning sunlight filtered through the tree line at the side yard, and I jogged in that direction. Out of sight of the house, I leaned against a tree and closed my eyes, breathing deeply to try and clear my head, putting my parents out of my thoughts. My focus was Simon. He was all that mattered.

What had I done? He was gone—disappearing from his bedroom like wisps of smoke from a campfire. After hearing my story, the investigators regarded me with suspicion and disbelief. Not surprising, given what happened. Who disappeared from a locked room? After repeating it several times without any variation, they'd allowed me to leave, and were now questioning my parents.

A gentle breeze blew leaves from the towering tree overhead as I lowered myself to the parched ground beneath, debating whether I should talk to Max. My fingers slid over the cover of my data pad while I reasoned it out in my head. After yesterday, it was obvious Simon and Max cared about each other, and had for some time. I winced, the stabbing, twisting pain in my stomach returning, reminding me of the secrets Simon had kept from me. Why wouldn't he have trusted me? What had I done to make him pull away?

If he wasn't found, I'd never learn the answer to that question. But what if Max knew where he was? Wouldn't Simon have told his boyfriend what was going on? And that brought on a whole new ache at the thought of Max knocking me down a rung on Simon's people-of-importance ladder, but my fingers whizzed across the data pad to pull up his contact information. It's what Simon would have wanted and was the right thing to do, no matter my own personal feelings.

Even though it was barely after sunrise, Max's stern face filled my screen in seconds. "I'm only answering this out of respect to Simon. What do you want, Evan?"

At the sharp tone of his voice, instinct pushed me to retaliate, but I fought against my nature, keeping Simon's needs at the forefront. "I need to tell you something."

He ducked his head, running his hands through his sandy blond hair, before meeting my eyes again. "I think you said everything last night. I've got nothing to say to you." He moved to disconnect us.

"Max, wait, it's about Simon." His hand froze over the button. "He's gone."

His head snapped back, brows drawn together in confusion. "What do you mean he's gone?"

"He disappeared last night, and the investigators are here. No one can find him."

His eyes widened, and with a catch in his voice he said, "I'm on my way." Before the screen went black, I saw him leap from his chair, and heard a clatter as it struck the floor in his haste to leave.

With a reaction like that, it was pretty evident Max had no idea where Simon was, either.

♊

Pulling at blades of dry grass, I grinded them between my thumb and forefinger while waiting under the tree for Max. I'd moved closer to the house and watched as the investigators paraded in and out, teams of them inspecting the yard and land beyond the fence out back, others no doubt headed to Scientific Innovations in search of Simon. I knew with certainty they wouldn't find him there. I'd contacted the lab hours ago, and the last activity on his ID card was from yesterday afternoon when he'd left to go home. There was no way he could have gotten back in without scanning it, and his lab was empty.

When questioned about Simon earlier, I'd only mentioned hearing him call out for me last night, assumed it was because of a nightmare, and the strange vibration that had shaken the house at its foundation. Leaving out Simon and Max's relationship hadn't been intentional, I just didn't see a connection between our argument and his disappearance. Although when 'argument' and 'disappearance' were used in the same sentence, it didn't shine a favorable light in my direction. Once Max got here and I explained everything, maybe he'd have something to add, or could point the investigators in a new direction.

I tossed the blade remnants to the ground when I saw Max running full speed toward the fence, leaping over it instead of wasting time with the gate. Standing and wiping my hands on my pants, I called out and gestured for him to come over.

"Where is he?" Max shouted, his chest heaving as he gulped in oxygen. I grabbed his upper arm and tried pulling him behind the tree where we'd have some privacy, but he shoved me off. "Let go of me, Evan, and tell me where he is, right now!"

"Keep your voice down," I hissed. The last thing I wanted was to draw attention to ourselves before Max knew everything. Or almost everything. "Just shut up, follow me, and I'll tell you what I know." His nostrils flared, but he tagged along as I led him to a grouping of large trees with low, overhanging branches. They allowed me to peer through them and keep an eye on the investigators to make sure we weren't approached before I was ready.

Once we were out of view, he spun me around and shoved me against a tree, the back of my head slamming against the trunk, as he kept his forearm across my chest to hold me in place. I growled and swept my right leg under his feet, knocking him to the ground, then quickly straddled his chest and pinned his hands above his head before he could regain his balance. I struggled to keep what Simon would want in the forefront of my mind, and was fairly certain it wasn't Max and me rolling around in the dirt taking swings at each other. "Max, stop!"

His hips bucked, trying to push me off as he fought to free himself, but I had him solidly pinned.

"Would you calm down? This isn't helping locate him, and we're wasting time. Is that what you want?"

His eyes burned with anger and he clenched his jaw, but my words had the desired effect, and he quit struggling.

"No."

Standing, I offered my hand to help him up. Max glowered at me, hesitating a few moments before accepting my gesture. "Where is he? What do you mean he disappeared?"

As with the investigators, I told him Simon had called out for me—leaving out the part about it being more than once, something that still brought on pangs of guilt, and a sick twisted feeling in my stomach. Max listened intently. The second I finished, he started pacing, combing his hands through his hair while mumbling to himself. "Did he tell you anything, Max? Do you have any idea where he is?"

He came to an abrupt halt and spun to face me. "Seriously? Do you really think I'd be standing here with you if I knew where Simon was? After the way you treated him last night, the things you said, you're the last person in the world I'd want to spend time with. He's your brother, and for reasons I'll never understand, you're his best friend. Your parents checked out years ago, so if *you* don't support him, can you blame him for leaving?" Max might as well have thrust the invisible dagger into my chest even further, and I collapsed against the tree, my legs no longer capable of supporting my weight.

"I was wrong." My confession was made quietly, nearly a whisper on the breeze, but I'd never spoken truer words. Shame and embarrassment nearly stole my voice.

"What was that, Evan? Admitting you're wrong? You're a little too late for that!" Anger at Max's accusations, crushing guilt and disappointment in myself, and overwhelming fear for Simon made for a volatile combination that set my blood boiling.

"Can you blame me, Max?" Pushing off the tree, I stalked toward him, and he felt threatened enough to back away. "Not so long ago, you used him as a punching bag." I snatched the collar of his shirt and yanked him toward me, inches from my face. "Now you expect me to believe you care about him? You're using him for something, probably to get back at me in some way, so why don't you just come clean and admit it. You're not good enough for him, and nothing will ever change that." I released my grip and shoved him backwards.

Max straightened his shirt and squared his jaw, his eyes blazing with anger. "Simon forgave me, and we put that behind us. If you believe I'm with your brother because I'm using him, then you have no idea how amazing he really is. Not everything is about you, Resnik, and I sure as hell don't need you to tell me Simon's too good for me—I've never deserved him. But for some reason he wants to be with me, and that should be good enough for you."

In a perfect world, maybe it would have been good enough for me, but Max had hurt my brother, something I was incapable of forgiving or forgetting. Simon had always been a better person than me, and if he'd accepted Max's apology, that was his business. I flexed my fingers, remembering the way my brother had looked when I'd found him, blood gushing from his nose and trickling down his face.

Max took a deep breath and spread his hands wide. "Look, can't we set this aside for a while? For Simon's sake? Like you said, we're wasting time, and it's clear you and I won't be agreeing on anything else besides that. People don't disappear into the night. It just doesn't happen." He shoved his hands in his pockets and leaned against a tree. "Simon told me about your freaky twin thing. Could that help us find him?"

Sighing heavily, I collapsed to the ground. Do it for Simon. "I've tried, but there's nothing. He's always been a part of me, like two hearts beating within instead of one, and it's the same for him. That's the way we're built, the bond we share. Since last night, the space where Simon has always been is hollow. There's no pain, fear, happiness—and that terrifies me."

"But why does that scare you? You wouldn't feel him unless he was here with you, right?"

I squinted up at him, the early morning sun forming a halo around his head. "It's hard to explain to people, but it's never mattered where Simon was. He could be in the same room or miles away, but there was always a constant...*awareness* of him, like a hum in the back of your mind you never noticed until it stopped. People don't just disappear into the night, but that's exactly what happened to Simon. That second heartbeat, the awareness...they're gone."

Max inhaled sharply. Before he turned away, I saw his eyes wet with tears. Maybe I was wrong about him, and he really loved Simon. For Simon's sake, I hoped he did. For Max's sake, he'd better, or I'd give in to my instinctive urge to cause him pain.

He wiped his eyes with the sleeve of his shirt and faced me again. "I think it's time for me to meet the investigators." This time he offered me his hand to help me from the ground. But I didn't take it.

Chapter 15
Evan
Present Day

I'd asked Syd to come home with me after we finished our shift, but I kept delaying our departure with the excuse that I needed to check on some things. The longer I kept the truth from her, the longer she'd stay with me. She'd finally gotten frustrated enough to forcibly drag me out the door.

Guiding her into the living room of my house, I dropped to the couch, pulling her down next to me, then draped my arm across the back of it and angled my body to face her. It was time to lay the cards on the table.

"Was Max just blabbing about another one of your stupid competitions over something? And they were dating? I know where he ranks on your scale of tolerance and likability, but how could you keep that from me? I'm tired, Evan, so just say what you need to say."

I closed my eyes and breathed in deeply, then exhaled. "We tell each other everything, right?"

Her whole demeanor did an about face, as her eyes dropped to her lap, cheeks blushed crimson, and she replied in a small voice, "Yeah, sure."

Well. Maybe Syd had some secrets of her own. Whatever they were, nothing could be worse than what I was about to reveal.

"What Max was talking about—I've kept something from you, and I can't do it anymore. Maybe I should have told you after it happened and things would be different. Maybe better. But if I had, I might have been alone for the past year."

Syd drew her leg up and shifted to face me, her forehead creased in concern. "Evan, what is it?"

I swallowed hard. "Something happened the night Simon

disappeared, something I've never told you, or anyone else. I need you to try not to judge me, because I'm afraid of the way you'll look at me once you know." My voice wavered. This was one of the hardest things I'd ever done, and my heart constricted thinking she could be out of my life in the next few minutes.

"Of course."

I took her hand in mine, wary of looking into her eyes and seeing the disappointment, disgust, and contempt that would be reflected after my confession. A trickle of sweat trailed down my back. "You remember the night Simon disappeared was also the same day we were accepted as Benders, right?" I glanced up as she nodded.

I blurted out the whole sordid, embarrassing story without stopping, tears blurring my eyes when describing how he'd pleaded with me to open my bedroom door, then later called my name, and I'd chosen not to help him because of my selfishness and pride. My own petty feelings of jealousy and insecurity had come before my brother.

Then it was over, and I was barely breathing, waiting silently for her to curse me and walk out the front door. Nearly identical to the exit strategy my own parents had used.

"Evan, look at me," she said quietly.

I shook my head. "I'm afraid to see that you think less of me. I can't lose you, too."

She moved to the floor and knelt in front of me, clasped one of my hands, and brought herself into my field of vision. Tears streamed down her face, but her eyes didn't reflect the disappointment and disgust I'd expected. Only heartbreak and pity.

"This explains so much. Your guilt, anger, and self-loathing caused you to push so many people away. And we could have helped you. I'm so mad at you for not telling me." She squeezed my quivering hand tightly, punctuating her words. "You kept this from me like Simon kept Max from you, and it hurts me deeply, but it also breaks my heart that you held this so close, letting it fester and eat away at the person you used to be."

"He'd still be here if I'd gone in his room that night." My voice broke on the last word.

Syd brought her other hand up to cup my cheek. "You don't know that. If you'd gone in his room, who's to say they, it, whatever, wouldn't have taken you too? Or killed you? You aren't responsible for Simon's disappearance. The blame is on whoever took him. And your parents? That's on them. They must have been devastated over losing their son, but good parents put their children before themselves, and they seem to have forgotten they have another son who's still here. It's not your fault."

My body deflated in relief at her words. I breathed easier, and even the air around me seemed lighter. Syd was still here, and she had no idea how thankful I was for that. I took her hand from my cheek and pulled it down, gripping both of her hands in my own. "Thanks for saying that, but no matter what, I'll always blame myself and wonder what if. Maybe both of us would have been taken. Or not, but at least we'd be together, and Simon wouldn't be alone to fend for himself."

She wiped her tears and moved to sit beside me. "So, Simon and Max, huh? Your brother has good taste. Max is hot."

I scowled at her. "Can we please not talk about my brother's love life?"

"Oh, come on, Evan. Max is a nice guy. All this bad juju between you came about because you're both too competitive for your own good. It's time to grow up and move past it."

"Yeah. Maybe." I grunted.

Syd giggled. "You look as exhausted as I feel."

"I've only been sleeping an hour or two at a time."

Her thumb traced the dark circles under my eyes.

"I'm too tired to go home, so do you mind if I just crash here?"

"Not a bit." I stretched out and pulled her down with me, my arm wrapped around her. She used my shoulder as a cushion, and I tugged a blanket from the back of the sofa over us.

Syd kissed my cheek softly. "No matter what you think, you're a good person, Evan." She nestled tightly against my chest, and I slept deeply for the first time in days, secure in the knowledge that she'd learned the worst thing I'd done, and had chosen to stay.

♊

"With Zia out tonight, we're uneven," I said, as the team's assignments downloaded to their data pads. Over the past few weeks, our caseload had unexpectedly exploded, and the number of nightmare cases alone had tripled. All the teams had logged extra hours, and I'd been working double shifts for days. Gabriel stated in all his years here, he'd never seen such a spike in volume.

"Syd, you pair up with Max. Dr. Quill is back and I can handle that myself." I'd also have a chance to ask him about the experience I'd had in Simon's bedroom.

She frowned. "But Evan, that's against policy to...."

"We couldn't bring anyone else in on short notice, and there are priority cases that need to be resolved. You know his cases are pretty routine. I'll be fine by myself."

Syd narrowed her eyes at me. "Does Gabriel know about this?"

I squared my jaw. "Yes, Syd, Gabriel is aware of the situation." Which was the truth. Because we were short-staffed and overloaded, he'd agreed to let me take care of a few usual cases alone, knowing I could handle them.

Syd eyed me skeptically, then she turned to Max to go over their assignments.

After Isaac, Max, Syd, and Amelia started on their cases, I went to lab C where Dr. Quill was being prepped. Flipping on my data pad, I again familiarized myself with the latest reason for his presence, then checked in with him to confirm some details. Seeing clients before cases wasn't standard operating procedure, but Doc was an exception. He waived the identity clause and always requested me.

"Ahh, Evan, so we meet again." Doc sat on the edge of the bed and smiled, as Ky placed leads on his temples and chest.

"Good to see you again, Dr. Quill."

"You've retrieved so many of my ideas, you could probably perform my job yourself," he chuckled.

"Believe me, Doc, there's not a chance of that happening. Getting into other people's heads comes easy to me. Science and math? Not so much."

"Well, the science and math are second nature to me, but when it comes time to find them? I guess we make a good team." He paused a moment, studying me. "The question you asked me, about someone disappearing from a locked room. That was Simon, wasn't it?"

"Yes, sir, it was. Nothing has turned up, and I just wondered if there was some kind of scientific explanation, anything that could help locate him. Something strange happened in his room a few days ago." As I relayed the story to him, he leaned forward, listening intently.

"You know, Evan, I never mentioned it, but I worked with Simon occasionally after he came to SI."

"I wasn't aware of that. I thought he only worked with Dr. Sebastian."

"Yes, Dr. Sebastian was his mentor, but Simon also worked with several of us. Such a brilliant mind. So many of us wanted to pick his brain and discuss ideas with him." He stroked his chin and squinted. "I wonder..."

"What?" I asked urgently. Did he know something?

His attention snapped back to me. "Just something your brother hinted at once. It's probably nothing, but I'll see what I can find out."

"Anything you can do, Doc, I'd really appreciate it."

He waved at me dismissively. "After all the problems you've solved for me, it's the least I can do." By now, he was lying down and his eyes were beginning to droop as the sedative took hold.

♊

Ky informed me that Gabriel had been called away from the control room to take care of something, but I chose to move forward on Doc's case without him. Ky wasn't completely on board with it, but since I'd been given clearance to handle this one on my own, he reluctantly agreed to prep me. Besides, I figured I'd be in and out of Dr. Quill's head before Gabriel finished whatever had pulled him away.

Today's conundrum involved a new idea for a synthetic protein. Standing in the familiar surroundings of Doc's information center, I was greeted with piles of papers and books falling haphazardly out of drawers, and scraps of paper attached to bulletin boards. Shaking my head, I chuckled, knowing how amused he'd be at a peek into his own mind.

I cocked an eyebrow. Here was something new. I'd seen pictures of these from decades ago. Small, square pieces of paper with adhesive on the back enabling them to be stuck on nearly any flat surface. And there were several of them in brightly colored shades of blue, yellow, pink, and green attached to the wall, files, and drawers. Could it really be this easy?

If I located the date of Doc's group meeting and the topics they'd discussed, the trail should lead me to his synthetic protein idea, but to have it front and center and so clearly marked? My job couldn't get any easier. Maybe he liked coming here because he enjoyed my company. I smirked. If that were true, he'd be the first.

Without a partner watching my back while I pilfered through Doc's information, I had to remind myself to sneak a peek every now and then. His dreams had never manifested anything threatening in the past, so the possibility of that happening didn't cause me much concern. Doc's mind seemed pretty comfortable with me being in here so often.

Starting on the third section of adhesive notes, it occurred to me I'd been so caught up in examining them that I hadn't checked the dome overhead. Looking up, I saw rows and rows of mathematical calculations flickering across the screen. Guess Doc even worked in his sleep.

Turning back to the notes, I plowed through what remained of the third section, when the word 'synthetic' caught my eye. Soon enough, the paper trail led me to what I'd been asked to locate, and after combining those notes with the others from his group meeting, I began my exit sequence.

Part of the exit sequence involved making sure the client's vitals were within normal range, and confirming they weren't suffering any adverse effects from a Bender's intrusion. In other words, their dreams should continue as usual. The average person had anywhere from four to six dreams per night, but that number could rise to seven or more, especially if the dreamer was the creative type, which Doc certainly was. Scattered and unorganized, but a confirmed member of the creative group.

My eyes drifted to the dome overhead where the mathematical equations continued. Ky confirmed the vitals were stable. I'd just turned to double check the notes once more, when an invisible force pummeled me square in the chest. My head snapped back and I dropped to the floor, hands reaching out to catch myself as I fell forward. The impact left me nearly breathless, and I fought to draw in oxygen. Was Doc attacking me? I'd always been welcomed before, but the mind was a strange and unpredictable place. Anything was possible. I was alone, and this could potentially be a bad situation. My eyes darted around the room, seeking a threat. What was happening?

I scrambled to my feet as quickly as possible, readying myself for whatever came next. The initial shock of being hit in the chest was fading, but something had been left behind, a soothing, comforting sensation, like falling into my bed after working a long night. I felt...whole again, complete.

Simon.

I pushed my eject button.

CHAPTER 16
EVAN
PRESENT DAY

My eyes shot open. Confusion, hope, disbelief, and excitement fought for dominance. Was he here? "Simon!" I ripped off the leads attached to my chest and temples, then called for him again. "Where are you?" Swinging my legs over the side of the chair, I sprang to my feet.

Ky came scrambling from behind the privacy curtain where he'd been monitoring Doc.

"Evan, what's wrong? Is there a problem? Are you hurt?" He scanned first me, then my vital monitors.

I grasped his upper arms. "Where is he?"

He gestured back toward the curtain. "He's still asleep."

Squeezing my eyes shut, I shook my head. "No, not Doc, *Simon*. Where is he?"

"Who? Who's Simon?"

I released his arms and charged around the room, shoving aside storage cabinets and upturning tables, searching for him myself, while Ky watched in confusion. My twin was still here. I felt it. A flicker of movement in the corner by the medical supplies had me darting in that direction. I was greeted with the shimmering silver light from Simon's bedroom, and this time no one could tell me it was from sunlight streaming through a window. It sputtered and danced, seeming made of energy, and the hair rose gently from my head.

His voice was the echo of a whisper, almost inaudible. But I knew that voice as well as my own. It was ingrained in me, and I'd listened to it since the day we were born. "Evan?"

"Simon, are you here?" Somehow, that light was connected to him, and I reached out for it. Bursts of static shock ran up my arm, and the floor rumbled beneath my feet, reminiscent of the night he'd disappeared. The air around me felt charged. Instead of fading away like before, this time the light emitted a resounding crack before it vanished, and I threw my arms over my face instinctively. Once again, everything that was Simon was savagely torn away. Staggering, I caught myself on a Bender chair, eyes closed, holding tightly to the fleeting sensation of my twin.

"Evan?" Ky asked hesitantly, his uncertain voice intruding on my pain.

The empty crater inside me erupted with anger and suspicion. Had he seen Simon before I'd ejected? Did Ky have something to do with the light or…I felt a sinking sensation in my stomach. Was he connected in some way to my brother's disappearance? Ky had to know something, and one way or another I'd get it out of him.

My eyes snapped open and bored into him. "What do you know?"

His face was empty. "About what, Evan? I don't understand what's going on."

"Stop lying, and tell me where my brother is," I growled, advancing toward him.

Ky scrambled backwards until he could go no further, his back pressed against the wall.

Clutching the front of his shirt, I stood inches from his face. "What happened to my brother?"

He shook his head rapidly and his questioning eyes bulged.

I tightened my grip. "Answer me!"

"Evan!"

Ky's gaze snapped to the doorway behind me, his body slumping in relief at Gabriel's presence.

"Release him immediately." My hand was still twisted in Ky's shirt, and I shoved him to the side, then turned to face the wrath of Gabriel.

His face was chiseled hardness. "My office, now."

"You don't understand—"

"Now, Evan." His tone was low and even, a sign I'd learned meant there was no option other than to obey him. Knowing Simon had been here, my every instinct fought against leaving the lab. With tremendous effort, I dragged myself away and followed Gabriel down the hallway. Halfway there, I tried again to explain myself but, keeping his back to me, he held his hand up. "Not a word until we're in my office."

He opened the door and stepped to the side, allowing me to enter before slamming it behind me. I sat heavily in the chair across from his desk, which was void of anything except his data pad. Gabriel's anger was a heavy cloud hanging overhead, and when he sat, clasping his hands together on top of the desk, his unwavering cold stare fell upon me. But I caught a flicker of something else before he became guarded again. Disappointment.

"Despite the fact you usually maintain cavernous personal distances between yourself and your team, they respect you as their leader. I know Ky to be an exemplary technician, so what would cause you to verbally and physically threaten him?"

Inhaling deeply, I tried to get a handle on my fluctuating emotions, and clenched my trembling hands. "Simon was here."

Gabriel's eyes widened in surprise. "I don't understand. Where?"

"I saw a light in his bedroom a few days ago and felt his presence. Just minutes ago when I was in Doc's head, I sensed him again and ejected. That same light was here, and Simon spoke to me. He called my name, Gabriel. He's alive."

He looked at me for a long moment, then cleared his throat. "I understand you and Simon were closely bonded and shared an unusual connection, but why, after little more than a year, do you think he'd suddenly reappear in a sleep lab?"

He didn't believe me—which wasn't surprising. Besides Simon and me, only our parents, Syd, and, as much as I hated to admit it, probably Max, understood the strength of the tether that joined us and how it operated. Seeing it in action was easier than attempting to explain the inner workings. "I have no idea why or how, but I never comprehended most of what he did, anyway." I leaned forward, resting my elbows on my knees. "But I'm telling you, somehow, he was there, and then gone just as quickly."

Gabriel leaned back in the chair and brought his index fingers against his lips in a steeple. His penetrating eyes searched my face as if looking for evidence I wasn't being truthful. Like I would make up something this huge. He brought his hands back to the desk. "Evan, how much sleep have you gotten over the past few days?"

I blinked. "What? You can't think I imagined this. I felt Simon—his emotions, his presence. It was real." The tone of my voice was insistent. He had to believe me.

"I'm trying to rationalize your behavior. With this backlog, we've all been overworked and, against my better judgement, I allowed you to handle this case on your own because of your familiarity with this particular client. Then I discover you standing over Ky, threatening bodily harm, and you tell me it's because your twin was there? You didn't see him, and Ky had no idea what you were talking about, so what other explanation could there be besides lack of sleep and exhaustion?"

Disappointment coursed through me, dampening my excitement, and I slouched back in my chair like a fifty-pound weight had been tossed into my lap. "How about the explanation that my brother's alive and found a way to make contact?"

Gabriel sighed and shook his head. "I want Simon to be alive just as much as you, Evan, but you have to see this from my perspective. Due to a spike in clients over the past few weeks for reasons unknown, we're all under heavy stress and overworked. Other than yelling at the occasional team member which, in your defense, is usually for a lapse in safety measures, you're an exemplary TL. But after several days of extra cases, longer hours, and very few breaks, what I witnessed between you and Ky was completely out of character, and you're confused and disoriented. What would you think? Do you have any proof?"

I rubbed my hands over my face, then raked them through my hair. My jaw clenched in annoyance. Sure I was tired, but the exhaustion took a backseat to the exhilaration of knowing Simon was alive. Somewhere.

Gabriel wanted evidence. What I'd felt was enough for me. "You know I don't have any physical proof. If we had cameras that monitored the whole lab, this wouldn't be an issue." Something nagged at the back of my mind, then it clicked. "What about my vitals? Wouldn't they show something?"

"I'm looking at your vitals from the case right now." He scrutinized his data pad.

"And?"

"Heart rate and respiration show no anomalies...." Gabriel paused, then rubbed his chin.

"What?" I shot up from my chair and planted my hands on his desk.

"Intriguing. Two minutes before ejection, your pulse and respiration rates shot up and nearly doubled."

"That's when it happened! There's your proof," I said, slapping my hand on the hard surface.

Gabriel sighed. "You know the spike in your vitals could have been caused by several factors. This is very subjective."

Staring down at him, I spread my arms wide. "So what now? You know I'm not giving up on this."

"And I would never ask you to," Gabriel said quietly, then cleared his throat. "But for now, you're irrational and too exhausted to be productive tonight. You need rest. After you apologize to Ky."

CHAPTER 17
EVAN
PRESENT DAY

I woke with a start, not realizing I'd even fallen asleep. After my half-assed apology to Ky, which I could tell he was too intimidated not to accept, I'd come home and replayed the whole incident with Simon in my head, hoping to find some clue I might have missed. Even though his room had been searched countless times by detectives, my parents, and myself, I'd again torn through his desk, data pad, and lab, but hadn't come up with anything new.

A year ago, the investigators had remarked how unusual it was not to find a trace of any designs or projects Simon had been working on. Knowing what an organized neat freak he was, I hadn't thought anything about it. Now that I knew his files had disappeared a few months before he did, it made me wonder if there was a connection. Everything was a little too immaculate—even for Simon.

One thing was for sure. This was beyond anything Deckard could help me with, and I mentally fired him. I'd find my brother on my own, bring him home, and we'd be a family again in this house, just the two of us.

Fatigue must have won out at some point, because I was lying crossways on Simon's bed, his data pad still beside me. Something must have woken me. And then I heard pounding on the front door.

Still in my black denim work pants, no shirt, barefoot, and hair dancing in every direction possible, I staggered downstairs. Opening the door, I squinted into the harsh late morning sunlight and rubbed one eye as the other identified the offensive door pounder.

"Hey, Syd," I croaked, my voice still coarse from sleep.

Her mouth was open and primed to yell at me, judging by the

annoyed look on her face. Before uttering a sound, her eyes widened, ran down my body, and her face flushed a deep shade of scarlet.

"What's wrong with you? You're blushing."

"I....what? Nothing, I'm fine." Syd ducked her head and tucked a strand of hair behind her ear, a nervous habit. Weird.

"Are you coming in or what? There must be some reason you're beating down my door."

With her eyes fixed on the floor, Syd practically wrapped herself around the doorframe to avoid touching me as she entered. Any other day she would have belted me one for talking to her like that. "You're acting more abnormal than usual."

She charged straight for the kitchen. After closing the front door, I followed to find her standing in front of the wide open fridge, eyes closed, holding a cold bottle of juice against her face while muttering. Leaning against the counter, I folded my arms over my bare torso and waited for her to say something intelligible. She quieted, slammed the fridge door shut, then spun to face me, eyes narrowed.

"I'm here because you threatened to beat Ky senseless last night." She shoved my shoulder. This was the Syd I knew. "Why would you do that, Evan? He's a good tech."

I didn't expect her to know the whole story—Gabriel would never break protocol and reveal what happened, and Ky was probably too scared to say much of anything. "Simon was there. He spoke to me."

She fell back hard against the fridge in shock. As I gave her the details, I saw the wheels turning in her mind. "This is...incredible. Simon's trying to come back from wherever he is. But Gabriel thinks you imagined it because of exhaustion?"

"Yeah." I reached around Syd to grab a bottle of juice for myself, then twisted off the lid. "He said he'd investigate some more."

Her eyes raked over me. "Why don't you go put on a shirt or something."

I glanced down at my chest and back to Syd, who was now quite interested in reading the label on the back of her juice bottle. "Why? You've seen me plenty of times without a shirt. You were there for my tattoos, so why does it bother you now?"

"It doesn't. I just can't..." She huffed, blowing a strand of hair away from her face and rolling her eyes. "Just put on a shirt, okay?"

"Fine, whatever," I shrugged. "Come upstairs and I'll show you what I've been working on." I was halfway through the living room before I realized she wasn't behind me. "Are you coming or what?"

"I'll be there in a minute."

I went on without her, wondering what was up with Syd. She was acting weird, like when she'd hugged me differently before going home the other night. Things felt—off between us. Before, she'd come in unannounced and unexpected, tackling me while I was lying on my bed listening to music or reading. We used to wrestle around all the time. Now that I thought about it, neither of those things had happened in a while, and I couldn't understand why, because Syd had always taken great pleasure in catching me unaware and pinning me.

I was just pulling on a semi-fresh t-shirt I'd found on my floor when she strolled into my room and leaned against the doorframe. "Better?" I asked, spinning slowly for her approval.

"Much. Maybe you could throw on some deodorant while you're at it. Wouldn't hurt."

I rolled my eyes, and she followed me to Simon's room. Stopping at the entrance, she brought her hands to her hips and surveyed the open drawers, clothes strewn over the floor, and ransacked closet. "Simon would kick you sideways if he saw what you've done to his room."

"He'll get over it." I sat on the bed and patted the space beside me. "Have a seat." I picked up Simon's data pad and opened it. We'd always shared our personal codes. "There's nothing here. No research, notes, observations. It's just empty."

She tilted her head and her brow furrowed. "Where is everything? That's not like Simon. I mean, he had a photographic memory, but there's no way he could keep it all in his head, right?"

"Exactly. I started thinking about his missing files, and it seems like he cleared out everything. I only know about his Posarius project because he mentioned working on it. So where's the information?"

"Good question." She caught a strand of hair hanging over her shoulder and twisted it around her finger, staring at the floor in thought. "You know, seems like Simon was always writing in a book the few times I saw him before he vanished. A blue one. I remember thinking how weird it was, because his data pad had always been like an extra appendage."

My eyes widened, because I could see him sitting at the kitchen counter writing furiously in a book, while I rushed to grab something to eat before leaving for Bender training. I'd nearly spilled a protein drink on it, and he'd yelled at me about being more careful. That memory stuck out in my mind, because I could count on one hand the number of times Simon had ever raised his voice. "I remember it now, but I didn't find it anywhere."

Syd raised an eyebrow. "So, where's the blue book?"

I grinned. "Exactly. We need to find it."

She stretched her legs out in front of her, then turned to face me. "I need to ask you something, and you're not going to like it. Have you told your parents about Simon?"

"What? You're joking, right?"

"No, I'm not joking. He's their son, and they'd want to know he's alive."

"Well, I'm their son, too, and they haven't made an effort to see if I'm still alive. They haven't contacted me in months." I flopped back on the bed in frustration, running my hands through my hair. If they didn't give a crap about what happened to me, why should I let them know about Simon? I was the one who refused to believe he was gone for good. I was the one who kept hounding the investigators, reminding them he was still missing and seeing what progress they'd made. I was the one who'd stayed and hadn't neglected my family.

"Yes, your parents need to be slapped for how they treat you, and it sucks they're all you have, but it is what it is. And in the depths of your heart, if you really believe he's alive, they deserve to...."

"No!" I snapped, springing up to a sitting position. "Don't tell me what they deserve. If Simon is able to make his way home, if I can get him back, then I'll let him tell them. I'm done, and we're not discussing this again."

I felt a strong urge to dodge the daggers shooting from her eyes. Both of us could be unyielding, but I wasn't budging on this. As far as my parents were concerned, I was nothing but collateral damage.

CHAPTER 18
EVAN
PRESENT DAY

Judging by the dark scowls cast my way when I arrived at SI that evening, the details about my altercation with Ky had gotten around. If the team were, at best, apprehensive but respectful before, now the vibes were more along the lines of afraid-to-speak-upon-pain-of-death or keep-my-head-down-and-he-won't-notice-me. Either of which could be beneficial, in my opinion.

At my evening meeting with Gabriel, he'd first gauged my mood, then warned me "Any further situations resulting in adverse working relationships could be detrimental to your position of authority."

If that wasn't bad enough, it felt like further punishment when he'd stated because of the spike in nightmare cases, Max's training needed to be fast-tracked, readying him in half the normal amount of time. I'd hoped to delegate his training to Isaac, but Gabriel insisted I handle it because of the urgency. That meant a lot of one on one time with Max, who barely tolerated me on good days. I had that to look forward to. Maybe it was selfish on my part, but I wasn't ready to tell him about Simon yet.

If pressed, though, I'd probably tell him before my parents.

Once everyone was gathered in my office for the evening briefing and assignments, I started off by clearing the air. "I'm sure you've all heard about what happened between Ky and me last night, but the details won't be discussed. I've apologized to him and it's over. We still have an overload of cases, and the majority of them are nightmares. Check your data pads for assignments."

"Why is mine blank?" Max asked.

"With the influx of nightmare cases, Gabriel asked me to accelerate your training, so you're with me for half this shift. Meet me in the training room in fifteen." Since Max had been anxious to work with nightmares, his expression was eager, but hesitant. He'd probably been hoping Isaac or Zia would handle his training. I knew the disappointment he felt.

I'd been counting on it, too.

⚎

"Rules, Max. It's crucial you understand all the guidelines about nightmare cases, not only for your safety, but also for your partner's. If you don't know them, you're useless and dangerous to everyone."

"I've already read the files. I know the rules, and I've been ready for weeks."

His arrogance had my hands curling into fists. Breathe deeply. If Simon cared about him, there must be a reason. Really deep down, somewhere. Buried underneath all the narcissism.

"Sometimes nightmares can be handled with a minor physical response, or even talking to the client and reassuring his subconscious. Those are the easy, level-one types. When it's intense and repetitive, affecting the dreamer's ability to function and their quality of life, it may require more strenuous intervention, and can be dangerous. You don't and can't know what kinds of creatures and situations you could be facing. The mind can be highly creative and capable of producing terrifying, unimaginable things. That's when we get into the higher levels."

Max nodded in understanding. "But what about the fear? No matter how much they talked about it at the academy, the simulations just weren't the same."

Simulations couldn't create terror felt by the dreamer. "It's our job to absorb any fear experienced by the client. It can also be frightening for us, so not only do we absorb their fear, we experience our own. That can increase the intensity, so it's imperative you maintain focus. Once the case is closed, before we're released from the lab, any residual anxiety can be downloaded so we don't project it into other clients.

"Some Benders download after every case of that type, some can wait a few, especially if it's not a higher-level nightmare. It's not healthy to carry it around."

Max tilted his head to the side and narrowed his eyes. "Then why don't you? Isaac said he can't remember the last time you downloaded."

I'd promised Gabriel to get around to it, but kept making excuses if he pinned me down. The last time I'd downloaded was a couple of months after Simon vanished. My Bender training had been accelerated because I'd shown such an affinity for it, and after starting nightmare cases, I'd held the fear close as penance for not saving my brother. Absorbing it for so long hadn't been difficult for me, because it was contained in a locked room of its own in my mind. "That's my choice and it's personal. I wouldn't recommend it to anyone else."

A dark shadow crossed Max's face and his nostrils flared. "It's because of Simon, isn't it? It has something to do with him. When they told me you never downloaded, he was the only reason I could think of to hold onto the fear, and I wondered why you'd do it. Remorse is all that made sense. What happened after I left that evening to make you feel guilty?"

Although my face remained carved in stone, my heart jolted, knowing Max was circling the truth.

"Or maybe it's what you didn't do."

He had begun to piece it together.

Despite the still heavy workload, Gabriel had forced me to take a couple of days off for his own peace of mind, strongly encouraging me to rest. Normally, I would have found some way around it, because my job kept me sane and gave me purpose, but due to recent developments, I didn't mind it so much. I'd just gotten home from a shift and was mentally planning a course of locating Simon's journal, when the buzzer let me know someone was at the door. I checked the feed from my data pad and saw Syd.

She looked up at the camera. "Let me in, Evan. I need to talk to you."

Upon opening the door, I knew right away something was different. Usually Syd walked on in. She was as comfortable here as in her own house. Now she stood in front of me fidgeting with the zipper on her jacket as she shuffled from one foot to the other.

"Hey. I didn't know you were coming over, but I'm glad you did."

"Yeah?" Her mouth curved into a smile. She entered, gently closed the door behind her, and eased past me toward the living room.

I trailed behind her and dropped onto the sofa.

She pivoted to face me, arms crossed over her chest as she bit her lip.

Since she didn't speak, I jumped in with what was on my mind. "I've been thinking about how to find Simon's journal, and—"

"Evan, wait. I need to tell you something, and if I don't get it out now, I'm afraid I never will."

"Yeah, sure. Okay." Whatever was running through her head was a mystery to me, but it seemed to have her tied in knots. "Why don't you sit down?" I patted the seat beside me.

"Um….no, I'll just stand." She started pacing in front of me and twisting the ring on her index finger. My eyes followed her path from the kitchen doorway to the window on my right. "I don't know if you've noticed, but things have changed between us."

"Changed?" My brows drew together in confusion. Guess she'd also sensed things had been off.

"Well, not with you, really. Something's changed with me. And I need to tell you about it, because it's gotten harder to be with you without you knowing. Or maybe you already know and just ignore it. Because you do that sometimes." She'd stopped with the pacing, but was now flailing her hands, as she spoke in circles about whatever she was trying to say.

"Syd, you're rambling. Can you just spit it out?"

She took a deep breath, and wrapped her arms around herself. "Evan, I love you." She closed her eyes briefly and her lower lip trembled. "I'm in love with you."

Time stood still for a moment as I processed her words. I forced myself not to look at her, instead keeping my gaze to the floor. Everything fell into place. Syd being uncomfortable around me when I wasn't wearing a shirt, not hanging out in my bedroom like we'd always done, the looks she'd been giving me. I'd been blind to it all. I was an idiot. We'd been friends for so long, it never crossed my mind she could ever feel that way about me.

"Evan, say something. Please." Her voice wavered, and I knew what it cost her to stand in front of me and open herself up this way. She was risking our friendship on the chance I'd feel the same way about her.

Something fluttered in the pit of my stomach. Did I love Syd? Of course I did. But was I in love with her? I'd never really thought about it, because Syd had always been here. She was as essential to my life as breathing.

I pictured what it would be like if we were together that way, and felt a tingling zip up my spine. Syd already made me happy—as happy as I was capable of being without Simon. But could I make her happy? She was such a good person, pure to her core. She'd always been here for me, stayed through all my drama, and called me on my crap. Her light balanced my dark. But what happened when that balance teetered more in my direction? In the give and take of our friendship, the curve was heavily skewed toward me taking, and her giving. She might be content for a while, but all my issues and insecurities would gradually taint her, eating away at the lightness inside her, pulling her down the rabbit hole with me. I'd keep taking until she had nothing left to give. And I couldn't do that to her. Ever.

Syd had said I was a good person, but she deserved someone who could commit fully to her, without holding anything back. Why she would want to be with me was a mystery, because I had nothing to offer, barely stumbling through life as it was. As past history had proven numerous times to numerous people—I wasn't enough.

I closed my eyes and clenched my jaw, knowing what needed to be done, but doubting I possessed the strength to do it. Whatever was left of my heart, anything worth saving inside me, would be shredded beyond repair. But it was for her own good.

"Evan?" she asked in a small voice.

Relaxing back against the couch, I looked anywhere but at her face. I was such a coward. "Well, this is awkward. What should I say, Syd? Thanks?" She sat down hard on the chair across from me. "I don't feel the same way. You're my friend, and that's it. If you've been hanging around hoping that changes, it won't, so stay or go. It makes no difference to me." I shrugged.

Her face paled and she shook her head slowly. "Why are you acting this way? If you don't feel the same way, fine, Evan, I can handle it. I knew it was a big risk telling you how I felt."

I picked at imaginary lint on my pants. "I don't love you. With all the problems in my life, the last thing I need is a clingy girlfriend wanting attention. If I wanted something more than a friend, I'd call one of those girls from my waiting list at school. I'm sure some of them wouldn't mind spending a couple of hours with me—no strings attached."

"No. This isn't you. What's making you say these things?" Hearing the tears in her voice, my impulse was to wrap her in my arms, and I crossed them before instinct won out. I couldn't keep up this charade much longer.

"Isaac seems to like you, so if you want a boyfriend so badly, why don't you go hang out with him? He probably comes with less baggage and can give you the attention you want." She'd never forgive me for this, and I'd never forgive myself.

"You're saying things that can't be taken back, Evan. You've hurt me before, but this is so far beyond that. If someone said you were capable of treating me this way, I never would have believed them. How could I have been so wrong?" When her voice broke on the last word, my eyes flicked in her direction.

And I instantly regretted it.

All the color had drained from her face, and her whole body trembled. I'd shattered her heart. If it were possible, I'd pick up one of the shards and stab my own to spare her this pain, but a wedge needed to be driven between us. Loving me would slowly crush her spirit, and I'd never be able to live with myself knowing I was the cause of it.

"Well, now you understand what I've been trying to tell you for years, Syd. So if you're finished, I've got some work to do. Close the door behind you on your way out." Somehow, I was able to lift myself from the chair and make my way past her on shaky legs. I stopped halfway up the stairs, hidden from her view, and sat with my head between my knees, listening as she released a sob. The thickness I felt in my throat gave way to tears rolling down my face.

Her feet shuffled in the direction of the door, and it closed gently behind her.

After checking to make sure she'd really gone, I bolted upstairs, lurched into the bathroom and vomited up the contents of my stomach, dry heaving for long minutes even after there was nothing left.

♊

Finding Simon's journal had fallen by the wayside. Since Syd had left, anything I ate came right back up, and sleeping became a distant memory. I was restless, bouncing from room to room and going out for runs, pushing harder and harder, trying to get away from myself. I heard someone once say, "No matter where you go, there you are." Now I fully understood the meaning of that phrase.

After finally falling into a restless sleep, I dreamed about ripping off my own skin, gripping chunks of it in my hands, peeling it away from my bones and muscles, and I woke up screaming, my face wet with tears. Didn't take a therapist to figure out the meaning behind that one.

I didn't want to be this person.

Chunks of time were missing, and I'd find myself holding my data pad, finger poised over the button that would contact Syd, wondering how I'd gotten there. I wanted to beg her forgiveness, and would do anything she asked of me, because my words had gone far beyond cruelty. How would I ever face her again?

On my first night back, I stayed in the restroom attached to my office as long as possible, staring in the mirror. I wore the professional, indifferent mask the world saw. Inside, I was a quivering pile of nerves, and wanted to hide in here like a child rather than face Syd. But it had to be done. I splashed cold water on my face and studied my reflection. Bloodshot eyes, dark circles, bags, and a couple of days' worth of dark stubble, because apparently I'd forgotten how to shave. I resembled some of the worst nightmares I'd encountered, but I needed to get out there for the evening briefing.

I tried the meditative breathing used before bending, but it did nothing to calm me. Only I was responsible for this situation.

After opening the door, I rounded the corner to see my team gathered at the conference table. Max studied his data pad, and Amelia and Zia were laughing about something, but my step faltered at the sight of Syd and Isaac. His arm rested on the back of her seat, partly draped over her shoulder, their heads bent together as they spoke to each other. Isaac's other hand reached up and tucked a loose strand of her hair behind her ear, and she smiled in thanks. It was such an intimate gesture—and I couldn't take my eyes off her.

Something inside strained at its bindings and broke loose, like a tidal wave flooding me with pent up feelings of jealousy, rage, and possessiveness. It took every ounce of strength I had not to climb over the table and throw Isaac through the window behind him.

It should be me sitting there with Syd. She should only smile at me that way. He shouldn't be touching her.

I froze. What was wrong with me? Where was this coming from? She'd dated other guys in school and I'd been fine with it, so what was different now? After what I'd said to her, I had absolutely no right to these feelings or any claim on her. Behind the massive, dominating cloud of jealousy, was a tiny shred of logic reminding me Isaac was good for her, and could offer her things I was incapable of giving.

But that didn't make it any easier. The place on my chest where Syd had lain her head as she'd nestled against me began to ache, and my hand drifted to that spot, remembering the feelings of contentment and peace that enfolded me when I'd held her.

"Evan? Are you all right?" My head jerked in Amelia's direction as her question broke my trance. How long had I been staring?

"I'm fine." My voice was gruff and harsher than I'd intended. "Let's get started."

The briefing was conducted on auto pilot. Detached was the only way I could function right now, and not once did my eyes stray in Syd's direction. The team had their assignments for the evening, and were trailing out the door when she spoke.

"Evan, I need a moment." Her voice was cold, impersonal, and very un-Syd-like.

Isaac threw a sinister expression in my direction before exiting the room.

She waited until everyone was gone before talking. "I'd like to request a transfer to another team." Like me, she wore a mask that disguised her true feelings, but knowing Syd for so long, I saw right through it to the suffering underneath.

"What are you doing?"

She refused to meet my eyes, instead, focusing on something to the right of my face. "I'm not sure what you mean."

"With him, Syd! What are you doing with Isaac?"

Her eyes found mine and she gaped at me in shock. "Are you serious, Evan? This is what you wanted. It's none of your business anyway."

I shoved my hands through my hair in frustration, pulling on the ends. "That's not what I...I didn't want you to..." What did I want to say? What was wrong with me?

"Didn't want me to what? You made your feelings about me crystal clear. You can't have it both ways." She stood up taller, chin jutting out in defiance. "About the transfer..."

"I won't approve a transfer," I growled.

"Your permission isn't needed. I was only asking as a courtesy—not that you deserve it. Gabriel approved it before the meeting. It will be effective next week, then you won't have to bestow any more of your valuable attention on me." She spun on her heel and walked out, slamming the door behind her.

Conflicting emotions surged through me. My impulse was to run after her, plead forgiveness, and keep Isaac away. But none of that was possible. She was doing what I'd asked. I kicked the chair closest to me against the wall, threw another one across the room, then planted my hands on the table and hung my head between my arms.

What had I done?

Chapter 19
Evan
Present Day

Most of this evening's session had been a battle of wills. Max's overconfidence grated on my nerves, and I sighed heavily in annoyance. He'd made minor mistakes in all four simulations, was argumentative, unyielding, and rejected any suggestions I offered. Sometimes people needed to learn the hard way. It was time to bust down his ego a few notches by kicking up the simulation a couple of levels. He was a coiled bundle of energy, hands clenching and unclenching at his sides, as he shifted his weight from one foot to the other.

"Evan, I'm ready and can handle this." He tilted his head side to side loosening his neck muscles. "I understand how to correct my mistakes from the other sims tonight."

Some people only learned after they were thrown into the deep end and told to swim. Max could be their poster child. I leaned against the control panel and folded my arms over my chest. "So, you think you're ready to ramp it up?" I asked, arching an eyebrow. "Because if you're certain, then I'll put you in at level four."

At the mention of the higher level, Max licked his lips nervously and swallowed hard. He shut his eyes for a moment and when they reopened, the overconfidence had conquered the doubt. "Definitely."

A shadow passed over his face, but he'd asked for this and insisted he was ready. Should I really be the person responsible for holding him back? I couldn't help the wide grin that spread across my face. "Then let's do it."

Max followed me down the stairs from the control room to the main floor where we each strapped ourselves in the chairs. Ky prepped us with the leads and intravenous line. We could easily have walked into the simulator, but to keep conditions as realistic as possible, the sedative was required during training.

The simulator was a freestanding, saucer-like structure, smooth to the touch, standing three stories high. Once inside, Benders were surrounded by three-hundred-sixty degree screens, including the domed ceiling, which could be programmed with an existing nightmare in the system or set on random, selecting actual nightmares from previous clients as reported by Benders. I found those more challenging. Within the simulator, three-dimensional creatures or people could also be created, and looked just as real as we did.

My gaze traveled to the window above us where I saw Charlie, the control tech on duty. "Take us up to level four sim, Charlie."

I heard the surprise in his voice from the com unit in my ear. "Confirming you said level four, Evan?"

"Affirmative, level four." Guess I wasn't the only one who thought Max wasn't ready.

I leaned back against the headrest and nodded at Ky to let him know we were ready. "Administering sedative." I felt the familiar tingling as it snaked through my veins.

Max's knuckles had turned white from gripping his armrests.

I smirked, then closed my eyes.

Soon I felt solid ground beneath my feet, and saw Max standing to my left. Beneath us was a deep, mossy green forest floor, and the air smelled of wet leaves and dirt. Towering trees flanked us, their lowest branches several feet above my head, and I heard crickets chirping in the distance. Through the foliage I could make out a full moon, but the light was diffused by the tree leaves, allowing only dim illumination. This sim promised to be challenging, and I grinned in anticipation.

Taking a step back, I nodded, letting Max know it was all him now. He crouched low, side-stepping around the clearing where we stood, readying himself for an attack that may or may not come. Sometimes the mind of a client looked threatening, but that's all it was—threatening, with nothing to back it up. In those cases, the conscious mind was suspicious of the intrusion, while the subconscious level permitted a Bender to be there.

Catching movement from the corner of my eye, I watched as vines snaked from beneath bushes, looping themselves around Max's ankles. Not very challenging, but some sims were more of a gradual build. He unsheathed a knife from his belt and easily sliced them away. While occupied with the vines, several of the overhanging tree branches lengthened toward him, winding their way downward, the smaller branches entwining and strengthening themselves as they drew closer.

The tips of the entangled branches moved forward to surround Max, then jabbed downward and buried themselves in the dirt. His head jerked up as one of the coils drove itself into the mossy soil in front of him. He spun around to run, realizing too late he was caged, and rammed his shoulder into a branch.

"That'll leave a mark," I muttered. He'd sport a painful bruise tomorrow to remind him of his mistake.

Max chipped away at the makeshift cage, and I assumed his strategy was to make an opening just large enough for him to slide through. Not a bad idea. The easiest escape would have been to fly, but his skills were still developing, and I guessed he'd either not thought quickly enough, or didn't trust himself quite yet. While silently observing him, grudgingly admiring some of his moves, a sudden wave of dizziness crashed into me. I swayed heavily on my feet, reaching for a nearby boulder to steady myself.

What was this? The sim was only programmed to interact with Max, and I was just a bystander. I took deep breaths and closed my eyes, concentrating on the rough, cool surface of the stone beneath my hand in an attempt to steady myself. Just as the vertigo started to pass, a burst of excruciating pain sliced into my head with an intensity that caused my eyes to roll back. I fell to the ground on my side, my body curling in on itself.

A ringing in my ears eclipsed all other sound. It felt as if glass shards were burying themselves in my brain, and I opened my mouth to scream, but was unable to draw breath into my lungs. My hands pushed against either side of my head to squeeze out the pain or keep the skin from slicing open and expelling the contents inside. I wasn't coherent enough to decide. Through the haze of unbearable torment, it occurred to me something must be happening to my body lying in the Bender chair, and I wondered if I was dying. Surely Ky or Charlie would get help.

As abruptly as the attack began, it ended, like a light being switched off, and I rolled heavily to my back, chest heaving. I lay on the mossy ground quietly recovering, trying to understand what prompted the attack, when the space inside me that housed Simon for more than sixteen years was filled with his calming, reassuring presence. I smiled in relief, knowing that somehow, somewhere, my brother was still near and had helped me. In seconds, the sensation was violently ripped away again. My chest shot upwards and spine arched, then fell back to the ground.

I was covered in sweat, my body feeling bruised and battered. A low buzzing emanated from the com unit in my ear, and as my hearing gradually returned, the buzzing became Max's cries for help, and Charlie's frantic voice trying to raise me.

"Evan, answer me! Can you hear me? Acknowledge, please!"

"Charlie?" I asked weakly, barely able to form words. The tension in Charlie's voice combined with Max's screams told me something had gone horribly wrong.

"Evan, finally! What the hell is happening to you and Max? Both of your vitals are off the charts. You need to get to him immediately. It's a Code One system malfunction. The sim won't shut down, and I can't override it."

I shook my head, trying to clear it. "T-tell him to eject."

"Don't you think I tried that?" he snapped. "He's in trouble, unable to eject, and I've lost contact with him."

A pit settled in my stomach. While I'd been struck helpless, Max had lost the battle with the sim. This could be catastrophic. A system malfunction of this severity was unheard of. Bender communication had never been lost, and a trainee never unsupervised during a nightmare sim—but all had occurred on my watch.

I pushed myself to a sitting position, grimacing as my body fought against me, then used a fallen dead tree to hoist myself to my feet. Max needed me, and although he'd been screaming moments ago, now there was only silence.

That scared me even more.

I unsheathed my knife, unsure of what awaited me, and lurched past the few trees separating us. Stumbling into the clearing, I found the situation completely out of control. Max was in imminent danger. Four of the larger trees had encircled him, their thicker branches now wrapped around his wrists and ankles holding him immobile and spread eagle twenty feet in the air, his knife lying useless on the ground below. Part of their trunks had twisted into something hideous that resembled a human face, and I heard a groaning sound, but it didn't belong to Max.

Not only were the trees moving on their own, they sounded as if they were alive, moaning in ecstasy at inflicting torture, while their branches continued to thread around Max's limbs and torso area like bandages around a mummy.

That I could handle, but the branch encircling his neck was cutting off his oxygen supply, and his face was colored dark red, bordering on purple. It was a miracle he'd been able to scream at all.

"Max!" But he was unconscious, blond hair curtaining half his face. Charlie was right. It would be impossible for him to reach his eject button, even if he were conscious. If I didn't get to him in the next few seconds, there was a real possibility he could die.

And it would be my fault.

Even though I'd been incapacitated by whatever had happened, he'd been my responsibility. Simon would never forgive me if something happened to his boyfriend.

The eject button was located on Max's left wrist, and blood trickled down his arm from where he'd struggled against the coarse tree branch. I launched myself into the air, my arm outstretched to press the button. Only inches away, a tree limb peeled away from his body and stabbed my left hand, piercing my palm. Blood spurted from the wound. I jerked backwards, hovering in the air just out of its reach, and it didn't seem inclined to come any closer.

What kind of screwed up malfunction was this? I shouldn't be recognized as a participant or threat, so why was I being assaulted? "Charlie, can you stop the sim yet? It's preventing me from helping Max."

"No, Evan, I've lost all control! The only solution is to delete the program, but you and Max have to get out first. If you're caught in the system, you know what that means." I heard the panic in Charlie's voice, and knew exactly what would happen if we didn't eject—Max and I would be lost inside permanently. Our bodies would still be lying in the Bender chairs, but our consciousness forever trapped inside a computer program. If we weren't killed first.

In an ideal situation, I'd be able to grab onto Max and push my own eject button, taking him with me. Unfortunately, only the person wearing the button was expelled. Seconds were precious, and Max's life was literally being choked out of him. I needed to act fast.

"Charlie, have medical standing by."

"Already here," he confirmed.

If the trees wouldn't allow me near him, I had to think outside the box. With clients, our utmost priority was to do no harm while in their minds, but this was a simulation. That allowed me some leeway. "Charlie, from the time you press delete, how long do we have to get out?"

"Evan, surely you're not thinking..."

"How long, Charlie?" I demanded.

He didn't bother suppressing a sigh. "By the time it cycles through, maybe ten seconds."

"Get ready." This had never been tried before, but it made sense. Physically, no one was actually inside the simulator. Metaphysically, Max and I were there. It stood to reason that if we could be injured within the simulation, our weapons could also harm the simulator. Or maybe my logic was all kinds of wrong, but my options were limited, and time was short.

Pulling the iron mallet from my belt, I launched into the air, soaring over the trees as their branches reached out for me. When I could go no higher, I began smashing the panels lining the walls and roof of the simulator. Shattered glass fell to the ground, and I could only hope none of it struck Max, or the branches entwining his body offered protection from the shards.

"Now, Charlie!"

"It's done. Get out, Evan."

The animated trees were faltering, some losing their strength, while others disappeared altogether as the simulation broke down. I dove toward Max, ejecting him just as the branches holding him splintered. Less than a second later, I followed him.

𝕀𝕀

I was greeted with total chaos as my eyes jerked open upon reentering my body. Charlie shouted program delete commands to other sim techs. The Bender emergency alarm echoed off the walls, nearly eclipsing all other sounds. Ky's voice was tight and clipped as he called out vitals.

Whipping my head to the right, I saw Max surrounded by medbots working frantically over his unconscious body. I ripped off my sensors and leaped out of the chair to get to him, but a medbot blocked my way.

To my left, Charlie rushed toward me, and I moved in his direction. "What happened in there? That malfunction may have killed Max!" Charlie stopped dead in his tracks as I stalked toward him. "What did you do, Charlie? Did you screw up the program somehow?"

"Me?" he squeaked, eyes wide in shock. "What about you? Where did you go? You were unresponsive to our calls. Why would you ignore your com?"

"Your rogue sim also attacked me, and I couldn't hear anything!" Worry for Max elevated my voice, and I was nearly shouting at Charlie. "Did you screw that up too?"

"Check it, Evan," he growled, teeth clenched. "And don't accuse me of not knowing how to do my job, when it was you who decided to throw a trainee into a level four nightmare sim and then abandon him."

Standing only inches from his face, I noticed a prominent vein pulsing in his forehead. I took a step closer, towering over him by several inches. "You're not putting your failure on me, Charlie. Before I was attacked, Max had things under control."

"I look forward to hearing that story." Gabriel. His voice dripped ice and accusations, his eyes cold steel and fixated on me. "Evan, get your hand taken care of by medical, and then go straight to my office."

Glancing down, I saw blood dripping from my left hand, leaving splatters on the floor. I'd forgotten about the wound inflicted by the tree branch. "I need to check on Max first."

"Now." The tone of his voice left no room for argument.

My gaze darted to Charlie once more as I stormed past him, the corner of his mouth twitching as he glared at me.

Looking over my shoulder, the last thing I saw was Gabriel bent over Max's still motionless body as he received status updates from the medbots.

Chapter 20
Simon
Present Day

"You'd make things easier on everyone if you'd allow me in, Simon. I know the key to the information is inside your mind somewhere."

I'd been correct in assuming Sebastian was responsible for my missing files on the Posarius Project. He'd managed to use that information and open a portal for a length of time that would have allowed him to escape back to Tage. Unfortunately, he knew regaining his place in society wasn't possible, and his ego was too large to accept anything less. As a consolation, he'd captured me instead, promising if I'd help him, he'd release me.

But I knew better.

Besides being unable to maintain the opening, he had no idea how to get to Posarius. It infuriated him that he'd come across something beyond his intellect.

Dr. Sebastian's ability to justify using innocent people for experiments had shattered any illusions I'd harbored about him as a brilliant man and inspiring mentor, but even in the Realm, he continued down a demented path. With his charismatic personality, authoritative manner, and promises of escape to Posarius, he'd recruited a loyal following naïve enough to believe his lies. If his plans ever came to fruition, I had no doubt they'd be left behind, but for now, they did his bidding, and kept me locked away.

"If you'd included your final sequencing with your files, this whole unpleasant situation could have been avoided. You'd be home with your brother, and I'd be celebrating my new life and carving my niche on Posarius by now. Instead, we're marooned in this godforsaken hell without the common luxuries of life, fighting for every morsel of food, if it can be deemed as such." He wrinkled his face in disgust, peering through the murky, dirt-encrusted windows of the room that had been my prison for the past year.

I huffed. Since the night Sebastian had captured me, my luxuries of life included a filthy mattress on the floor, and the chair I was tied to. With nothing to occupy my mind, another of his torture techniques, my sole purpose had become developing ways to communicate with Evan.

I'd been aware Sebastian had identified a need and created the Mindbender Academy years ago. However, discovering he was a gifted, accomplished Bender was an unexpected and unwelcome surprise. Since he'd brought me here, he'd practiced stringently on other convicts, entering their minds, planting suggestions, and manipulating them after threatening to expose their secrets. So far, he'd come across only one mind with impenetrable barriers—the one containing the information he needed to escape the Realm.

It was mine, of course, and he was correct in deducing the information was safely locked away in my inner recesses. All those years of barricading Evan's mood swings—constant, distracting music in his head that drifted over to mine and giddiness to anger in the blink of an eye—had been the perfect training for obstructing Sebastian's attempts.

"My suspicions about you were the sole reason I never completed the file, and if my captivity prevents you from being unleashed into another world and destroying it, then I'm content with my choice."

He clenched his jaw in frustration. Any form of intimidation he'd attempted had no effect on me. Yes, he'd hurt me physically, but he'd never incapacitated me...because he needed me. Since Evan and my parents were unreachable, using them as leverage wasn't a viable option, and he didn't know of Max's existence, an unforeseen and fortunate benefit of keeping our relationship a secret.

Max. Just the thought of him made me want to withdraw to the world I'd created in my mind, where we were still together and Evan was accepting of our relationship. More than that, he and Max were friends. With nothing to occupy me other than my thoughts of escape, ways to outsmart Sebastian, and edible food, I created scenarios of what our lives would be like together, the three of us a family, and Tage once more a habitable planet. The constant physical ache in my chest from missing them flared up. That imaginary world and the thought of being with them again were the only things that kept me from giving up. I'd consciously avoided thinking about Max moving on in the year I'd been gone. I wouldn't blame him if he had and only wanted him to be happy, but in my fictional world, he was waiting for me.

Sebastian moved away from the window and sat across from me in the chair he'd brought in with him, crossing his ankle over his knee. Any indication of frustration had vanished. Instead, he radiated confidence in every movement, from the way he raised his chin to the calm, matter-of-fact manner in which he observed me. Threats and withdrawal of comforts and food hadn't been effective, so perhaps this was a new tactic he was testing. I regarded him with suspicion, but a small part of me held of sliver of doubt, wondering if he actually held some unknown advantage.

He studied his hands, no doubt offended by the dirty, ragged nails, and missing his weekly manicures. "Since our supply of sedative was so low and my contacts on Tage have been unable to send any more, I've been experimenting with a new bending technique. Did I fail to mention this earlier?"

His relaxed stance and casual remark about bending set off internal alarms, and my stomach clenched. Sebastian never discussed anything without a reason. I'd known the sedative supply was nearly exhausted and was hoping that would put an end to his continuous attacks on my mind.

"I've been gradually tapering the amount administered, and made a remarkable discovery. I can now successfully bend without any sedative." My heart tightened. This wasn't a positive development, although I'd been expecting it. If there was such a thing, Evan was a natural Bender, first entering my mind without the use of sedative when we were children. Perhaps some of it was because of our connection, but my own endeavors had failed. I'd long suspected he had an innate ability, and knew he'd found his calling when the Mindbender program was created. Upon learning of Sebastian's bending, I correctly guessed he also possessed a natural ability, and it would only be a matter of time before he came to the same realization.

"Without that restriction, I wondered what else I'd be capable of. And it's beyond what I'd imagined." He leaned forward, elbows resting on his knees, gaze never leaving mine. "I'm able to journey past the Realm and into the minds of people on Tage." Trails of ice crept down my spine. If he truly was able to do this, and if Tage's scientists had somehow found my work and been able to continue it, Sebastian could retrieve the missing information from their minds.

"I've kept your brother busy over the past few weeks." At the mention of Evan, my heart ceased beating from fear of what this could mean for him. "While searching through our fellow scientists' thoughts for information on portals, I left behind several terrifying nightmares that will result in an increased workload for him. Tired, overworked, and challenged, he may inadvertently let down his guard and allow me to slip in." A menacing smile slid across his face, as I calculated all the ways he could harm my twin.

"Just imagine the damage I could do, Simon. Nightmares would be a waste of my time. I was thinking more along the lines of permanent damage." He sat back in his chair and tapped a finger to his chin. "But a recurring nightmare about your brutal death, a death Evan caused, would be something he'd relive every night. Not a bad place to start."

"You'll never reach him," I retorted, my voice flat and even. "Evan is as strong a Bender as you, maybe even more so."

He laughed bitterly. "You can't be certain of that. Give me the information I want, and spare your brother pain and suffering. The choice is yours." His expression was arrogant, knowing he'd cornered his prey. Although an undeniably brilliant man, one of Sebastian's downfalls was the assumption he was always the most intelligent person in the room. He might think he'd accounted for every possible outcome of a situation, but that was only if he possessed all the relevant information.

Which he didn't.

With all my energies focused on communicating with Evan, I'd finally had a breakthrough, coming very close to speaking with him. I may not bear his Bender abilities, but our twin connection and my unrelenting desire to escape Sebastian, this prison, and the Realm were the driving forces behind my success. And returning to Evan and Max. On Tage, Sebastian knew my brother and I were close, but he was unaware of the extraordinary bond we shared. A bond which gave us a distinct advantage.

"I have every confidence in Evan's abilities, so do what you will. It makes no difference, because I'll never tell you how to sustain a portal or get to Posarius." I smiled. "How frustrating for you that a man of your intellect is at a standstill because of not one, but two challenges you can't overcome." Casting doubt on his intelligence had the desired effect of infuriating him and knocking him off balance. His expression of content twisted into one of hatred.

"You will regret those words, Simon. No challenge is too great for me. While I infiltrate your brother's mind, I'll allow you to watch and suffer, knowing you're the cause of his destruction."

Sebastian closed his eyes and calmed his breathing. Evan had explained Bender techniques, so I understood what was required. Right now, Sebastian was picturing my twin's face and preparing to separate from his body. I'd indicated my complete faith in Evan's abilities as a Bender, and hoped he wouldn't disappoint me. For both our sakes.

My own eyes snapped shut as I also conjured my brother's face and searched deep within myself for the root of our connection, confident that was the key in leading me to him. I'd barely achieved this only a couple of times, but my fear for him was a powerful force. Failure wasn't an option. He'd need my help. I focused on the feel of Evan, the storm of emotions and noise in his head, both his quick temper and joy of life. His intense desire for acceptance by our parents. My body was light and flew quickly through hazy clouds and swirling colors while searching, and I concentrated more intently, nearly dizzy from the momentum. Suddenly he was there, surrounding me, and the familiarity was so overwhelming I nearly cried out.

While his mind instantly accepted me, it simultaneously battled an attacker, and I felt Evan's confusion, along with his strength and determination as he fought against Sebastian. This was a situation he'd never experienced. Nightmares and the occasional person who thought they'd penetrate his barriers were nothing compared to an unusually talented and driven Bender, and while Evan's body was in physical distress, his mind continued to defend itself.

Not being formally trained in barricading my mind, I resorted to my own technique in blocking Evan, aligned myself with his defenses, reinforced his walls, and pushed against Sebastian, refusing him entry. I shared the crippling agony my brother experienced. It was like being miles below the ocean's surface, the intense pressure of tons of water above, and I wondered how his body avoided succumbing to the torment.

Evan was weakening under the unbearable, continuous attack. I couldn't let him fail. With one last forceful thrust against Sebastian, he withdrew and was gone. I'd depleted nearly all my energy, but had just enough to allow myself to settle inside my brother, missing our 'twinness' as he'd called it. For one brief moment, I experienced the serenity of knowing my soul was home, and nearly sobbed in relief.

Then I was snapped back to my body, imprisoned in the Realm.

CHAPTER 21
EVAN
PRESENT DAY

I paced the floor while waiting for Gabriel in his office, alternating between staring through the window overlooking the common area below, and studying my surroundings. What once seemed a sleek, methodical area void of clutter now felt cold and indifferent to me, lacking any personality or insight into who Gabriel really was. If I hadn't known him for the past couple of years, based on his office, I'd assume he was detached and incapable of any genuine feelings. But more than once, Gabriel had demonstrated that he cared for me as more than a subordinate. About the welfare of my team, too. We weren't just employees to him.

But the way he'd looked at me in the lab had me wary, and the longer he kept me waiting, the more anxious I became. There was no way I could have predicted a system malfunction. What if Max was seriously injured or hadn't survived? What if he'd lived, but was permanently disabled physically or mentally? No matter what I'd said to Charlie, this was on me. Attacked or not, I'd left Max in a potentially dangerous situation, with no backup or guidance.

And what was that, anyway? Now that the danger was over, I had time to examine it. Charlie had said my vitals were off the charts, and I'd felt like my body was being pummeled with a sledgehammer. Then there was the brief sensation of Simon. Whether it had been seconds or hours, I knew with unshakable certainty it was him. But the question remained—where was he?

The click of the office door brought me out of my head, and I prepared to make my case to Gabriel. He entered the room with the momentum of a crashing wave, strode behind his desk, leaned over and planted his hands on the flat surface, fixing his gaze on me.

"Gabriel, I—"

"Not. A. Word." His rage was barely restrained, and it grew in the space between us. "Sit." He pointed at the chair behind me.

I backed up until the chair hit my knees, then I dropped into it. Which was probably a good thing, because I felt a little weak. This wasn't the Gabriel I knew.

He closed his eyes and inhaled deeply, his nostrils flaring when he exhaled. Then he slowly opened his eyes. "What were you thinking? Or were you even thinking? You shirked your responsibilities as a team leader and mentor, deserted your trainee, and left him in a level four simulation, knowing the dangers he could be facing." His voice was level and controlled, but laced with fury.

"Gabriel, something happened to me..."

He slammed his fist on the desk. "You do not have permission to speak!" His hands now gripped the back of his chair, knuckles white. "What's worse is that the sim controller attempted to contact you not just once, but numerous times, and you disregarded your com while Max fought for his life, all the while calling for help.

"I'm aware of your history with him, but I never thought you capable of deliberately putting his life in danger. I trusted you to demonstrate the maturity and integrity required at your level, and had the utmost faith in you to rise above any personal feelings."

A vise gripped my chest, and the longer Gabriel fumed, the tighter it squeezed. But the disappointment I saw reflected in his eyes cut worse than his fury.

He spun around, his back to me, and stared out the window. I swallowed hard and wet my lips. "May I speak?"

His back stiffened and he turned slowly to face me again. "You may."

"How's Max?"

He raised a brow. "Now you're concerned about his welfare?"

"Please, just tell me. Is he all right?"

"Max is conscious and doing well, considering the trauma he suffered."

Exhaling loudly in relief, I ran my hands over my face. Max was alive.

He might never forgive me, but that's something I could live with. I leaned forward, elbows on my knees. "Gabriel, not that I'm shirking my responsibility, but something happened to me in the sim. Maybe it was because of the malfunction or something else, but it left me incapacitated when the situation got out of hand with Max."

It was subtle, but I saw a hint of concern, before the stoic expression returned. "Evan, you're an experienced Bender. You've handled precarious situations many times, so what could possibly have kept you from assisting Max?"

"Excruciating pain in my head, loss of hearing—I wondered if my body was being attacked in the lab, but when Charlie said the program had gone rogue, that would have been the logical conclusion. Except for one thing."

"Which was?"

"Simon. It was Simon, Gabriel."

Because of his flawless posture, most people wouldn't have noticed his imperceptible slump upon hearing my words. But I did. "I thought we were finished with this and agreed the last time was a hallucination brought on by exhaustion."

I shook my head. "No, technically I never agreed—I just didn't correct you. Yes, I've been working double shifts and haven't been sleeping as much, but after sixteen years of having a part of Simon buried inside me, I know when he's near. It was brief, but he was there. And almost like he'd been helping me fight off the attack."

Gabriel closed his eyes and shook his head, then sat down heavily in his chair, as if he could no longer carry the weight of his responsibilities. "I wasn't going to mention this, but Syd was in here earlier, and asked for a transfer. I'm not sure exactly what transpired between the two of you, but when your own partner, a best friend who's been fiercely loyal to you, doesn't want to work with you anymore, it's an indicator your problems are more serious than I'd imagined."

"It's not like that."

He held up a hand to silence me. "Evan, if you need counseling, you know we'll provide it, and get you the help you need. In hindsight, perhaps that's a path you should have taken long ago."

I fell back against my chair. Not this again. "What do I need to say to get you to believe me? I'm not hallucinating." My voice rose an octave, to which Gabriel cocked an eyebrow in silent warning. "Simon was there, just like the last time. It's our connection, and I'm certain he's trying to communicate with me."

Gabriel's eyes tightened. He smoothed his hair back to where it was gathered at the nape of his neck, then clasped his hands together on top of the desk. "Evan, in light of everything that's happened, not just today with Max and Charlie, but also with Ky and Syd, you've left me no choice. Effective immediately, you're suspended."

His words knocked the wind from me, and it was an effort just to reply. "Gabriel, please..."

"I can't have you endangering and threatening team members. You're obviously overworked, and under a tremendous amount of stress. Some rest and time away would be beneficial to everyone."

"Gabriel, you can't..."

He raised his brows. "I assure you, I can."

My head dropped and my hands ached from gripping the arm rests. This couldn't be happening. After Simon was gone, I'd clung desperately to Syd and my job—they'd given me a reason to get out of bed every day. Now I'd lost both. Tears threatened to brim over, making me angry with myself, and I refused to raise my head and let Gabriel see them. "You know how important this position is to me. It's all I have left." My quivering voice made me even angrier. "Please...Gabriel, reconsider your decision."

His silence stirred a grain of hope inside me, but upon peeking through the hair that had fallen over my forehead, I was met with something like pity, and his mouth was set in a fine line. "Evan, we'll investigate the malfunction and take statements, but the bottom line is, you endangered Max's life. Fortunately, he's fine, but the outcome could have been very different, and your actions can't go unpunished. Please clear out your office until further notice. That's my official answer.

"My unofficial answer," he cleared his throat and my head snapped up. "is that, if all goes well, provided you seek help with anger issues and get some much needed rest, you may request to be reinstated as TL within a reasonable amount of time."

Gabriel rose and walked around the desk to stand beside me, placing his hand on my shoulder and squeezing it. "You're more to me than just an employee, Evan, and I care about you as if you were my own son. I know how much you miss Simon, and although you'd never admit it, even your parents sometimes. If there's anything I can do for you during your suspension, you know where to find me."

"Why won't you believe me? The machine, the pain. Simon..." It wasn't fair that, once more, no one took my side.

"Evan." He squeezed my shoulder again. "I'll be checking in to see how you're doing."

So it was done. I'd trusted Gabriel, allowed him to get close after offering to mentor me during Bender training. He'd seen me through losing Simon—forcing me out of bed, making me eat, pushing me to work. Knowing he didn't believe me gouged a new wound deep inside. Considering the number already inflicted, including the recent devastation with Syd, I'd have thought the intensity would lessen. I was wrong. Gabriel was just another adult I'd disappointed, someone else who'd lost faith in me.

Time to reengage shields.

I swiped my eyes with the cuff of my shirt, squared my jaw, then stood to face him. "I'll be out in ten minutes," I said, my voice flat as I turned toward the door.

"I'll be in touch soon, Evan."

"Don't bother." And I pulled the door shut behind me.

CHAPTER 22
EVAN
PRESENT DAY

I ignored the accusing stares and whispers from other Benders I encountered on the way to my office. Their opinions held no weight with me. No matter the truth, they'd gossip and exaggerate events, and I was mature enough to admit it was partly my fault because of the 'Keep Out' sign Syd swore was hanging around my neck.

Gabriel had said a temporary suspension, but the fact that I'd been told to clean out my office hinted at a permanent decision, and someone else would replace me. Thinking of another TL taking my place, giving out assignments to my team, and moving into my office was like a punch to the gut. I wouldn't give it up without a fight.

Like Gabriel, my office wasn't littered with personal effects, and after surveying the room, I realized my only possession was a picture of Simon and me. We'd been about seven-years-old, playing in a sandbox in our backyard. While I bulldozed and plowed through sand with my vehicles, Simon carefully carved out structures, weighing and measuring the portions, even then creating things beyond my grasp. The corner of my mouth turned up at remembering how he'd only spared our mother a minute to take the picture, anxious to get back to his creations. I shoved that and my data pad into a bag, then looked once more around the room that had been more of a home to me than my own. At least here, there was activity, laughter, noise, and camaraderie. Maybe I was never in the center of it, but if given the choice of observing it from the sidelines or sitting alone in my lifeless house, I'd choose the sidelines every time.

But my empty, lifeless house was all that was left, so I slung my bag over my shoulder, squared my shoulders, and flung open the door. No way would I let these people see me crawling away with my tail between my legs, even if that's the way I really felt inside. Pride was one of the few things I had left.

♊

Tossing my bag over the back of a chair, I trudged to the couch, and allowed my weary body to collapse onto it. Both mental and physical exhaustion warred with the other part of me that wanted to stay awake and plan my next move. How could I connect with Simon? Where was his journal? I lay staring at the ceiling, the stillness of the house like a roaring in my ears. What would I do now?

I must have drifted off, because the next thing I became aware of was standing in a stark white room—white walls, white floor, white ceiling—just a white nothing. Maybe I wasn't even standing, but something felt solid beneath me. There was no sound at all, almost as if I were in a vacuum. If this was a dream, it didn't promise much entertainment. Turning in a circle, I searched for a door, stairs...anything to lead me out. Nothing.

If this was a lucid dream, maybe I could kick it up a notch, add some action, or jump off a cliff for fun. A second before completing a circle, I knew he was there, and came to an abrupt halt. Simon stood so close to me, I could touch him. I gasped. But if this was a dream, that wasn't a possibility.

He lunged at me, throwing his arms around my neck and pulling me toward him as I embraced him. My brother was solid, real. He was here, and that sense of peace missing since the second he'd left was returned, like a warm blanket draped over my shoulders. Whatever stupid insecurities I'd let come between us, no matter how big of an ass I'd made of myself, all was forgotten. Simon was alive.

I released him. There were so many questions, apologies, and plans to be made. His appearance was haggard, like he hadn't slept in days—or weeks even—and he was so thin. His hair had grown longer and he had dark circles under his eyes, but the air around him vibrated with urgency.

"We don't have much time, Evan. The connection could terminate at any time, and there are things you need to know."

"How are you here?" My voice was unsteady, hovering somewhere between an overjoyed shout and sob of happiness.

"It's like when we were young. It's taken a year for me to do what you succeeded at on your first attempt." He smiled, shaking his head slowly. "The strength of your mental barrier is something to be proud of. I managed to penetrate it only because of our connection."

"Where are you?"

"I'm in the Realm because of Dr. Sebastian. He opened a portal and pulled me through."

"Can't you open it again and come home?"

He shook his head. "I'm being held prisoner. The project I was working on when I was taken..."

"Your files were lost or stolen, Max..."

"It's why Sebastian kidnapped me. Find my journal and you'll understand—" Simon cut off mid-sentence and cocked his head sideways as if listening to something. "Someone's outside the room. The journal, Evan."

"But I've looked everywhere. There's no journal. How can I help you?" I was terrified he'd disappear at any moment and leave me with no answers.

"Ask Max about it. Tell him to take you to our place. He'll know."

"Isn't there another way?"

"I have to go. You need to know Sebastian is a Bender. He tried to attack you earlier, and someone on your side helped him when I was taken."

"What? Who?"

As he dissolved in front of me, his final words were like stones shattering the last remnant of support system I clung to. "Don't trust Gabriel."

♊

I jerked upright from a deep sleep, still slumped on the couch littered with dirty clothes. The sterile, white, windowless, doorless room, along with Simon, were all gone, only existing temporarily in my subconscious. Sitting up, I leaned over, elbows on my knees, and rubbed my face.

It couldn't be true. Simon had to be mistaken. Sure, I was harboring some ill feelings toward Gabriel after my suspension, but for the past year, he'd been a constant. A safe place. He'd helped rebuild pieces of me when I was unable or unwilling. He'd provided an alternative home. He'd been a friend to me.

Besides Syd, there was no one I trusted more.

And Sebastian could bend? He'd nearly gotten in my head, and I cursed myself for not recognizing an attack. Focusing on the level of complication accompanying that revelation was too much of a stretch for me right now.

Simon said Gabriel had known all along where he was, and was responsible for him being taken. He'd watched as I drowned in grief, only half existing, and cutting myself off from nearly everyone around me.

But my brother wouldn't have made a statement like that without proof—that's the way he operated. He'd repeated it over and over, stressing that you never drew conclusions without all the information, and could make a statement based on fact. Hard, conclusive evidence.

He'd never lie to me. I realized that now. But much too late.

How could Gabriel, the man who'd been closer to me than my own father, have deceived me for the past year? He was above reproach, embodied integrity, had a work ethic that put most everyone to shame. Why would he help someone as demented as Sebastian?

Gabriel said he was proud of me, said I was like a son to him. How could he have said those things and meant them? Answer—he didn't. All lies. He'd had a front row seat, watching me become a shadow of the person I'd once been, grieving for the brother who'd meant more to me than anyone in my life. And all along he'd known everything.

Panic and nausea came in waves. I felt something rip open inside me, like my soul was being split in half. Rolling to my side, I folded my body into a fetal position, hoping to find relief, but the deep ache inside me only grew. Pain careened through my chest, wrapped around my heart, then shot through my limbs, striking every nerve ending in my body, and my head dropped back as my mouth opened in a silent scream.

I was alone.

I had no one left.

And I'd probably failed the only person who cared about me.

It was too much to bear, and the weight of emotion threatened to snap me in half. I lay motionless in a ball, staring at the wall behind the chairs, but not seeing anything. Minutes, hours, or days could have passed—I'd lost track of time.

Knowing I was truly alone, losing the only three people I'd cared anything about, had drilled a chasm so vast inside, I pictured my limbs separated from my body, internal organs scattered on the couch beneath me. Whatever had been holding the pieces together had dissolved.

Then, a tiny spark deep within reminded me there was someone who'd stood by me through everything, as I'd erected walls and withdrawn behind them. Someone who'd never lied to me. Someone who'd rubbed my nose in the blunt truth no matter how much I hadn't wanted to hear it.

Syd.

But I'd sent her away with my cruel and heartless words when she'd offered me her heart. A gift any man would be incredibly lucky to receive. I needed her, and I could only hope that once again, she hadn't given up on me.

⁂

I had no memory of going to Syd's house. One minute I was thinking about begging and groveling, wondering if she'd even speak to me, and the next, her front door stood before me. Miraculously, it was raining for the first time in months, and water streamed down my face. Considering my pruny fingers and water-logged clothing, I'd been outside for quite a while—and I hadn't noticed the downpour. I silently prayed the rain wasn't the only miracle on the agenda tonight.

Trudging up the stone steps of her porch, the sound of her muffled laughter echoed from inside, and my feet stopped. I had no right to infringe on whatever happiness she'd found. Syd deserved everything good life had to offer. And that didn't include me.

Guilt and disgust warred within. It was a hard truth to face, but I was selfish and desperate enough to intrude anyway. Studying the planks beneath my feet, I watched as rainwater dripped from thick ribbons of hair snaking down my face and splashing the surface, forming rivulets trailing back toward the steps I'd just climbed. I was undeserving of her help, her time. Her. But I couldn't do this alone.

Closing my eyes briefly, I inhaled deeply, then knocked. Faint footsteps approached and the door swung open. "Evan?" I didn't have it in me to meet her eyes, afraid of what I'd see—anger, disappointment, pity. Judgement. But Syd's voice was heavy with concern. She knew something was wrong.

"What is it?" My throat closed. The words wouldn't come. She tilted my head up and pushed the rain-soaked hair from my eyes. "You're drenched." She grabbed my hand and pulled me inside. "Come in and tell me what happened."

I waited in the foyer while she hurried to get a towel. My body trembled all over, but I was unsure if it was from my chilled skin, the shock of Gabriel's betrayal, or my fear of Syd tossing me back into the rain. She returned and helped me dry off as much as possible, then she guided me into the living room.

"Syd?" Isaac rose from the couch, a wary expression on his face. His presence shouldn't have come as a surprise, since I'd practically pushed her into his waiting arms. "Evan, what are you doing here? I don't know exactly what happened between the two of you, but I know how much you hurt Syd. And after what happened with Max, I think you should leave."

Any other day, I would have made Isaac regret saying those words, but right now, I didn't have the strength to meet his gaze, and kept my own fixed on the floor.

"Isaac." Syd's voice had a warning tone.

"You said you were done with him, and wanted to give us a chance. Can't you see what's happening? Evan's on a slow spiral of destruction, and he's trying to drag you down with him. I've been right here waiting for months. With me, it would be so easy, Sydney."

I heard the pleading in Isaac's voice. Lifting my gaze slightly to Syd's face, I saw a quiet conversation pass between them. Isaac was asking her to choose. If I were her, it wouldn't be me. By all the laws of the universe, it *shouldn't* be me. My head dropped down once more.

"Isaac, I told you all I could offer right now was friendship, and maybe there would be a chance for something more later. But right now, no matter what happened between us, my best friend needs me, and I won't desert him. That's not who I am, and I'm sorry if that's a problem for you."

She moved to face me, placing her hand under my chin and gently raising it to meet her eyes. "Evan? Talk to me," she said softly.

Isaac's heavy steps pounded past me as he barreled toward the front door, slamming it on his way out. She'd made her choice.

I couldn't contain it. Everything inside me was being folded and crushed, and it was too much, too big. Knowing I might fail Simon, Gabriel's duplicity, losing my family, my position. Nearly losing Syd. My face was wet again, but not from the rain.

"Come here." She opened her arms to me.

I lowered my head to her shoulder, wrapped my arms around her, and let it all go. Deep, gut-wrenching sobs wracked my body, and I clung tightly to her, silently begging her not to let go, to stay with me, help me through this, all the while knowing she had every right to turn me away at any moment.

She held me until I'd quieted, then drew me over to the sofa. I dropped down and rested my head back, wiping the tears as best I could. Syd sat beside me, stretching an arm across the back of the sofa, tucking one leg beneath her, and faced me. "Tell me."

So I poured out everything that had happened. Seeing Simon—to which her reaction was to practically launch herself into my lap—and my fear of failing him. Telling her about Gabriel was difficult.

"No." Her voice was flat, her expression disbelief. Like me, Syd respected and looked up to Gabriel. "He couldn't do that to you, Evan. He wouldn't."

"If it came from anyone but Simon, I wouldn't trust it. But you know he's never stated anything without information to back it up."

She nodded, looking down at her lap while she absent-mindedly ran her fingers through my half dry hair with the hand behind me. "But why? Why would he help Sebastian? It's like something Gabriel's evil twin would do if he had one."

"I haven't done so well at processing since Simon told me, but Gabriel's not built for deception like this." Bringing it up again would reopen the deep gashes in both our hearts, but I couldn't live with myself if I didn't. I picked up her hand and held it to my chest. "You know I didn't mean most of what I said to you." I flinched uncontrollably, remembering the soul-crushing words I'd spewed. "I'm broken and damaged, but thought you'd be happier if you were away from me and all my darkness. That hasn't changed, but I'm still the selfish bastard who needs you in my life."

Her eyes were damp. "I know. You cut me, and I won't lie and say it didn't hurt. I called you a ton of names I won't repeat. Not yet, anyway. But once I got home and had a chance to think about it, I understood why you did it. I'm an expert at the Psychology of Evan." She smirked, but it didn't cover the sadness underneath.

Knowing I'd put it there would gnaw at me forever.

"You're the only good thing in my life, Syd, and I'm sorrier than you'll ever know. I'll probably say that to you every day, but it will never be enough." I swallowed hard. "You could be happy with Isaac. He seems to really care about you, and I didn't want him to leave because of me. I probably screwed that up, too."

Syd brought our clasped hands to her lips and kissed my knuckles. "Isaac is a good friend, but I've never felt any other way about him. He's fun to hang out with, but my feelings haven't changed. It's you that I love."

My vision blurred, and I felt a tightening in my chest. "You deserve better than me. I'm empty. I've got nothing to give you right now."

She tilted her head slightly and gave me a half-smile. "Don't you know? I've known you since we were children, seen your best and worst days, and stood beside you through the dark and the light. I know what's inside you, the good and the bad, and everything you don't know that you are. You're worth waiting for. I'm not going anywhere." She leaned in and lightly brushed her lips against mine, then sat back.

The pain in my chest loosened its hold. Not completely, but enough. She had no idea how her words affected me. Hearing someone say I was worth the wait meant everything.

"All I need from you is a promise you won't push me away again. Let everything else happen organically. Or not. Right now, Simon is the priority."

"I promise." I squeezed her hand, reinforcing my oath.

"So, where do we go from here?" she asked.

I grimaced. "Simon said I need to work with Max. To trust him."

In contrast to my feelings, Syd was all smiles. "Seems like a sort of symmetry in that, don't you think? Maybe the two of you can finally learn to play nice with each other. Aren't you glad you didn't get him killed?"

Her last statement was said with a grin that challenged me to respond, but I held back. It was totally appropriate.

CHAPTER 23
EVAN
PRESENT DAY

"What the hell do you want?" Max stood in the doorway of his house, clearly unhappy at seeing me. Bandages covered his wrists from where the nightmare trees had held him prisoner, and his face bore several scratches, with one deeper gash displaying a line of stitches.

I squared my jaw and gritted my teeth. 'This is for Simon' was the mantra continuously running in the back of my mind. "Can I come in? I need to talk to you."

He barked a laugh. "You're kidding, right? You almost got me killed, and now you want to talk to me? The only thing I want to hear from your mouth is an apology, and I don't care if you think I'm being insubordinate. I was your responsibility, and you let it happen."

"You're right, Max, and I'm sorry, but when you hear why—"

"It's like you weren't even there, Evan." His voice rose, and the veins in his neck bulged like thick rope cords. "Or maybe that was your plan all along. It's no secret to anyone that we aren't friends. Maybe this was your opportunity to take me out and then blame it on a training accident. A convenient way to rid yourself of a complication in your life and a constant reminder of Simon."

I rolled my eyes. "Don't be an idiot, Max, I wasn't trying to get you killed, but yes, I was distracted. That's on me, but—"

"You were distracted? That's your excuse? I know you didn't think I was ready, but Gabriel moved up my training. Was this your way of making a point? Are you really that self-absorbed?" He stepped back, and moved his arm as if to slam the door in my face.

Honestly, I was surprised he'd waited this long.

"It was Simon. That's why I was distracted. Simon is alive, Max."

He froze. For a long moment he was silent, staring at the floor, with one hand resting on the door knob, and the other against the frame. When he raised his eyes, they pleaded with me. "Don't you … You'd never …please." His quivering lips couldn't finish the sentence, and he swayed. Lunging through the doorway, I got an arm around him before he dropped, guided him to a sitting position on the tile floor of the foyer, then closed the front door behind me.

"Get away from me!" He slapped at me, but the shock had zapped his strength. I lowered myself to the cool tiles, my back leaning against the wall opposite him. Max drew in his knees and ducked his head between them, his heavy breathing the only sound in the room.

I sat silently in the narrow foyer, our knees almost touching, knowing my words were a heavy load to drop on him. When he raised his head, his expression was pained, as if every breath hurt. He regarded me with suspicion. "Evan, please say you're not making this up and using Simon as an excuse for me to forgive you. If you are, then you're without a soul." Behind the suspicion, I detected a faint tinge of hope.

"No. No way. I'd never use my brother like that."

His hand shot out and clutched my forearm, fingernails digging in. "Where has he been? Where is he now? You have to take me to him."

I gripped his hand and peeled it off my arm, noting the indentations he'd left. "I don't know all the answers yet, all right? And he's not here physically. Something has been going on over the past few weeks. It all started when I was working with Dr. Quill." I explained the flashes of light, hearing Simon's voice. "A couple of nights ago, Simon appeared in my dream. I mean, that's nothing new, because I dream about him a lot. This was different, like he was a Bender in my head."

"But that couldn't happen, though, right? We're trained to block entry into our minds. You've even had the advanced training because of higher level cases."

I shook my head. "He said he's been practicing for a while, but only got in because of the twin thing."

Max nodded. "Yeah. If anyone could break through your barrier, I'd guess it would be him. What did he say?"

"He didn't have long, but it was something about a journal. Do you know what that means?"

"That blue one he was writing in before he disappeared? The last couple of months, it was like it was attached to him. Even more than his data pad, and that's saying something for Simon."

"Yes! That's exactly what I've been searching for."

"After his files were gone, it became an obsession for him to write down everything he could remember about his project. Whatever he'd been working on was high level and pretty important. He was determined to remember everything and record it all in that book. The thing was practically attached to his hip. Or his hands, I guess."

"He never mentioned the files." I tried to keep the hurt from my voice, but by the expression on Max's face he'd picked up on it.

"It was while you were studying for the Bender program, and he knew how important that was. He didn't want to dump his problems on you, because you'd drop whatever you were doing to help him."

His words were like a punch to the gut. Simon had complete faith I'd sacrifice anything to help him and be there when he needed me. But I hadn't. "Yeah, that sounds like him. He wouldn't have wanted me to worry and get distracted." The corner of my mouth turned up as I remembered how he'd always downplayed his goals over mine.

Max ran his hands through his hair, exhaled, and looked at me intently. "I want to believe more than anything he's alive, and I know you do too. Are you positive this wasn't a dream or hallucination?"

My head banged back against the wall in frustration. Again with the doubt. I was so tired of people questioning my judgement over what I perceived to be real or imaginary. Before saying something I'd regret, I put myself in Max's place. We were about as far from friendship as Tage was from Posarius. Even civility was hard to come by most days. At best, we tolerated each other. Our only common ground was our love for Simon. And that had to be enough.

"Remember the morning after he disappeared when I told you I couldn't feel him inside me anymore, like there was a void in his place?"

Max nodded, his eyes hopeful.

"When I saw him in my dream, and during your training, that space was filled again. It's the first time I've felt whole since he left. In the past year, he's been in my dreams nearly every night, but I've never felt his presence. Until now."

Max looked to the side and his lip quivered. "I've just been afraid to hope until now, you know?" His voice cracked and he ducked his head. "I didn't think I was allowed to hope."

"I know. I never gave up, but it was getting harder and harder to stay positive."

He glanced up sideways at me, his mouth turned up into a half smirk. "Are we bonding, Evan?"

I snorted. "Don't get your hopes up, Delacort. Not a chance. But we need to call a truce long enough for you to help me find his journal."

He shrugged. "I don't get it. How am I supposed to know where Simon kept it?"

"He said to tell you to take me to your place."

"My place? What does he—" Max stopped abruptly and his eyes widened. Then the corner of mouth turned up. "I know where Simon's journal is."

Chapter 24
Evan
Present Day

I followed Max along the streets of city center, the towering buildings around us housing various businesses and retailers, but also a fair share of private residences. People flitted about us, intent on getting to their destinations, and I overheard snippets of conversations as they passed. Water supplements, protein alternatives, rationing. As always, the survival of Tage was the major topic of conversation. SI had announced just this week that the soybean crops were nearly gone, and the few remaining were diseased. Rationing had become even more severe.

The day was cloudless, and I squinted up at the sun, nearly blinded as it reflected off the mirrored surface of the building we'd stopped in front of.

"This is where Simon and I would meet when we couldn't go to your place." Max ducked his head and looked up at me sideways. "When you were home. Sorry, Resnik." At least he showed some remorse for hiding their relationship from me.

I nodded. "What is this place?"

"My parents aren't together anymore. I live with my mom and stepfather, but my dad lives in this building. He's away on a long term assignment, kind of like your parents, but didn't want to give this up. Simon didn't want our relationship to be public until you knew about us, and Dad's apartment gave us some privacy." Max scanned something on his data pad, and the double doors in front of us slid open. "It's on the tenth floor, so we'll take the tube."

The open lobby area was a lofty three stories tall, and in earlier years had no doubt been stunning. We passed hollowed stumps of dead trees that had been cut down so as not to be a safety hazard, and a massive water feature that hadn't been turned on since rationing had begun. It remained bone dry.

Max led us back to the tube, and the door opened automatically as we approached. "Ten," he said. The door snapped shut, and there was a whooshing sound as we shot upwards. It reopened to a vacant hallway infused with natural light from a wall of windows along the left side. I traipsed behind Max until he came to a stop at the sixth door on the right.

His handprint was scanned on the panel on the right side of the door, there was a faint buzzing sound, and the door popped open. Max stood unmoving at the threshold, quietly staring into the apartment. Wondering if there was a problem, I looked past him into a room lit only by sunlight streaming through the windows. It was full of comfortable-looking furniture, and I saw no immediate threat. "Is something wrong?"

He turned, seeming surprised I was standing there. "Uh, no." He ran his hands through his straw-colored hair and swallowed audibly. "It's just that I haven't been here since Simon went missing. Too many memories, you know?"

I winced and looked away. Coming home to an empty house every day—a house that once upon a time was filled with Dad's laughter over his own stupid jokes, and the tantalizing smells of Mom's cooking competing with the odd aromas emanating from Simon's lab—was incredibly hard. The first night on my own after Simon was gone and my parents had left me again, I'd barely slept, alternating between listening to music and wandering through the hushed rooms, each bringing back bittersweet memories. I was more comfortable with people and noises of everyday living, but I had no place else to go. So yeah, I understood why Max hadn't been back.

"Guess we're not going to help him by standing in the hallway, are we?" He straightened, inhaled deeply, and entered. We walked through the large living and kitchen area, then turned left down a short hallway. The quiet seemed so—large in this place, like it was a physical being that took up space. It reminded me of my own home, only this place was much cleaner and looked less 'lived in'.

"Even though I live with my mom full time, I have a bedroom for when I'd spend nights with my dad if he was in town. If Simon hid anything, it would probably be there." There were only two closed doors along this hallway, and Max stopped at the first one. I assumed the other was a bathroom. He swung open the door to reveal a medium-sized room. Besides the bed, it contained a desk, chest, and bookshelf that held some personal items. And a picture of Simon and him on the bedside table.

Max moved slowly to the bed and sat down, his quivering hand reaching for the picture frame. The two of them were laughing, clearly comfortable and happy together. His arm was draped across Simon's shoulders. "My dad took this picture of us before he left on his last assignment. It's also on my data pad, but I haven't been able to bring myself to look at it. Not for a long time." His voice was nearly a whisper. Raising his head, he studied the room, a faint smile on his face.

I didn't want to intrude on his private memories, but we'd come here for a reason. I cleared my throat. That seemed to do the trick, because his head snapped back in my direction, then he placed the frame back on the table. "The last time we were here was about a week before Simon disappeared, and I know I didn't see the journal then."

"There must be something here, or he wouldn't have led me to you." I scanned the room. Think like Simon, I told myself. If he wanted to hide something, where would it be? In a room this small, there weren't many options. Drawers and the closet were too obvious, and the floor was a solid slab of natural stone. The ceiling offered no possibilities, either.

Thinking like Simon wasn't getting me anywhere, until a childhood memory flashed through my mind. When we were much younger, he'd had a serious sweet tooth. Mom always monitored our treats, and although I never cared much for them, I pretended I did and would give my share to my twin. He had to hide them, because Mom would have cut us off completely if she'd known. And she'd never discovered his hiding place.

"Max, what's under your bed?" He'd been occupied with pulling out drawers and searching behind furniture.

"Nothing but dust, probably. It's low to the ground, so there's not much room to hide anything." He dropped to the floor, lifted the bed covers, and peered into the darkness underneath. "Grab my data pad." I retrieved it from the desk and placed it in his outstretched hand. He turned on the spotlight setting and scanned the small area beneath the bed. "There's nothing here, Evan. Empty." He switched it off, sat up, and leaned back against the bed, slumped in defeat.

Simon wouldn't be so obvious as to simply hide something in plain view. I dropped to my knees and lifted the bed covers, but instead of looking on the floor, I felt up against the supports that held the mattress. I elbowed Max in the side. "Move over so I can see."

"I just looked, Resnik, and it's not there," he snapped.

My fingers glided across the cool metal mattress supports, searching for anything that felt out of place, but nothing seemed to fit that requirement. "I need to get under this bed."

"Well, good luck with that. Hope you're not claustrophobic."

Lying on my back, I wiggled inch by inch under the bed, but not without difficulty. I had to exhale the air from my lungs so I'd fit underneath the frame, and then take only shallow breaths. Max hadn't been kidding. The mattress was only a few inches from my face, but enclosed spaces had never really bothered me. "Can you open my data pad, turn on the spotlight, and hand it to me?" Max slid it under the bed, and I shined the light on the surfaces close to me, changing positions until I'd covered the whole area. Just when I was about to give up, I noticed a slight bulge in one support compared to the others.

When I brought the light to that section, a smile crept across my face. Simon had wedged the book between the supports, just like he'd done with the bag of extra sweets all those years ago. I maneuvered my body in that direction, and freed a blue, leather-bound journal. Once I'd wiggled back out, I brushed away the dust and held it up to show Max.

"You found it!" His eyes were wide with excitement. "How did you know?"

"His favorite hiding place when we were little. I guess some things never change." I leaned against the bed beside Max, blew more dust from the cover of the journal, and opened it. Two envelopes slid to the floor, one labeled with my name and the other addressed to Max. Both in Simon's handwriting.

Chapter 25
Evan
Present Day

Evan,

If you're reading this, then A, as I suspected, something has happened to me, B, you're working with Max, and C, you remembered my favorite hiding place.

Even before my files disappeared, I became aware of some strange occurrences. It all started shortly after I anonymously reported Dr. Sebastian. There was evidence someone had accessed my files, but I was unable to track the person's identity. It was obviously someone very familiar with the inner workings of the system, because they'd covered their tracks quite well. A couple of times while working in the lab, I sensed I wasn't alone. No, I'm not talking about an otherworldly presence, but there was a level of energy, something almost tangible. I had a suspicion of what it might be, but didn't discuss it with anyone because, frankly, I didn't know who to trust. Sebastian had been receiving help.

When my data disappeared, I knew my suspicions were correct, and I formed a contingency plan. And now you've found it. I couldn't hide anything in the house or on my data pad, because I don't think our house is safe, and with my files already stolen, a handwritten account is the only trustworthy alternative. Read my journal, and you'll discover what might have happened to me.

Hopefully, I was able to tell you about Max and me before whatever brought you here, because at the time of this writing, I haven't. I'm fairly confident of your initial reaction, and I'm uncertain at this point if I should gradually introduce you to the idea, or just push you into the deep end. That was your favorite approach in getting me into the pool when we were younger, so perhaps that would be best. Either way, I don't see it going well. But know this, Evan—Max isn't what you think he is. He might have been once, but people are never one thing. They're made up of different layers, hidden mysteries, and barriers, but once you find your way through all that, you reach their core, who they really are at their most base level. And Max is a good person. He's brought something to my life I never knew was missing, and because there's no science to it, the only proof is what I feel for him. Please give him a chance. For me.

Simon

I exhaled loudly. Simon had known all along something wasn't right, but he'd never told me. Maybe, like with Max, he just hadn't found the right time to let me know. Maybe he thought he'd have more time before whatever happened to him.

Max's breath hitched, and I turned to see a single tear slicing down his cheek as he folded his letter. "What did he tell you?" I asked.

"That I should try to look past your anger, because your instincts are usually on target. That I should follow your lead, but help you keep focused." He wiped his cheek with the heel of his hand. "There was also some stuff you probably don't want to hear, so I'll spare you the details."

"Much appreciated." I grimaced at the thought of what else my brother might have written. Simon in love was going to take some getting used to.

"Well?"

"Well what?"

Max sighed heavily. "What did he tell you?"

Bonding with Max wasn't something I saw myself doing, but for my brother, I'd have to make some allowances. Didn't mean I had to like it. "He said we needed to read his journal."

"I could have guessed that on my own, Evan. Did he tell you anything about me?"

I folded my letter in neat fourths, slid it in the inside pocket of my jacket, and turned to look directly at Max. "Yeah." I opened the journal and began reading.

"Fine, don't tell me," he shrugged. "I can probably guess what it was anyway."

I ignored him and continued reading, flipping pages back and forth—

and quickly came to the conclusion that it would be easier to figure out the hidden secrets of the universe than interpret Simon's notes. All this science-speak made no sense to me. Max had been watching me intently, but at least he hadn't tried reading over my shoulder and getting in my space.

"Uh...how much do you know about science?"

"Judging by the biology course we had together, a lot more than you. Give me the journal." Max skimmed several pages, nodded his head occasionally, and upon reaching the last page, gasped as he reached over and gripped my forearm. "Simon discovered a way to Posarius. Portals."

"Portals? All the way there?"

He removed his hand and studied the pages once more, shaking his head. "He's a genius. This could change everything, and it's been hidden under this bed for a year."

"One world to another. We could travel to Posarius and they could travel here. We could share resources." A grin split my face. That news didn't surprise me at all. Not coming from Simon. "He saved all of us." But that still didn't tell me what I needed to know. "So, how do we get to him?"

Max laid the journal to the side and rubbed his face. "I don't understand how it works exactly. His calculations are far beyond what I'm able to comprehend. Can we open it and bring him back? How do we open it? How do we locate him?"

With all the progress we'd made in just a couple of days, we'd come to a grinding halt at our next step. This close to bringing him home, and the two of us weren't smart enough to close the deal. It was maddening and unfair after what we'd been through over the past year. There had to be someone who could help us understand Simon's language. Someone we could trust.

And then the answer seemed so simple, I felt like an idiot for taking so long to think of it. My highly unorganized, frequent flyer, Dr. Quill.

ⅠⅠ

"Fascinating. Utterly profound." Dr. Quill sat at his cluttered desk and flipped through the pages of Simon's journal, occasionally making calculations on his data pad and muttering to himself, while Max and I stood in silence, waiting to hear if it was possible to find him. "Evan, what your brother has discovered will change life as we know it. It will transform the lives of millions, possibly billions of people."

"Well, Doc, I'm glad you figured out what Simon's saying in that book, because we really need your help." I drew up a chair and sat facing him, while Max pulled one up beside me. "We know Sebastian stole Simon's data and took him. We need you to tell us how to reopen the portal to bring him back."

"Yes, I see," he nodded. While Doc studied Simon's journal, I noted the papers scattered about his office, signaling his next session with me was most likely only days away. Assuming I was working again, and Gabriel...I needed to shut down that line of thinking for now.

Max leaned forward, just as anxious to hear what Doc had to say.

Finally, he sat back in his chair, propped his glasses on his forehead, and rubbed his eyes. "That, Evan, is where the problem lies."

"Problem?" I should have known this wouldn't be easy. The fact that it had taken a year to contact me should have been an indication, but I hoped it wasn't another year before we could retrieve my brother.

"Yes. What Simon discovered is absolutely brilliant, no question. However, it's not as simple as reading his journal, learning how to open a portal, then have him home for dinner. I only wish it were."

I glanced over to Max to gauge his reaction.

He chewed on his thumbnail, eyes glued to Doc, while waiting for him to continue.

"In the simplest terms, a portal cannot be randomly opened into an unknown destination. If you're unaware of what's waiting on the other side, you could be opening the door to anything from a peaceful grassy field, to invaders from another planet, to a black hole.

"Think about it in terms of the tube you entered to get to this floor when you arrived today. You entered, the door closed, and you stated the floor number. The tube then took you to your destination. What if you hadn't stated a floor? This building is a known quantity, so the worst that could have happened is that you'd be taken to the wrong floor and have to backtrack. The likelihood of coming face to face with imminent danger isn't really a factor. You're safe in this environment.

"Portals are an unknown quantity. Simon understood that he'd need a door on the other side of the portal, and he'd have to know the exact location where that door would open. In this case, the site would be Posarius. Since we have established lines of communication with them, it wouldn't be a problem to schedule a portal opening." He paused to take a sip of his drink. Doc was explaining things in simple terms, but I didn't like the direction we were heading. Judging by the scowl on Max's face, he felt the same way. Simon might as well have been across the universe.

"We know Simon didn't open the portal himself, as he was in the beginning stages of trials and knew the dangers. What disturbs me is that Dr. Sebastian needed Simon's exact coordinates to locate him."

Now I really didn't like the direction this was going, and I was pretty sure what Doc would say next.

"Someone here, on Tage, someone who was very familiar with Simon and his whereabouts, assisted Sebastian. Unless your brother can tell you exactly where he is, and I have to assume he can't, or he would have already done so, the only person capable of knowing that information is responsible for Simon being gone in the first place." My fists clenched, and I slammed them on Doc's desk.

Gabriel.

He knew where we lived, and could easily have found out Simon's schedule. That's why I'd been told not to trust him.

Chapter 26
Evan
Present Day

I scowled in Syd's direction, a direct contrast to her own expression.

"Can I just go on record and say how weird it is you two are getting along? Weird, and yet, kind of sweet in a karma-ish kind of way." Syd was curled up in her favorite chair to my left, and her gaze darted between Max and me. "Aren't you glad you didn't get him killed, Evan? Simon really would have been upset with you when Max wasn't waiting for him when he got back, don't you think?"

She was positively beaming, excited at seeing the two of us being civil to each other, and actually working together for a change, but my scowl toned down the wattage a couple of notches.

The three of us had gathered at Syd's house in hopes of brainstorming a plan to deal with Gabriel. As relieved as I was over the truce with Max, having Syd here took some of the pressure off me in case I started backsliding into my old habits. Which was probably only a matter of time.

"Why would Gabriel help anyone open a portal to take Simon? I've turned it over in my head a thousand different ways, and I'm at a loss." Max threw his hands up in the air. "I'd always gotten the impression Gabriel was like a surrogate father to you, Evan, so it makes even less sense when you look at it that way."

I nodded. "Yeah, I've been thinking about that. He's been there for me from the beginning, but knowing what we do now, I think it was more out of guilt or spying on me than actually caring about me." Even with his betrayal, saying that statement aloud hurt more than I'd thought. Made it seem real. He was family—well, the family I'd made, not the abandoning one I'd been born into.

Syd reached over squeezed my arm. "Don't say that, Evan. Remember, he had a relationship with you before he helped Sebastian. I always felt like Gabriel really cared about you. He's always oozed goodness and integrity. Maybe living with what he did has been tearing him apart all this time."

"Well, he sure didn't act like it." I sighed. "When have you ever seen Gabriel ruffled? He's always calm, controlled, and in command. Doesn't look like he's in pain to me."

Syd pulled her hand back. "Well, you don't know what he's like when he's home behind closed doors. Maybe he falls apart every morning after work, and barely makes it through the days."

Max shook his head and propped a leg on the table in front of us. "I'm with Evan on this one, Syd. I've never caught a whiff of anything that smelled like guilt around Gabriel. Why are you defending him, anyway?" He narrowed his eyes accusingly at Syd.

Syd undid her ponytail and shook out her hair. "I'm not defending him, I'm just trying to look at the whole picture from different angles, maybe get an idea of why he did it."

"Well, he had to have gotten something out of it, right? If anyone is caught helping criminals, they can be sent to the Realm, so what would make Gabriel help Sebastian?" Like Max, I'd wracked my brain trying to think of a reason he would have done this. Personal gain? Revenge? Blackmail? Nothing seemed to fit.

Syd twirled a strand of hair, eyes unfocused as she turned things over in her mind. Max might have been suspicious, but I knew she wasn't defending Gabriel. That's why she'd always been good at balancing me. Sometimes my mind shot to a conclusion at warp speed before considering all aspects of the problem—especially when it involved people. Syd had reined me in more times than I'd like to admit.

"Too bad we can't get into Gabriel's head and have a look," Max said. "I'd take great pleasure in dragging him into the lab, strapping him to the chair, then stabbing and missing a vein several times before getting the needle in."

Not a bad idea at all. Maybe we were more alike than I'd thought.

Syd stopped twirling, gasped, and sat up abruptly. "That's it."

"Seriously?" Max's eyes widened. "I was just joking. Seems like we'd need more people to help us..."

"No, not dragging Gabriel to the lab. Getting in his head, yes, but we don't need to sedate him."

Max looked as confused as I was when we both asked, "What?"

"Evan can do it. He doesn't need the sedative to get into Gabriel's head and find the information."

"Syd, why would you think that?" I'd never gotten into a client's head without a sedative, nor had I ever tried.

"If you can do that, it's a miracle you didn't get me killed months ago. I'll be more careful about what I think from now on." Max took a swig from his drink.

I shot an annoyed glance in his direction, but he just shrugged.

"Come on, Evan. I've heard the techs say you never take the required dosage. You told them months ago to cut it in half."

"That's because the full dose left me with headaches that lasted for hours after the case was finished. I'm still using the sedative."

"I heard Ky say he'd misread a number and gave you even less than that, but you still got into the client's head with no issues."

My forehead creased. "Ky gave me the wrong amount? Why didn't he say anything?"

Max snorted. "He probably thought you'd slam him into the wall again, and it was better to just keep his mouth shut."

Well, there was that. I genuinely liked Ky. He was a nice guy and good at his job, and I felt bad for making him think he couldn't talk to me.

"But Evan, don't you see? If you can bend with only a third of the sedative and not have any problems, you can probably do it without any at all if you'd practice." Syd had that intent gleam in her eye, her body leaning forward in excitement, and I knew she wasn't going to let this go. No matter how improbable it was. I'd done it with Simon when we were little, but that was only because of our connection. Wasn't it?

I leaned my head back against the sofa and rubbed my face. "Maybe I didn't have trouble with a partial dose, or maybe it was psychological, with my mind thinking I'd received the usual amount. I'm not sure when that happened, but I've never needed extra sedative. Trying to bend without any is unheard of. As for practicing—I can't just go up to a client and ask them to let me in. It's a total invasion of privacy."

Syd tilted her head and smiled gently. "So, practice on me."

Max was so excited he dropped his foot from the table and practically bounced on the couch. "Awesome idea!"

"No, Delacort, bad. It's a bad idea, and I'm not doing it. How did we make the jump from me taking a lesser dosage to plundering around in Syd's head?"

Syd rolled her eyes. "Come on, Evan. You know everything about me, anyway, and I'd be a willing participant. No barriers or walls to worry about, no subconscious fighting back. It's ideal."

"She's right. Like I said, you sure don't want to be rolling around in my head. Besides seeing some of my not-so-nice thoughts about you, there are some memories of Simon you may not want to witness." Max waggled his eyebrows.

I closed my eyes and groaned. "As happy as I am my brother found someone, I absolutely don't want a front seat to his love life. Even twins need their distance."

"Exactly. That's why Syd is perfect to practice on."

"Don't encourage her."

Syd moved from her chair to the spot beside me on the sofa and placed her hand on my thigh. "What would it hurt to try, Evan? If it doesn't work, fine. We'll think of something else. But if it does? You could slip into Gabriel's head tonight or tomorrow and get the answers we need. And he'd never be the wiser until we confronted him."

I exhaled loudly. Syd had a point. What would it hurt to try? She was willing, and it would solve a lot of problems for us. But if I was being honest with myself, it made me a little nervous thinking about what I might see in her head. She'd admitted how she felt about me, but knew I wasn't in a place to offer her anything right now. Yes, she understood, but that didn't mean it wouldn't be painful to see how much she cared about me, all the while knowing I wasn't good enough for her. Then there were all the devastating lies I'd told her. She said she forgave me, but there had to be some painful wounds. Wounds I'd caused.

With my head still tilted back against the sofa, Syd brought her hand from my thigh to my cheek, turning my head to face her. "I know what you're thinking," she whispered so Max couldn't hear, "and I'll try to hide that part. I don't want to hurt you anymore than you want to hurt me, okay?" I searched her face for any sign of doubt but, as always, she was an open book. She wanted to try this. So I nodded, but she was in no hurry to remove her hand from my face. And it felt really nice.

Max cleared his throat. "Yeah, well, glad that's settled. Should we move so Resnik can stretch out and begin his meditation?"

Syd broke eye contact with me and stood. "Absolutely." She tossed pillows to the floor. "Max, dim the lights. The control panel is on the wall behind you."

I lay prone on the couch, a cushion supporting my head. Syd eased herself into the chair Max had been sitting on directly across from me. "You can do this, Evan. Relax, get into your meditation, and I'll open my mind to you. Easiest case you've ever had." She grinned.

I wanted to give her a reassuring smile, but the muscles in my face hadn't moved that way in so long, they'd forgotten how.

Lying back, I let my body go limp, or as much as I could under the circumstances, closed my eyes, and began my deep breathing. Inhale four counts, hold two, then exhale four counts, letting my mind drift. With no sedative, prep work, or case file, I kept my mind focused on Syd and pictured her face. Breathe in four, hold two, breathe out four. Rhythmic, steady breathing. Muscles gradually relaxing. Mind wandering, lifting, and pulling away from my body. Syd. Her face. Getting inside her head.

And then I was floating above us, looking down at my body stretched out on the sofa, feet hanging over the armrest on one end. Max sat quietly in the chair by my head, the foot crossed over his knee twitching rapidly as his eyes flicked between us. Syd's head was tilted back, her face relaxed, like she was actually enjoying this. It was working—I'd traveled out of my body without the use of medication.

And instantly snapped back into it. Idiot, I thought, angry with myself for losing concentration.

"Did it work?" Max asked.

Without opening my eyes, by the closeness of his voice, I sensed him kneeling by the sofa at my shoulder.

"Back away, Max. Just sit in your chair and quit bothering me."

He mumbled something unintelligible, but put some distance between us.

Shifting my body, I found a comfortable spot and started over. Breathing deeply, quieting my mind. In. Out. Soon I felt myself detach, floating again, but this time, I remained calm and fixated on what needed to be done.

Syd. Focusing on her, I willed myself to sink closer, stroking her face with my finger. She smiled gently, as if she'd felt it. But that was impossible. No way she'd be able to sense my touch. Max stared at her, but showed no signs of recognizing my presence, then his eyes moved back to my body on the sofa.

Focus, Evan. Focus on the mission. And the mission was to get into Syd's head, so I closed my eyes and concentrated on moving forward, penetrating the protective barriers of her mind, and entering her subconscious.

I opened my eyes to vibrant colors, flashing lights, and joyful giggling—a sound that nearly brought tears to my eyes, because it was the laughter of Sydney as a little girl. In front of me, a carousel spun a lazy circle, while festive music floated through the air in the background. It was a perfect representation of Sydney. She lived life wide open and enjoyed the rides, thrills, journeys, and everything they had to offer.

Moving cautiously toward the carousel, I caught movement out of the corner of my eye. Spinning in that direction, I crouched in a defensive position. Syd said she'd welcome me, but previous experience proved that the subconscious might not be as willing as the client, and could take any form of protection.

The form it took in Syd's mind, was Syd herself at roughly seven years old.

"Hi." She held a box of popcorn in one hand, tossing kernels into her mouth with the other. "What are you doing here?"

Allowing my body to relax, I stood upright again, assuming there was no immediate danger. Young Syd studied me while chewing her popcorn, eyes wide as they examined me from head to toe.

"Uh...I came to see you."

She regarded me with suspicion. "Do I know you?"

"Yeah, you do." I crouched down to her level. "You've been my best friend nearly my whole life."

She chewed her popcorn a few seconds more, then her whole face lit up. "Oh, yeah! It's you, Evan. Just bigger." Syd skipped over and put her small hand in mine. "Want some popcorn?" She offered me the bag.

Her face alternated red, blue, green, and white from the colored lights of the carousel, but the freckles sprinkling the bridge of her nose were still visible. As she'd matured, they'd disappeared, and I'd nearly forgotten about them.

I smiled. "No, thanks."

She looked back to the bag, shrugged her shoulders, and tightened her grip on my hand. "Come with me and I'll show you around. This is a fun place to play, and you can ride the carousel any time you want. It stops if you ask it to. Do you want to ride?"

"Well, I don't think I'll be able to while I'm here, but maybe another time. Would that be all right?"

"Sure. There are games here, too." She gestured over my right shoulder where I saw stalls that held several stuffed animals and brightly colored objects as prizes. Adjacent to that was a small building, but it sharply contrasted the vibrant and inviting structures around it. Instead, it was dilapidated and a weather beaten gray, slanting slightly to the left. Even stranger was the thick chain wrapped around the structure and looped through the door handle. The end links were held together by the largest padlock I'd ever seen.

I stood, keeping her hand in mine. "What's that building?"

Her face clouded over as she frowned. "I don't like to go there. It's not a fun place."

"Why isn't it fun?"

"It's where the bad things stay. That's why it's locked, so they can't get out."

Bad things. With a heavy, padlocked chain around the door. I scrutinized the building closer. "What kind of bad things, Syd? People? Monsters?"

She rolled her eyes. "There's no such thing as monsters, silly. It's where sad things are kept so I don't have to think about them and can stay happy. When something bad happens, I take time to be sorry, then lock it in the building where it can't bother me anymore. Don't you have a place like this?"

I stared wistfully at the padlocked building, knowing the hurt I'd caused Sydney with my lies was stored in there. I'd do anything to take them back, but at least now I knew it was locked away—still in the back of her mind, but not on display where she could relive it or turn it in every direction and examine it constantly. I turned back to her. "I wish I did, but I'm afraid mine would need a lot more space with stronger chains. It's good that you have this, Sydney. You shouldn't have to think about sad things all the time. You deserve to be happy."

"So do you, big Evan. And we mostly are."

My brows furrowed. "We?"

"Us. You and me. Don't you know?" Then I heard another child laughing. But it couldn't be. I turned in the direction of the giggling and saw a dark-haired boy around the same age as Syd. "You're always here with me."

"Syd, come on, let's go on the carousel!" the younger me called.

"Well, I have to go now, big Evan. Come and visit again so we can play games, okay?"

"I will. I promise." Then Syd dropped my hand, skipped toward the grinning younger me waiting impatiently, and took his.

I lost sight of them when they scampered around the other side of the carousel.

♊

My eyes opened to Max looming over me with an inquisitive look on his face, again asking, "Did it work?"

It felt surreal. I'd gotten into Syd's head without meds, all on my own. Which meant I might be able to get inside Gabriel's mind and learn exactly where Sebastian had taken Simon in the Realm.

"Well?" Max repeated in a louder voice.

"Yeah. I think it did." Pushing up on one elbow, I looked across the table at Syd, wondering whether it would be awkward between us now that I'd been nosing around her innermost thoughts. Giving permission required the highest level of trust, and although she'd given it, I'd never been inside the mind of someone I knew. Especially someone I knew as well as her.

She studied me intently, then gave a lopsided grin. "You're always with me, silly."

And I knew everything was fine between us.

CHAPTER 27
EVAN
PRESENT DAY

"Now that we know Evan can get inside Gabriel's mind, there shouldn't be any problem getting Simon's coordinates, right?" Max couldn't sit still. He alternated between pacing, then sitting for a few seconds, only to shift around so much, be began pacing again. His nervous, anxious energy needed an outlet.

"It was pretty easy getting in Syd's head, but it won't be that simple with Gabriel. She gave me permission and lowered her walls. His mind might be an impenetrable fortress."

Max stopped his pacing and clasped his hands behind his head, keeping his gaze to the floor. Syd stared into space as she resumed her hair twirling. I knew that look. It was the 'I'm getting a big idea' expression.

"What is it, Syd?"

Max's head shot up in interest at my question.

"We know Gabriel will have strong defenses, so I was thinking about alternative ways. What if he was asleep? His walls would still be up, but maybe not as solid. Think about it. When has anyone tried to get into Gabriel's head? Certainly none of us, and no one outside of SI. At least, not that we've heard of."

Slide in when he was sleeping. If bending in Gabriel's mind was even possible, that could be the best time to try. After all these years, maybe he'd let the barriers slip a little, and wasn't as vigilant as he once was. No one had discovered how he'd helped Sebastian, so maybe he was feeling a little overconfident, and relaxed just enough for someone like me to get in. He'd never suspect anyone could gain access without meds, and I was the last person he'd expect. As far as he was concerned, I trusted him blindly. And I didn't have access to the Bender lab anymore.

Picturing him laughing behind my back at what a fool I was for believing in him made me clench my hands, the anger threatening to shoot through the pores of my body. I made a silent promise to Simon that I'd get in, one way or the other.

"I like that idea."

"So do I," Max agreed. "He'd never suspect someone while he's sleeping. Or any time, really. We're all trained Benders, and he'd have no reason to think we'd even try."

"Exactly." Syd grinned. Just as quickly, the grin was replaced with a frown. "Does anyone know where he lives?"

Max shrugged, looking worried again. "Evan? If anyone did, it would have to be you."

"Yeah, I do." After my parents had left again, Gabriel had invited me for meals at his house more times than I could remember. Being with him had given me a semblance of family, and kept me from being swallowed by loneliness at my house for just a little longer. Because of my practically nonexistent relationship with my parents, I'd needed someone to believe in me, be proud of my accomplishments, and understand my connection to Simon. And that's exactly the role he'd assumed. Never again would I allow myself to be deceived by someone. Especially someone I cared about.

"Is it possible for you to get close to him?" Syd asked. "I'm not sure how easy it would be for you if he were miles away as opposed to just a few walls, you know?"

Max nodded. "That's logical. So what kind of place does he live in? Please tell me he doesn't own a ten story building and live by himself. Are you good enough to get through ten stories?"

I rolled my eyes. "Geez, Delacort, I'm not sure I'm good enough to get through one wall. Syd was sitting five feet away. Adjust your expectations."

"Expectations. Right. Okay."

"So where does Gabriel live, Evan?" Syd asked, steering the conversation back on track.

"It's not too far from SI. Just a few blocks. He wanted to be close if he was called in for emergencies. It's a freestanding structure, and I know where he sleeps, so maybe I can set up outside the house along his bedroom wall. One wall shouldn't be too much trouble, right?"

"We'll help you. Someone has to stand watch while you're out of your body."

Max had been quiet for the last couple of minutes, something I'd discovered was unusual for him. How had Simon had tolerated his incessant talking? It wasn't long before he broke the silence. "Guys, what if we get caught? What if Evan can't get in Gabriel's mind? What happens next? We can't just leave Simon out there." All the uncertainty had gotten Max worked up, and the pacing started again, while he muttered to himself.

Syd leveled her gaze on me. "All good questions. We could get caught."

"Which is exactly why I need to go alone. If we're all caught, we could be sent to the Realm. I can't let that happen to either of you."

"Evan—."

I held up my hand to stop what I knew would be her disagreeing with me. "If I get caught or if something goes wrong, you have to promise me that you won't give up on Simon. You'll keep trying to locate him and bring him home. I know Max will never stop looking for him, but he'll need help."

"Evan Resnik." Syd squared her jaw in determination. "You know I'd never give up on Simon. I love him like a brother. But you also know me well enough that it won't come as a surprise when I say I'm going with you whether you like it or not. It's my decision."

"And mine," Max chimed in. "If something happens to us, we'll tell Dr. Quill to get Simon's journal to the right people. I'm all-in on this."

Syd shrugged. "Well, looks like you're stuck with us."

♊

"Are you talking about that clump of bushes back there? Are you sure no one could see you from the other buildings?" Syd gestured to a grouping of flowering bushes that had been imported from Earth before it had fallen. I didn't know all the technical terms, but they were drought resistant, something I only knew because it was one of my Mother's projects years ago.

"Obviously I haven't been inside every building to look out the windows, Syd, but the bushes should provide enough camouflage. I seriously doubt anyone will be paying attention to a clump of unsuspecting shrubs." While Max and Syd had been at work last night, I'd staked out the area around Gabriel's house to search for the best place to hide myself while I ransacked his thoughts. He was home now, off for the next twelve hours, and I was anxious to get started.

This section of the city wasn't too busy, but not exactly in the middle of nowhere, either. Three teenagers hanging around shouldn't draw suspicion. Nighttime would have provided more cover, but it wasn't like we had much choice. It was the nature of Benders. At least I wouldn't be lying in a clump of bushes alone, where anyone snooping around could stumble over me. Syd and Max were my lookouts, and could run interference if someone got too curious. I needed as much uninterrupted time as possible, unsure of how long it would take to get into Gabriel's mind. Or if I even could. His mental barriers were still a big concern, but I'd deal with things as they came. It was time to begin.

Max sat on a bench in the park across the street where he'd have full view of the front of the house, on the off chance someone decided to visit during the day. A common area behind Gabriel's house was shared by several surrounding homes, and Syd sat underneath a tree with her data pad. Nothing out of the ordinary if someone questioned why she was there. Taking a last glance around and seeing no sign of anyone suspicious, I hunkered down and slunk into the bushes against the outside wall of Gabriel's bedroom, making myself as comfortable as possible on the straggly brown patches of grass. Fortunately, the shrubs were grouped such that I had room to stretch out completely and stay hidden from view.

Once I was settled, I fell into the familiar routine of deep breathing, clearing my mind of anything but inhaling and exhaling. The moment of losing focus and falling back into my body when practicing with Syd crossed my mind, but I shoved it to the side and slammed the door behind it.

In minutes, I pulled away from my body, but kept Gabriel as my target, not even peeking at my outstretched form lying on the ground beneath me. My subconscious effortlessly passed through the exterior wall and into the stillness of his darkened bedroom, where he lay prone in bed. He was unmoving, other than his steady, even breathing. This was the first time I'd seen him since learning of his betrayal, and I had to bite back the animosity and the urge to do him bodily harm. Which wouldn't have been possible in my state, anyway. Still, I wanted to hurt Gabriel like he'd hurt me. But now wasn't the time. I had a goal.

I slowly descended toward him, watching for any indication he was aware of my presence. Wanting to test his defenses, I pressed gently against his mind and met resistance, unlike with Syd when she'd welcomed me in unobstructed. But I'd expected this. Gabriel was extensively trained in guarding his mind, so any initial attempts at penetration wouldn't be successful, but I needed to get the lay of the land before continuing.

Withdrawing, I ascended a couple of feet and studied the situation before me. When I closed my eyes, Gabriel's barriers appeared as unyielding iron gates extending up as far as I could see. Intimidating was an understatement. And this was most likely just the first of many obstacles. Trying again, I pushed harder this time, but still not at full capacity. The gates gave minutely, but held firm.

Giving up wasn't an option.

There had to be a way in, a secret passageway, or an open window. I'd heard the computer guys talking about back doors in programs, a way they could get in if all the usual ways failed, or were locked out for some reason. That's what I needed—a back door.

Be like Simon. I needed to somehow channel his logic and think about this from a different angle. My brother was more rational, but he wasn't a Bender. Or maybe he was now. Either way, I needed to combine our minds—his logic and my abilities.

What did Gabriel allow through his protective walls? Everyday work activities, of course. Case reports, client requests, debrief files from team leaders, course of action preparations. All routine things that didn't require screening. People he dealt with on a daily basis he trusted not to breach his defenses—his subordinates, employees in other departments, familiar clients—all friends and coworkers that didn't require his barriers to be on high alert. Someone like me. Especially me, because Gabriel dealt with me nearly every day. And we were friends. Or, at least I'd thought we were, recent developments notwithstanding.

So it stood to reason that his mind should trust me, and lower his guard to allow me entrance. I needed to make him think it was a typical night at SI, and my presence was no threat. Seemed like a rational conclusion to me, so how could I trick his mind into believing it?

The times Simon had helped me with homework popped into my head. Really, there were too many to count, but he'd mentioned I had a tendency to make things harder than they were. Something about the simplest explanation usually being the correct one, and that I needed to take a step back and look for the most straightforward approach.

If I wanted Gabriel's mind to believe this was a nonthreatening encounter, then I should do something familiar, like give him a client report. Simple and straightforward. And I sure hoped it worked.

My subconscious began reciting what I remembered from Dr. Quill's latest visit, just like I'd done so many times before with Gabriel. While part of my brain rattled off an ordinary followup report, another gently tested the barrier, poking and prodding ever so slightly.

And there was no resistance. It was working.

I continued reciting the report and pushed harder, slipping through nearly as easily as with Syd, and in seconds, I'd stepped into his inner recesses. I'd have to tell Simon I really had been paying attention during lessons. Maybe not all the time, but at least when it had been important.

Surveying my surroundings, I noted that Gabriel's mind resembled his office—neat, orderly, clean lines. Everything in its place. There was even a water feature in the middle of the room, the gentle gurgling creating an atmosphere of peace and serenity. A mixture of cinnamon and vanilla permeated the air, which I found to be very weird.

To my right, a long, rectangular table resting against a golden-hued wall held three data pads, each connected to a large screen. All looked identical, so I chose the first on the left and discovered it contained unrestricted access, with no password required. The files displayed on the screen appeared to be from Gabriel's younger years, each labeled his age or year of school. Nothing really caught my eye, so I went on to the next pad, which also didn't require a password. Although it would be strange to have a password on a data pad in your subconscious, I wouldn't put it past someone like Gabriel as a final layer of protection.

All the information appeared to be work-related—names of clients, co-workers, and cases he'd handled. Seeing a file labeled 'Evan', I opened it, anxious to see if it contained any information about Simon or Sebastian. After scanning several pages, all very clinical and non-detached, with no personal comments or remarks, I closed that file. It had the feel of Gabriel at work—calm, controlled, and professional.

While closing the second data pad, my forehead creased when I noticed the color of the walls. I was sure they'd been a warm golden color when I'd arrived, but they were more of a dull mustard yellow, and the room appeared somewhat dimmer. Not a good sign. Gabriel's subconscious could be aware something wasn't right. I needed to hurry before things got ugly.

I quickly moved on to the third data pad, knowing my time was more limited than I'd thought, but was surprised to see that it required a passcode. An added layer of security. Which told me there were more sensitive memories inside—exactly what I'd been searching for. But I couldn't even begin to come up with a password Gabriel might have used. Knowing the chances of it working were slim to none, I entered his birthdate. Which failed. Too easy, but I honestly didn't know many personal details about Gabriel. The passcode was probably some random mixture of numbers, letters, and symbols that I'd never crack, especially in such a limited time frame.

Stepping away from the table, I scanned the room, frantically searching for any hints of the passcode. And that's when I saw it. There was no way I would have missed this before, so it must have just appeared. In the corner of the wall opposite the data pads, there was a crooked, dilapidated door that was out of place in this neat and orderly environment. The surrounding wall was a dark, muddy brown, not even close to the original golden hue of the room. Cracks lined the door's surface, and chunks of it were missing, as if someone had tried breaking through, until I noticed the door swung inward toward me, instead of outward into whatever was behind it. Maybe the missing wood chunks were the result of someone on this side preventing things on the other side from getting in.

Like suppressed memories. Things you didn't want to know or admit about yourself. Dark secrets.

Approaching the door slowly, I noticed slivers of angry red light seeping through its cracks and the narrow space between the floor and bottom of the door, a sharp contrast to the serene atmosphere in this room. I reached toward the knob, halfway expecting the door to be locked or to require its own passcode, but with it being shoved to the corner, away from the calm of the rest of the room, it felt like a someone was trying to ignore what was behind it, or at least sweep it to the side in hopes of forgetting its contents.

The knob turned easily and the door swung wide, as if the weight behind it was too heavy a burden to contain. Memories rushed out in pint-sized red clouds, swirling through the air and surrounding me, eager to be acknowledged and heard. And I *could* hear them as they flitted about, some speaking in Gabriel's voice and others in voices I didn't recognize, revealing the secrets he'd been keeping. Everyone was talking at once, as if I were in the midst of a crowd. The memories needed to be isolated so I could listen to them individually, and hear and understand what they were saying.

Reaching out, I tried to hold one of the tiny clouds in place. It was intangible, but as my hand passed through, the red vaporous fog latched onto me, wrapping itself around my forearm, and I heard Gabriel speaking to someone so clearly, it was as if they stood before me as I witnessed their conversation.

"Please, she did nothing wrong. I promise you, Sasha was oblivious to the type of heinous experiments Dr. Sebastian was conducting."

"I'm sorry, Gabriel, she broke the law, and it's out of my hands. We've discovered evidence proving Sasha had recently become aware of the nature of Dr. Sebastian's studies, but did nothing with that information. She'll be sent to the Realm immediately."

"I'm begging you. She's my wife. She'll never survive the Realm." Now I understood why he'd never discussed his wife. Until now, I'd never even known her name. The pleading tone of his voice told me that no matter what she'd done, Gabriel had loved her a great deal.

After playing itself out, the memory detached from my arm, and before I could reach out for the next one, another cloud descended and locked around my forearm, immediately drawing me into its recollection.

"How is it even possible you're contacting me from the Realm?"

"Who do you think was responsible for establishing communication with Posarius? We have matters to discuss, Gabriel. How I'm able to communicate with you is the least of your concerns." I froze. That voice. I recognized it immediately as Dr. Sebastian's but, like Gabriel, I'd thought it an impossible act to reach out from the Realm, other than the way Simon had contacted me.

"After what you did to Sasha, lying and allowing her to be sent away instead of telling the truth about the nature of her involvement, what makes you think I'd want to have anything to do with you? I'm terminating this connection and reporting you immediately."

"If you care about your son, you'll listen to what I have to say."

Son? I didn't think Gabriel had any children. He was silent a moment before replying. "I don't have a son. Sasha and I never had children, so don't try inventing excuses to prevent me—"

Sebastian interrupted. "Sasha was pregnant when she arrived."

There was a sharp intake of breath, and when Gabriel spoke, his voice wavered. "You're lying. She would never have kept something like that from me."

Sebastian huffed. "She was unaware of the pregnancy, but in spite of the living conditions here, Sasha recently gave birth to a healthy baby boy. So yes, Gabriel, you are indeed the father of a son."

Gabriel paused, and I could imagine him sitting at his desk, eyes wide in shock. "I n—n—need proof from Sasha. You can't expect me to believe something like this based on your word."

"Of course. She's right here."

After a few seconds, a woman spoke, her trembling voice full of tears. "Gabriel?"

He released a sob. "Sasha, sweetheart, is it true?"

"Y—yes. He's telling the truth. We have a son and he's beau—"

Her voice was cut off by Sebastian. "So, there's your proof."

Despite what Gabriel had done to Simon and me, I couldn't help but feel sorry for him. Not only did he lose his wife, he was a father who'd never meet his son, let alone known about him. That was a heaping pile of pain to deal with.

"What do you want from me, Sebastian? Why are you telling me this?"

"What if I told you there was a way to get your son out of the Realm?"

"I'd say it was impossible. There's no coming back from there. Everyone knows that."

"That's what everyone has been told and, up until now, it's been true. I've found a way, but I require help from you. What would you do to be with your wife and son?"

Gabriel's voice was eager. "Anything. But I don't understand why you think I can help you."

"Through some information I've acquired, I have the ability to open a portal between the Realm and Tage. Unfortunately, the doorway can't be sustained for long, and I need someone on your side to assist me in keeping it open for an extended period of time."

"I know nothing about portals, so I don't —"

"It's not you I need," Sebastian scoffed. "It's Simon Resnik. I need to know the exact coordinates of his whereabouts at a specific time to communicate with him. He's the only person who can do this."

"You want me to tell you the location of Simon Resnik? What makes you think I'd know that? I have no contact with him. We work in completely different areas of SI."

"But you work with his brother, Evan. You know where they live, and can tell me when Simon is home so I can consult with him."

Gabriel was silent for a moment. "Just consult with him? You said the portal isn't open for long, so how would that give you enough time to speak to him?"

"Under my supervision, Simon worked on this project for two years, and it's because of his research that I'll be able to create the doorway at all. It will only take seconds to confirm some calculations with him."

"What makes you think Simon will speak to you after everything that happened? Like everyone else, he must have been repulsed by what you did. I heard one of the victims was a previous lab partner of his."

"Simon understood the necessity of those experiments, and that I'd only chosen subjects who couldn't contribute to Tage's survival. He was always supportive of me."

The liar!

"But then what? What's to stop you from coming back to Tage and bringing every convict with you? For the safety of everyone, they can't be given their freedom."

Sebastian chuckled. "I have no desire to return to Tage, and of course I'm not giving the convicts their freedom, Gabriel. What kind of person do you think I am?"

"The kind that experiments on humans and kills them. The kind that incriminates innocent people. I know exactly what type of man you are, Sebastian."

"You have no idea what you're talking about! Don't presume to know me. Returning to Tage isn't an option. I can return your wife and son. All I need from you is Simon Resnik's location at a specific date and time. It's as simple as that. Make your choice."

Gabriel was quiet as he thought over his decision. "You only need Simon's location to confirm calculations with him? Nothing else?"

"You have my word."

"Which means nothing to me." Exactly what I was thinking.

"Coordinates for your family, Gabriel. You've already missed precious months of your son's life, and who's to say how much longer he can survive here?"

Although it was clear what his answer would be, I couldn't help but hope for a different outcome to the events that had already taken place. "You can guarantee the safety of Sasha and my son?"

"Of course. I've been watching over them as long as we've been here."

Gabriel sighed heavily. "Yes, I'll get you the coordinates."

"Wonderful. I knew you'd make the right decision. I'll be in touch soon."

The memory's grip on my arm released its hold, bringing me back to Gabriel's mind. After what I'd just witnessed, two things were certain. One, Gabriel had made a deal with the devil, who had coerced him into helping by using his family as leverage. He'd never really had a choice. Two, he'd had no idea what would happen to Simon. Sebastian had betrayed him as much as us.

Chapter 28
Evan
Present Day

When the memory freed me, I immediately noticed the color of the walls had changed from a mustard shade to a dark brown, and the previously smooth texture now had a rough, patchy appearance. Vibrations ran up my legs as the floor below shook threateningly. Gabriel knew something wasn't right, and I needed to withdraw right now. There was no time to sort through the other memories, but I'd gotten what I needed. It's almost like he sensed I was here, and his subconscious wanted to confess.

When I retreated from his mind, I studied Gabriel's troubled face while hovering over him. His sleep was restless and he kicked at the blankets, tossing and turning in agitation.

Passing through the bedroom wall, I settled into my body still lying in the shade under the clumped bushes, and sat upright with a gasp. My chest rose and fell rapidly as if I'd just run a marathon instead of lying here unmoving for the past several minutes. Once my breathing was under control, I peeked through the shrubbery, and after seeing no one but Syd, I jogged over and took her arm, pulling her behind me. We needed to grab Max and get out of here before Gabriel woke and became suspicious.

♊

"You're saying Gabriel is just as much of a victim as you or Simon? He really thought Sebastian just wanted information." Syd shook her head in disbelief as she sunk into my sofa. "I can't believe Gabriel trusted him. He should have known better. He's smarter than that."

Max shrugged. "I don't know, Syd. If I'd been in his position and someone told me they'd bring Simon home, I'd have done just about anything I was asked."

I nodded in agreement. "And now Gabriel's got a son to think about."

"Yeah," Max said. "Love and family are pretty powerful motivators."

"They are," Syd sighed. "But he's still not off the hook. He went a year without saying a word to Evan or anyone else about what really happened. What's he been waiting for?"

Max leaned forward and rested his elbows on his knees. "Maybe he's afraid of what could happen to his family. Gabriel's at Sebastian's mercy. Sebastian may still be contacting him. Who knows?"

"Exactly why we need to confront him," Syd said, tucking her feet underneath her. I sat to her right. The cushions shifted as she leaned over and placed her hand on my shoulder. "Why are you so quiet, Evan? You've hardly said a word since we got back."

I shrugged, but kept my gaze fixed on the floor, pulling at a loose thread on my pants. Some sort of unspoken conversation must have passed between Syd and Max, because he stood, saying he needed to get going. Something about things to take care of before work this evening. Syd had correctly guessed my thoughts, knowing I needed to talk to her alone.

The front door shut, and she turned to face me, legs crossed.

"So what's up? You should be ecstatic right now about having the ability to get into people's minds, and we're a step closer to bringing Simon home. Gabriel didn't intentionally deceive you, and—there it is."

"What?"

"I saw your eyes flick toward me when I mentioned Gabriel's name. So quit being all melodramatic and spill what's bothering you."

"I'm not being melodramatic." I rolled my eyes. "I've been thinking that with the way he was tricked into helping Sebastian, maybe all of this hasn't been an act, you know? Maybe he's really cared about me all along, and wasn't just pretending so he could get information."

She grabbed my hand and pulled it into her own, entwining our fingers. "I think deep down I always knew Gabriel cared about you, Evan. When you told me what Simon said about not trusting him, it didn't feel right, like trying to force a puzzle piece to fit into the wrong space. It hurts knowing he's kept all this to himself over the past year and had no one to confide in. At least I assume he didn't." Syd cocked her head to the side and furrowed her brow. "You know, when I think about it, I really don't know that much about him. I've seen him nearly every day for more than a year and spent countless hours with him, but other than our team, what else does he do with his life?"

That was a good question I didn't have an answer for. All I knew about him was that he seemed to work constantly, went home to rest, and came by my house to check on me occasionally. Knowing there was a family he couldn't be with all this time made me wonder how he'd lived with that knowledge and kept it hidden. He'd covered the pain and suffering well. If I hadn't had Gabriel and Syd, especially Syd to pull me out of my misery and solitude, I don't know what I would have done. I'd needed them. Now Gabriel needed us.

"I think we're all he has." I sighed. "I need to talk to him, tell him I know what happened." I looked at our entangled fingers.

"Do you want me to come with you?"

I shook my head. "This feels like something I need to do on my own. We've both been hurting for a long time. Maybe together we can do something about it and get our families back. But I'll let you know if I need you." I pulled her hand to my lips and kissed the back of it, finally understanding my feelings for her ran much deeper than friendship. Things were still left unsaid and undefined between us, but when I was with her and saw the way she looked at me, it gave me hope that maybe someday I'd finally be enough.

Chapter 29
Evan
Present Day

Gabriel stood behind his desk staring through the window overlooking the operations floor below, but by his reflection, I saw the way his eyes were glazed over, and wasn't sure he really saw anything. He gave no indication he'd even heard me come in. When I cleared my throat, he tensed slightly and turned to face me.

"Evan, what are you doing here? You know you're not supposed to come in during your suspension."

"We need to talk, Gabriel. About a lot of things."

"We've already discussed the steps you need to complete before being returned to active status, and until then, I can't allow you to resume your position."

Holding his gaze, I closed the door behind me. "I know about Sasha and your son."

It was if I'd physically punched him. His body slumped, and he leaned onto the desk for support, face nearly as white as the carpet. He choked out a feeble, "How?"

He wasn't going to like my answer, but the time had come to share all our secrets. "From your memories."

He lowered himself into the chair and shook his head. "That's impossible. There's no way you could have accessed my memories."

"How else could I have known about them?"

He continued shaking his head in denial, then raised his eyes to mine. "Are you saying you took sedative out of the lab and somehow used it on me?"

"No." I shuffled my feet and threaded a hand through my hair. "See, that's the thing. I don't need the sedative anymore. I've been able to access Syd's mind, and now yours."

Despite the initial shock of learning I knew about Sasha and his son, Gabriel now looked indignant. Which I totally understood. "You pilfered through my mind without my permission?" And then the impact of what I'd said washed over his face. "What do you mean, you don't need the sedative anymore?"

I grabbed the nearest chair and pulled it up as close to his desk as possible, then dropped into it. "Maybe I should start at the beginning."

"Yes, Evan. That would certainly help."

I began with what Simon had told me after I'd been suspended, including the parts with his journal, and ended with what I'd discovered during my intrusion into his most private memories. Gabriel listened closely, his expression blank. "I'm sorry I did it without your permission, but after what my brother said, I had no choice. I hope you understand."

He was silent for some time, staring at his clasped hands atop the desk. "No, Evan, I'm the one who should apologize." His face was creased with sorrow and shame. "If I'd only been smarter and taken the time to think things through, maybe Simon would still be here. I'm so, so sorry for keeping it to myself all this time, but I was afraid Sebastian would harm my family if I told someone."

"It's your wife and son, Gabriel. I get it. I'd do the same for my brother."

"Another thing. You need to know that my feelings about you weren't a sham. During Bender training, I recognized your talent, a natural ability for this kind of work, and wanted to mentor you. Once I understood the situation with your parents, I knew you needed a support system and wanted to be that for you.

"You see, Evan, you saved me, too. After Sasha was sent away, I was lost, and couldn't bring myself to tell anyone what happened to her. Mentoring and taking care of you, helping Syd bring you back...it was both my penance and purpose. All the time we spent together was genuine, and I always thought if I'd been fortunate enough to have a son, maybe he'd have been a little like you."

I felt lighter and breathed easier knowing it hadn't all been a lie. "Just with less attitude?" I smirked.

He gave me a wan smile.

"But you do have a son." Even through the sadness in his eyes, he beamed with pride at my statement. "And we need to find a way to bring our families home."

"That we do, Evan. Do you have a plan?"

"I've been working on one, and if you have the location on Sebastian, Dr. Quill says we can open a doorway."

A slow smile snaked across his face. "I have the location."

♊

We met in Bender lab C. Syd, Max, and Dr. Quill were already there when Gabriel and I arrived. My default mode had always been action over words, and I was ready to slice open the portal, pull my brother through it, and then deal with Sebastian. During my downtime from SI, to keep myself occupied, I'd come up with over a dozen different ways to inflict pain and suffering that wouldn't end well for him, but would make me feel a hell of a lot better. Luckily, more practical minds were in on this plan, and I'd await instruction from them. But no one said I had to be patient.

Syd's face was the first I saw upon entering the lab, and I naturally gravitated in her direction, kissing her cheek lightly when I reached her. When I turned to face the others, Max smirked at me and waggled his eyebrows, to which I returned a stony glare. Truce or not, we weren't at the stage where he had any right to make statements over whatever was happening between Syd and me.

Gabriel shook Doc's hand. "Paul, Evan tells me you need Simon's location to open the portal, and I can provide that information."

Doc nodded quickly. He was a hive of excitement. "That's good news, and we may need to rely on that information, but in speaking with Sydney, I may have a better idea."

I looked at her in confusion. Did she know something about portals she wasn't telling me? Possess some latent scientific genius ability?

"Evan, Syd has been telling me about your highly unusual connection to Simon, one I find utterly fascinating. If I'd known about this before his disappearance, I'd have spoken to you both about participating in a study."

I nodded, urging him to continue.

"Are you familiar with the term quantum entanglement?"

"Can't say that I am, Doc. What does it have to do with Simon and me?"

"Quantum entanglement occurs when pairs or groups of particles are generated or interact in ways such that the quantum state of each particle cannot be described independently of the others, even when the particles are separated by a large distance."

My jaw slid sideways and I blinked at him in confusion. Some of those terms were familiar, having heard Simon mention them occasionally, but they didn't make any more sense now than they did then. Doc and Simon definitely spoke a common language. I didn't.

"I'm gonna need some simpler terms on that one, Doc. Simon got all the science genes."

He held his hands up, closed his eyes, and shook his head. "Of course, of course. I'm just a little overexcited about your twin connection. This tether that allows you to experience each other's emotions and know what might be happening to the other when separated, it's very similar to a quantum entanglement. When you're separated, as you are now, with Simon in another world as it were, the connection between you isn't severed."

"Right, it's not. I thought it was, until Simon was able to contact me, almost like he was a Bender." I wasn't sure exactly where Doc was headed with this, but so far it seemed like a good thing.

Syd slid her hand in mine and squeezed it, smiling up at me.

"With quantum entanglements, when the particles are separated, they're still connected by what you may know as a wormhole."

"Yes!" Max exclaimed. He'd been quiet, but radiated energy clamoring to be released. The two of us seemed to share the action-over-words viewpoint, but he definitely edged me out with respect to science knowledge. "Simon mentioned something like this to me, said he had some suspicions, something about a bridge, and wanted to look into it after he wrapped up what he was working on."

"Hmmm," Doc said, rubbing his chin. "I'm not surprised, which confirms I may be on the right track if Simon suspected the same thing."

"Can we slow down a bit? What does a bridge have to do with Simon and me? You're losing me, Doc."

"The technical term for wormholes that connect entanglements is Einstein-Rosen bridge, a concept hypothesized many years ago by brilliant Earth scientists. We've known for a while that some twins experience unique relationships, but what you and your brother have is far beyond anything I've heard of, and I have a hunch a bridge such as this may connect the two of you."

Doc's explanation was just getting stranger by the minute. Some kind of weird bridge between us? "Okaaaay. Say this bridge exists. How does that help us?"

"If I'm correct in my assumptions, you and Simon are both gateways to this bridge. Once we determine the entry point, you can literally travel across the bridge and retrieve him."

Stunned was too mild a word to describe my feelings. "I need to sit down." Syd led me over to a Bender chair, where I sat on the level end that wasn't reclined and combed my hands through my hair. "So, you're saying that all this time we've been connected by a bridge, and Simon could have just come home when he felt like it, or I could have just hopped across, fetched him, and all this drama could have been avoided?"

Doc chuckled. "It's not quite that easy. First, we need to locate the entry point. Even though Simon may have suspected its existence, if he's been held captive, and assuming it even exists in the Realm, he wouldn't have been able to get to the equipment needed to find the entrance. If I'd been aware of your connection with your twin, perhaps we could have moved to this conclusion sooner, but there are several variables. With you, I can put something together that will let us know within minutes if this bridge exists. If indeed it does, this would be the safest technique for everyone. With Simon's calculations, we can certainly open a portal, but my concern is that Dr. Sebastian, or anyone else in the Realm, may also try to enter."

"That was a concern of mine." Gabriel had been silently listening to our discussion, until now. "I'm not sure if you're aware, but my wife and son are also in the Realm. If this bridge exists, would it be possible to bring them across as well?" His expression was so hopeful, I was afraid a negative answer would literally shatter him right in front of us.

"From what I understand with my research, if Simon brings them through on his end, they should be able to pass. But if Evan enters the Realm from Simon's door, and through some unfortunate event Simon cannot come back, Evan would be unable to bring your wife and son across the bridge."

"You mean if Simon dies," Max said, his voice unsteady.

"Yes," Doc replied quietly.

"That won't happen." Being this close to getting Simon, there was no way I'd let anything stand in the way of him coming home. Even if it meant sacrificing my own life. "So, what you're saying is, you do some kind of science stuff, locate the gateway, and I can cross the bridge and grab him, right?"

"In the simplest terms, yes."

"I'm going with you." Syd and Max spoke simultaneously.

"No to both of you. I'm going by myself." I rose from the chair. As the two of them ganged up on me, stating my denial of their offer only confirmed my level of stupidity, I countered with threats of physical restraint.

Doc interrupted the three of us.

"Scientifically speaking, Evan can be the only one to cross. Bringing back one adult and a small child shouldn't upset the balance of things, but two added adults could collapse the bridge."

I threw out my hands in front of me. "There you go."

Syd scowled darkly at me, while Max reverted to his mumbling and pacing.

"Gabriel, I promise we'll bring back your family."

His eyes were wet when he answered. "I know you will, Evan."

I'd carried the burden of guilt and pain for over a year, and it was exhausting. I'd blamed myself for so long, and allowed our parents to do the same. But not anymore. I was going to bring Simon home. Me. Not my parents. With him here, our empty house would become a home again, and we'd be a family, just the two of us.

"All right, Doc, what do you need from me?"

CHAPTER 30
EVAN
PRESENT DAY

While I stood in front of a white screen, Doc bustled about, setting up some kind of lens in front of me that would show the entry point of the bridge between Simon and me—if it existed.

Syd and Max had continued to pout, until Gabriel brought up the point that arrangements had to be made for Simon, Sasha, and Gabriel's son's arrival. Sebastian hadn't allowed Sasha enough time to even tell Gabriel his son's name. We didn't know what kind of shape they'd be in, if they'd require medical treatment, or even be able to walk unassisted.

I was essentially going in blind.

"When I shine light through on this side, the gravitational lens will bend, or refract the light before it reaches you. Any dark space around you that doesn't accept the light will be the gateway to the Einstein-Rosen bridge."

Trying to imagine a bridge connecting Simon and me, let alone dragging around an entrance behind me, or wherever it was, seemed totally bizarre. But I could live with heaping amounts of bizarre if it got me to Simon quicker.

Unsure of what I'd be walking into, I'd put on an actual utility belt—not the dreamworld type Benders used—loaded with a couple of bowie knives, rope, a hatchet, and zip ties. Simon said he was kept in a room by himself, but that didn't mean he'd be alone when I entered. And I had no idea where Sasha and Gabriel's son were being held. I could only hope it was close, and they'd be easy to get to.

While Doc got everything in place, I observed Gabriel, Syd, and Max. Gabriel's expression, as always, was stoic even during extreme stress, but the tightness around his eyes said it was just a cover. Max was going to climb the walls if he didn't burn off some excess energy soon, and I knew he was just as worried about Simon as I was. He needed to calm down, because we'd need his help when we returned. Syd was completely absorbed in what Doc was doing, moving and adjusting things as he called out instructions. She'd always said keeping busy was a helpful distraction when she was nervous.

Doc finally stood back, hands on his hips, and surveyed the equipment. "I think we're ready. Evan, do you have any questions?"

Considering no one had ever done this before, as far as Doc knew, I should have had enough questions to fill a book, but all I could think about was Simon's safety instead of my own. "When I get to him, what prevents Sebastian or anyone else from following us back across the bridge?"

"In order to enter the gateway, someone would have to be in physical contact with either you or Simon, so it's imperative that Sasha and her son stay close."

"Good to know. Any idea what this bridge looks like? If I fall off, do I just drift off into space?"

"That, Evan, is something I can't answer." Doc shrugged. "My expert advice would be to stay on the bridge and watch where you're going."

I smiled. "Excellent input, Doc."

"Ready when you are."

My gaze roamed over the people closest to me. I never thought Max would be part of that group, but over the past few days, I'd seen a different side to him. Or maybe I finally paid attention. If my brother loved him, he couldn't be that bad of a guy. He stood watching me, arms folded over his chest. "Simon said you had good instincts, so make sure to use them, all right?" His eyes softened. "And tell him I'm waiting for him."

A hug from Syd would have been a comfort right now, but Doc had instructed me not to move. "Don't make me have to come after you, Evan." She smiled warmly. "But you know I always will."

"I hope you'll never have to." My gaze traveled to Gabriel, who could only muster a reassuring nod. The fate of his family was in my hands, and the magnitude of that weighed heavily on me.

I gave Doc a thumbs up. "Let's get started."

With Syd, Max, and Gabriel gathered behind him, Doc flicked on the white light and I stared fixedly as its intense beam struck the lens, but as he'd stated, bent to the right in my direction instead of passing straight through. Being told not to move, I was unable to see the end result when the light shined on me, but judging by loud gasps from the observers, it must have been pretty revealing.

"What? Can you see something? Is it the entrance?" Syd's hands covered her mouth as she nodded, while Max's mouth just hung open.

"Simon and I were correct." Doc walked toward me, staying to the side of the light, carrying a large mirror. He stopped a couple of feet away from me and held it up. My reflection was anxious and haggard, and I doubted a solid week of continuous sleep could cure the dark circles under my eyes. Behind me on the white screen was the outline of my soot-colored shadow. Nothing out of the ordinary.

But to the left of me, only inches from my shadow, was something I'd never seen before and very much out of the ordinary. Standing nearly my height and a couple of feet wide, was an arch of sparkling darkness. The gateway to the bridge that joined Simon and me. My smile beamed brighter than the white light. "Doc, you're a genius. I don't know how I'll ever thank you. If there's anything you ever need...."

"Well," he interrupted, "if you could persuade Simon to let me work with him on the portal to Posarius, I'd be eternally grateful."

"Done. So, what happens now?"

He gestured toward the dark arch behind me. "Go get your brother."

Yet another connection to my twin, but one we'd been unaware of our whole lives. Or I had, anyway. Simon had apparently suspected its existence. Can't say that shocked me. I pivoted slowly to my left, and with one final backward glance at Syd, watching with her clasped hands tucked under her chin, I stepped through the mystifying doorway into the unknown.

My feet hit solid ground, and glittering, infinite darkness surrounded me like a cloak. I heard nothing, and the air felt heavy against my ears. When I snapped my fingers, the sound was muffled, as if it came from the room beside me. Dropping my eyes to the bridge that connected us, I was greeted with a long, straight walkway made up of every color in the rainbow continually churning below me. It was awe-inspiring, intriguing, hopeful, thrilling, and precarious all at once, and from where I stood, the end wasn't visible.

I needed to move, so I took my first cautious step toward Simon.

CHAPTER 31
SIMON
PRESENT DAY

Sebastian hadn't made any more attempts to get into Evan's mind, as far as I knew. He'd been furious upon discovering that one, Evan was a much stronger Bender than he'd believed, and two, my twin and I shared a connection Sebastian had been unaware of. In addition to his relentless interrogations for the portal calculations, he now questioned me about what our connection entailed. As if I'd reveal any details about that, either.

I was mentally and physically weary from being constantly vigilant about him slipping into my mind. With so much of my focus on Sebastian, I lacked strength to contact Evan and hoped he was making headway on his end. I had faith in him, enough for both of us. Most of his life, he'd been told in one way or another that he wasn't good enough or smart enough, but I knew better. He was so much stronger than he realized.

Through the locked door of my cell and across the hallway, I heard the wails of Sasha's son, Alex. There had been some kind of commotion earlier, with scuffling in the hallway and voices shouting, but I hadn't been able to determine what had happened. Whatever it was, I was sure Sebastian would visit me soon enough to gloat about it.

Rising from the bare mattress, I moved toward the tiny window that offered my only view apart from the room I'd been held in for so long. It was a depressing sight of a shabby, narrow street lined with drab buildings, but at least it was something different. I occasionally saw people in the street and conjured stories about their lives as a form of entertainment. But they were just that. Fictional stories. The reality was that every day was a fight for survival—food, adequate shelter, safety. Hope didn't exist in the Realm. You slept, only to wake and begin the same struggle the next day. Surrender was easier for some.

My shoulders slumped and I sighed, grateful for the momentary reprieve from his attacks, but also wondering how much longer I could survive here. Food was considerably scarcer than on Tage, and although I was given rations, hunger was a constant companion. I was thin, and my clothes loose and baggy, but had no way of knowing how much weight I'd lost. Thinking maybe sleep would improve my outlook, I turned back toward the bed.

And ran into Evan. He wore a lopsided grin, with one eyebrow raised mischievously.

"How are you....? What did.....?"

"Never thought I'd see you incapable of completing a sentence, brother. How about we get the hell out of here?"

I threw myself against his strong, unwavering body, hugging him tightly, while also warning him to keep his voice down, as we could be interrupted at any moment. The missing pieces inside me clicked into place, and I felt whole for the first time in over a year.

Evan pulled away first.

"It's the bridge. Dr. Quill said you were right about your suspicions."

"The Einstein-Rosen bridge?"

He nodded. "Yeah, whatever you call it, but it's how I got here and the way we're leaving. Do you know where Gabriel's wife and son are? Sebastian lied to him about you. I promise we can trust him."

Of course he did. Gabriel was just another victim of Sebastian's manipulations. I could still hear the baby's faint cries. "They're across the hall. My door is locked, but I don't think it's guarded regularly. Sebastian correctly assumes I can't escape from this room. When I was first abducted, I was permitted supervised trips to his on-site lab, and that's how I learned of Sasha and Alex. She's just another innocent victim of Sebastian's and doesn't deserve to be here."

"Gabriel said the same thing, and I promised I'd bring them back." He hurried to the door, hunkered down and peeked underneath it, then stood and examined the lock. "There's no one outside, and I can get us through this door." He reached into a small bag attached to his belt for something, but I placed my hand on his arm to stop him. "Simon, we have to—"

"I'm sorry, but it's been over a year and I have to know." I needed the answer, but dreaded what it might mean. "Max?"

Evan smirked and rolled his eyes. "He's waiting for you on the other side. It's possible he's not as big of an idiot as I thought."

I couldn't contain my smile. Maybe the fantasy I'd created wasn't so far-fetched after all.

"Now, will you let me do my job and get us out of here?"

He squatted in front of the lock and began working with slim silver tools.

"Are you picking the lock? Where did you learn to do that?"

"Part of a Bender's job. Do you have any idea how many nightmares hide in locked closets? You'd think some of them would be more creative."

I heard a faint click, then Evan stood and placed his ear to the door. He brought his index finger to his lips to silence me, slowly cracked the door open, and peered out into the hallway. After looking both ways, he motioned for me to follow him, pulling the door closed behind him. Alex's cries continued, and I wondered if there was a problem. Babies weren't my area of expertise, but the cries seemed different from his usual hunger wails—more desperate somehow.

"You keep watch while I open their door," he whispered. "It won't take me long." The hallway remained empty while he worked, and I thought perhaps a crying baby worked in our favor, driving people away. Out of the corner of my eye, I saw the door swing open as Alex's pitiful howls carried into the hall. Evan and I rushed in, closing that door behind us, so to anyone passing, everything would look normal.

What I saw upon entering the room tore my heart apart. Sasha lay on the bed with Alex screaming in her arms, but her eyes saw nothing. They were fixed and staring into space.

Evan gently pulled the baby from her and tried to quiet him, while I knelt at the bedside and checked her pulse, knowing none existed. Her body had already started to cool. While our food wasn't plentiful, it had been enough to keep us alive, but Sasha's body was dangerously thin, while Alex looked relatively healthy. I stood and ducked my head in sorrow, knowing she'd sacrificed her own life by giving her portions to her child so he could live.

The feeling of a warm body, even if it was a stranger, had calmed Alex, and by the look in Evan's damp, feral eyes, having the baby in his arms was the only thing preventing him from tearing the place apart and hunting down Sebastian himself. "I was too late. If I'd gotten here even one day earlier, I could have saved her."

I shook my head and grabbed Evan by his shoulders. "No, even if she'd been strong enough to cross over, she wouldn't have survived more than a day or so. She starved herself to save her son. Take Alex to his father."

He held my gaze, and I could see him warring with himself, wanting desperately to make Sebastian pay for all he'd done, yet knowing we needed to get to safety. Once I crossed over, this doorway would close permanently, keeping Sebastian out of his reach. And Evan would have to live with that.

He nodded once. "Doc said you need to have physical contact with anyone entering through your side." He carefully transferred Alex, who had thankfully fallen into an exhausted sleep, into my arms.

The door burst open, crashing into the wall behind it, startling both of us, as Alex let out a blood-curdling scream. Sebastian stood in the doorway, a murderous look on his face that quickly slid into confusion upon seeing Evan, me holding Alex, and Sasha's dead body. Before I could draw a breath, my brother was on him.

Evan spoke no words. He was a physical storm of rage, and Sebastian nothing more than a helpless leaf caught up in his intensity. He charged at Sebastian, grabbed his neck, and slammed his head against the wall hard enough that cracks spidered out behind him. His eyes bulged in fear as Evan tossed him to floor, where he lay helpless as Evan straddled his chest, fists raining down relentlessly.

I cradled Alex's head to my shoulder so he couldn't witness the abuse, then gasped in surprise as three men appeared in the doorway, watching in shock as their ticket out of the Realm was assaulted.

"Evan, we have to go!" I worried he was too far gone to hear me, but he looked up in acknowledgement as the men advanced in our direction. He stood and moved backwards toward me, blood dripping from his fists, never taking his eyes from the men.

"The door is directly behind you to the left," he said quietly.

Tucking Alex against my chest with one arm, I grabbed Evan's blood-covered hand and spun around, pulling him behind me through a doorway I couldn't see, but had to trust was there.

I won't lie and say it didn't feel good to let go on Sebastian. Honestly, it was really cathartic. But I would have preferred a little more quality time with him. My knuckles would have survived it.

But Simon was right. We needed to escape while we could, and get Alex to Gabriel. Simon to Max. Me to Syd.

No matter what Simon said about Sasha not surviving, I'd always blame myself for not getting to them sooner. I couldn't imagine what she'd gone through. Knowing her child was hungry, listening to him cry—any parent would have made the same decision. Well, most, anyway. I had to content myself with the knowledge that she didn't die in vain—we saved her son.

Simon grabbed my hand and pulled us through the doorway. Not knowing what to expect, he was a little dazed and off balance at seeing the bridge and surrounding glittering darkness for the first time. Alex had calmed after all the commotion, and was lying quietly against Simon's shoulder, eyes wide open and thumb in his mouth. Maybe he sensed he was going to a better place, a home with a father who loved him.

"Just stay on the bridge and we'll be fine. Only took me a few minutes to get to you from my side." I walked forward, but Simon wasn't following. Turning, I saw him staring past me as he absently patted Alex's back. "Look, Simon, I know this is like science porn for you, but we really need to move. Can't you study this later?"

He shook his head. "It's not that. After over a year, I'm finally going home. I'd started to give up."

If I'd been tuned into him, I would have known. That place inside me hadn't been filled for so long, maybe I was out of the habit of checking in. Up until a year ago, it had been second nature, a reflex.

I smiled softly. "Well, it's real and they're waiting for us, so let's get across this bridge." Although Doc had said it wouldn't be possible for anyone to follow, that didn't prevent me from checking behind us every few seconds. When I looked forward again, the silver arched doorway back to the SI lab was only a dozen feet away. Maybe it was because Simon and I were together, and I'm sure he could provide some long, detailed explanation that wouldn't make a bit of sense to me. But I didn't care. My brother was thin and malnourished, but alive. And I was bringing him home.

I placed a hand on the door and looked back at Simon. "Ready?"

He grinned, still patting Alex's back. "More than you can imagine."

Pulling open the door, I was met with four anxious faces full of hope and relief. When Simon stepped out from behind me, Max let out yelps of joy, and I managed to take Alex a second before he crashed into Simon.

Wanting to give them privacy, I turned to Gabriel. His questioning eyes brimmed with tears, but without me saying the words, he understood about Sasha. Squeezing the lids shut, he bowed his head a moment. When his gaze met mine again, his eyes were filled with both sorrow and love as he reached for the squirming baby in my arms. "Gabriel, meet your son, Alex." Gabriel cradled him against his chest, as Alex's small hands reached for his face.

"I'm sorry about Sasha. She saved Alex."

He nodded. "We can talk about it later. I don't know how to thank you, Evan."

"You'll never have to."

A warm hand slid into my own, and I turned to find Syd gazing up at me. A puzzled look crossed her face, and she lifted my hand and studied it.

"Evan, you're bleeding. Are you all right?" Her voice carried a hint of panic.

"Yeah. It's not mine. Well, some of it is, but most of it belongs to Sebastian." I felt a certain amount of satisfaction at having drawn his blood, but even more blood and suffering would have enhanced my mood.

"Is he...?"

"He's still alive," I replied in a flat voice. My gaze drifted in Simon's direction. Max's hands were on either side of Simon's face, their foreheads touching while they spoke in low voices to each other. "But Simon is safe and he's home." The sheer scope of his happiness made me feel almost lightheaded, and I wondered if I'd ever feel that way myself or only experience it secondhand. Shifting my focus back to Syd, my heart nearly jolted to a stop. Had she always looked at me this way? Like I was the only thing she saw, with such profound love and trust so clearly evident to anyone who cared to notice? I blinked, stunned anyone could feel that way about me.

A strange fluttering rose inside me that hadn't been there before. Strange, but somewhat familiar. I wondered if the feelings I'd kept locked up over the past year were easing their way through cracks in the door. It had been so long since I'd allowed myself to feel anything other than guilt, anger, and self-loathing, that most other emotions were a distant memory. But this felt good. Simon was safe, and it was time to let go of the heavy emotions and experience what was right in front of me. Someone that had always been there for me. Feelings I was beginning to suspect I'd suppressed for quite a while.

I pulled Syd to me and wrapped my arms around her, tucking her head under my chin. Her warm body fit against mine perfectly, filling in all the contours and crevices. This felt right. Natural. Maybe these feelings wouldn't be secondhand after all. She'd said I was worth the wait, and I silently promised to make sure her wait had been worthwhile.

A gentle touch on my shoulder brought back my awareness, and Doc's questioning face appeared before me. I reluctantly let go of Syd, but kept one arm around her.

"I'm sorry to interrupt," he said, a sheepish grin of embarrassment covering his face.

"No problem, Doc. I wanted to thank you. Simon wouldn't be here without your help. We—"

"Evan!" Max's panicked voice called my name.

The floor tilted sideways and needles sliced through my head, causing my eyes to roll back. Syd's arm tightened around me, and Doc leaped forward to help her. My vision swam as my head rolled in Max's direction to see Simon's limp body in his arms. What was happening to us? And was this happening to him or me?

I needed to think, but the haze of pain, confusion, and fear clouded everything. Simon was down, lying on the floor with Max leaning over him, pleading for him to wake up. Syd and Doc staggered under my weight while trying to support me. The sensation was nearly indescribable, like my mind was twisting sideways inside my skull.

Simon needed me. I shook my head to clear my thoughts. What was this? I had to go beyond the pain and get inside him, see which of us was truly experiencing this. Sinking into myself and finding that part within me that was all him, I latched onto it.

And immediately knew something was very wrong. It was like biting into a strawberry and discovering it was filled with mustard. Simon wasn't alone. Someone else was in there with him.

It had to be Sebastian.

Why hadn't this occurred to me? I was a trained Bender, one of the best, and should have recognized a mental attack. Especially when I was nearly the target. Simon was weak, and didn't have the strength to fight off an intrusion. I immediately reinforced my own barriers, and that seemed to sever our connection. The agonizing pain and disorientation disappeared just as quickly as they'd started, and I stood on my own, pushing away from Syd and Doc.

Syd looked at me questioningly. "Evan?"

Max cradled Simon's head in his lap. "What's wrong with him? What's happening?"

"It's Sebastian. He's in Simon's head, and can bend from the Realm without sedative. Simon's been blocking him for months, but now he's too weak to stop him." My voice wavered. He could do irreparable damage to my twin, twisting and manipulating his mind to the point that he'd become a different person. My brother would disappear forever. If he even woke again. Sebastian could potentially destroy the gifted mind that held the key to saving Tage. I looked at Gabriel. "We need a tech to draw his blood, and we'll need more Benders. Syd, get the rest of the team."

"On it," she replied, her finger already moving over her data pad to alert them.

"I'm going with you," Max stated.

I shook my head. "Stay with him. You're too close."

"And you're not?"

I clenched my jaw. "Fine. Grab a chair and get prepped."

Max carried Simon to the bed reserved for clients, and lay him down gently. Doc immediately began attaching leads to him, knowing exactly where to place them because of his own history. Ky had already arrived, and was pulling on latex gloves as he elbowed Max out of the way. Before he left Simon's side, he bent over and kissed his forehead, pushing his hair away from his too thin face. He whispered something before dashing over to a Bender chair.

Syd and Isaac strapped themselves in, while I grabbed a com unit, then took the last chair beside Syd. Gabriel transferred Alex to Amelia's waiting arms so he could run communications, and Zia attached leads to us. Glancing back in Ky's direction, I saw him mixing a small amount of Simon's blood with the sedative.

I turned my head toward Syd. "I don't need Simon's blood or the anesthesia. I'm going in now."

"Evan, no, you should wait for us."

"I can't. You know what could happen." I pulled her hand to my lips and kissed it. "See you soon."

Chapter 33
Evan
Present Day

I faced a massive, red-tinged wall, deeply gouged from claw marks where Simon's barriers had been relentlessly attacked. He'd fought so hard to keep Sebastian out. Looking up and to either side, it extended further than I could see, which left me no other option than to punch my way through. Judging by how thin and fragile the walls were in some places, it wouldn't take much effort. The ground rumbled and vibrated beneath my feet, either from Sebastian's anger or Simon's feeble last attempts to bar him, I couldn't be sure. If Sebastian had complete control of my brother's mind, any number of things could be causing the rumbling.

Maybe I wouldn't have to use force to break through. As with Gabriel, Simon's defenses should recognize me. The second I placed my hand against the battered wall, it surrendered to me and crumpled, either welcoming me or pleading for help. After teaching Simon how to compartmentalize thoughts, his mind had always been a tranquil, orderly place. But no more.

I stepped through into an open field shrouded in gray mist, the wispy clouds swirling around my feet and spiraling up past my knees. Streaks of lightning danced in the distance. I needed to stay alert. Even something as seemingly innocent as fog could be a threat. My eyes flitted in all directions. Without the other Benders here, I had no one to cover my back.

In the distance, a dark figure approached, moving rapidly toward me. It appeared to be a man, and my hand darted to the knife on my belt. I sincerely hoped it was Sebastian, so I could finish what I'd started.

Wanting to get the upper hand, I leaped into the air and landed a dozen feet in front of the man, confirming my suspicions that it was

Lucas Sebastian.

He sneered, looking like he'd already won. I'd never let it happen, but until I understood exactly how deeply embedded he was in Simon's mind, I needed to hold back.

"You don't seem surprised to see me, Evan."

"Not at all. We have unfinished business." My voice had a warning edge to it. I wanted him off balance.

"Admittedly, you're stronger than I'd believed. I'm still unsure exactly how you took Simon, but it's of no matter now. I'll retrieve the information I require. Unfortunately, my efforts may permanently damage some areas of your brother's mind."

"Don't bet on it."

"You may be a talented Bender, but don't forget it was I who created the program. The odds are heavily in my favor, and you don't stand a chance against me." My hands trembled with the need to forcibly wipe the haughty expression from his face.

From the com unit in my ear, I heard Gabriel's confident voice. "They're all launched, Evan."

"Sure I do." Syd, Max, and Isaac appeared at my side, poised and ready. "Don't ever underestimate me, Sebastian."

His eyes widened briefly, then gleamed malignantly.

Max and I shot into the air on either side of him, weapons drawn. Sebastian drew one arm back and fired a throwing star in Max's direction. Max spun away in the other direction, but not before it nicked his shoulder and drew blood.

Syd and Isaac, both armed with bowie knives, charged at Sebastian. At the same time, a flick of his other hand erected some sort of transparent shield in front of him, and the two of them plowed heavily into it. The shield was new to me, and I heard their grunts of pain over the rumbling thunder as they ricocheted back to the ground beneath the mist. Losing track of Syd threatened to distract me, but I knew she could take care of herself for now. The shield wouldn't keep her or Isaac down.

Sebastian drew a bowie knife from his belt and launched himself straight up to meet me. I rolled right, dodging his blade. Hurling my own knife into his heart, assuming one actually beat within his chest, would be effortless for me. His body back in the Realm would die quickly from the wound. But with this many of us, and Sebastian being unpredictable, I couldn't be certain my knife would hit its intended target and not one of my team.

Max hurtled through the air behind him. An animal snarl clawed its way up his throat as he drove his shoulder into Sebastian's back, forcing him to the ground. Max was too inexperienced to understand his mistake, and Sebastian drove the knife back into his thigh. They landed hard, and blood gushed from Max's wound as he howled in pain.

"Max, eject!" I yelled. If the knife had sliced into his femoral artery, he might not live long enough to hit the button.

I heard Gabriel's voice in my ear. "Eject Max."

"On it." I nodded at Syd. She threw herself in Max's direction and pushed his button over his loud protests.

The eject button. It was something only SI Benders possessed. Sebastian didn't have one—that could give us an advantage.

Sebastian quickly got to his feet, and Isaac was at his back. It looked as if he'd lost his knife in the mist, which was rapidly dissipating. Isaac hooked an arm around Sebastian's neck and kicked at the back of his knee, forcing him back down to a kneeling position.

Syd stood several feet in front of them, knife in hand, ready to throw. The shot wouldn't be difficult—she had the highest accuracy rate of any Bender.

She flung the knife, aiming dead center at Sebastian's chest.

Sebastian gripped Isaac's arm, bent, and threw him over top of him, effectively blocking Syd's target. The knife embedded itself in Isaac's upper right shoulder. His roar of pain echoed through the air, but was nearly eclipsed by Sebastian's hysterical laughter.

"Isaac, eject," I yelled, my voice coarse from barely contained frustration, anger, and fear. He'd already taken out two of us. I could have Gabriel launch Amelia and Zia, but this fight might be over by the time they reached us.

Our surroundings were growing darker, and the thunder and lightning had all but ceased. Simon was losing his ability to battle with whatever fight he had left. I needed to help him. Sebastian fought us with one part of his brain, while the other burrowed into my twin's subconscious, searching for the portal information. Just as he'd undervalued my Bender capabilities, he was also unaware I could split my mind in the same way he had.

While part of me joined Syd in sparring with Sebastian, the other reached out and located the core of Simon's mind, jarred at how little strength remained. I bound myself to him, wrapping my subconscious around his own, hoping to hold off Sebastian just a little longer. With my added fortitude, thunder bellowed overhead, rain fell in torrents, and lightening split the air, striking a tree only feet away.

Syd and I charged, attacked, and bombarded Sebastian with every tactic in our arsenal, and he dodged or outsmarted all of them. His ability to elude us was maddening, and I was growing weary from essentially being in two places at once.

I held the heavy iron mallet, hungry to hear it collide with Sebastian's head. Syd flew over top of him as a distraction, while I came at him from the other direction. Before I could reach him, Sebastian shot into the air, locked an arm around Syd's waist, and threw her to the ground, keeping his hold on her. My heart stuttered as he brought them both to a standing position, one arm still hooked around her waist, and the other holding one of her own knives at her throat. Syd's hands gripped his forearm across her neck, her eyes glittering jewels of anger and defiance.

"Stop whatever you're doing, Evan. I know you're helping Simon somehow."

I shook my head. "I'll never abandon him. Not again."

At my refusal, Sebastian smirked, then drew the knife across Syd's neck, but not deeply enough for a mortal wound. She clenched her jaw in pain, unwilling to give him the satisfaction of hearing her scream. At the sight of her blood spilling, completely at his mercy, my world narrowed to a single focus, and something shifted inside me, nearly bringing me to my knees. The need to protect her was so overpowering, it threatened my link with Simon.

"No!" I charged in their direction, but he held the point of the knife at her carotid artery, halting my attack.

"Release Simon and she's yours. If not, she dies in front of you. Make your choice."

Simon or Syd. He had no idea what he was asking. There *was* no choice—I'd never give up either of them.

Syd's eyes met my own, and my gaze flicked to the eject button on the cuff around her left wrist. During all the chaos, it had slipped Sebastian's mind. The imperceptible shake of her head went unnoticed, as her lips drew into a hard line. She didn't want to leave me here alone, but the thought of Syd suffering was more than I could bear. I needed to know she was safe.

"Your time is up. Simon or Syd?"

I tilted my head slightly, begging her to trust me. Her eyes reflected everything she felt—fear, love, resignation, and faith in me—before she closed them and disappeared.

The astonishment and confusion on Sebastian's face was laughable, but I used the opportunity to my advantage, lunging and tackling him to the ground. We scuffled, each of us trying to gain leverage, but in the end, I was heavier and stronger. Sitting astride his chest, I pinned his arms above his head, preventing him from reaching any weapons. My chest heaved from exertion, and raindrops sluiced down tendrils of my hair, splashing onto his face.

Simon was still protected, and Syd was out of his reach. Sebastian was all but defeated.

But he gave me a sinister smile, his eyes sparkling in amusement.

What was I was missing?

"You think you've won?" He was enjoying this.

I experienced a stab of doubt and prodded at the barrier protecting Simon, finding it secure. Sebastian hadn't penetrated it, so what could be filling him with confidence?

"How are you going to kill me, Evan? You have no weapons left in your belt, and the knife I was holding isn't within easy reach. You'd have to free one of my hands to seize it. Who's to say I won't get to it first?"

I grinned in triumph. "I know I've won. You once referred to me as dead weight, Sebastian. Even then, you underestimated me." I gathered all the fear, anxiety, and terror I'd held onto, both personally and absorbed from clients in every level of horrifying nightmare, everything

I'd never downloaded, joined with more than a year of crushing guilt and misery, and released it into Sebastian where my hands connected with his wrists. It surged through my body, gathering speed, energized at sensing a new host to feed on and devour. Sebastian shrieked in horror and agony, eyes rolling back into his head, body convulsing, as he foamed at the mouth. His body and mind were unable to absorb the colossal impact of such intense emotions all at once.

His body stilled, but his eyes remained open, fixed and unfocused as he disappeared from beneath me. Even if his physical body in the Realm had survived, his mind was unhinged. The brilliant intellect behind Scientific Innovations that had both helped and killed so many was destroyed. It seemed a fitting end. He'd never be a threat to anyone ever again.

Chapter 34
Present Day

SIMON

Ahh. Magnificent cushioning underneath my body. After lying on a paper thin, filthy mattress for a year, my body was unaccustomed to such comfort. Tense voices surrounded me, yelling and arguing, but one in particular rose above the others.

"I don't care if I leave a trail of half the blood in my body, I'm moving over to this bed and you can treat me there!"

The mattress beneath me dipped, and I shifted slightly. My eyes fluttered open and locked on his stunning amber gaze that first caught my attention. Max raised his hand to lightly stroke my cheek. "Simon? Are you hurt, baby?"

A slow smile spread across my face. The muscles hadn't been used in so long, I was sure they'd atrophied. "I'm really here. It wasn't a dream." His lips met mine in a gentle kiss. Perhaps the muscles hadn't atrophied after all.

"It's not a dream. You're home."

"What happened to me?" Then Max explained how Evan had yet again saved me. Saved all of us.

♊

EVAN

I opened my eyes to Syd's anxious expression as she hovered over me, her hand pushing the hair back from my face. A bandage from the knife wound encircled her neck. Zia, Amelia, and Gabriel—who held a sleeping Alex—stood behind her. "Simon?" I croaked.

She released a breath of air in relief. "He's fine. We're all fine.

Sebastian?"

"Done." Syd helped me to a sitting position, then to stand, and I winced from invisible bruises that would show tomorrow, if they weren't already glorious shades of purple and black. I draped my arm around her shoulders, partly for support, but mostly because I needed her close, to know she was unharmed.

Medbots tended to Isaac. He was grimacing in pain and lying on his side in the Bender chair.

"You know it was an accident, right?" Syd asked.

Isaac snorted. "There are so many responses that come to mind, but I don't have the energy. We're good, Syd. Your aim's better than that."

I put a hand on his shoulder. "I know it's your job, but thanks for helping."

"Yeah, it's my job, Evan, but that's not why I did it. He's your brother, man." His gaze darted to Syd, then back to me, his eyebrow arched in question, and I pulled her closer, letting him know he didn't stand a chance.

Yes, it was a little possessive on my part, but I honestly didn't care. I'd lost too much time with her already, and didn't plan on wasting any more. Over the past year, I'd taken considerably more than I'd given, but that was about to change. I had so much to make up to her. To so many people.

Across the room, Max reclined in the client bed beside Simon, holding tightly to his hand while his wound was treated. I was truly happy to see he hadn't bled out. Amazing the difference a couple of weeks made in how you perceived people. Doc stood at the bedside talking animatedly to Simon. The two of them had a lot of work in their future. They'd make a good team. Maybe he could even help Doc with his organizational skills.

Immense joy and happiness overflowed from my twin, settling in the space inside me that had been hollow for the past year.

While imprisoned, Simon's life had been a nonstop clash of wills between him and Sebastian. He'd been unable to let down his guard, always needing to stay alert to protect both himself and me. Although emotionally and physically exhausted, he'd never given up. And he'd done it all on his own. He was so much stronger than me. Despite my stupidity and insecurity on the night he'd been taken, Simon had faith in me, and knew I'd bring him home. That meant everything.

He smiled widely, looking between Syd and me as we approached the bed. "I'm sensing a change in relationship dynamics between the two of you. Is there something you'd like to share?"

"You're sensing correctly, brother." I bent down to brush Syd's lips lightly with my own.

I knew we'd have to contact our parents—it was inevitable—but maybe they'd change their opinions about me after learning what I'd accomplished without them. Maybe they wouldn't. I wasn't holding my breath, because what they thought didn't matter anymore. My self-esteem was no longer tied to their perception of me. I'd created my own family with my brother, Syd, Gabriel, and even Max. And I could be kind of a big brother to Alex, too.

I finally knew I was enough.

Thank you for choosing to read my work, and I hope you enjoyed *The Gemini Connection*. I'd be grateful if you could take a few minutes to leave a review at Amazon, Barnes & Noble, or Goodreads.

About the Author

Teri Polen reads and watches horror, sci-fi, and fantasy. *The Walking Dead*, *Harry Potter*, and anything *Marvel*-related are likely to cause fangirl delirium. She lives in Bowling Green, KY with her husband, sons, and black cat. Her first novel, *Sarah*, a YA horror/thriller, was a horror finalist in the 2017 Next Generation Indie Book Awards.

Visit her online at www.teripolen.com

View other Black Rose Writing titles at <u>www.blackrosewriting.com/books</u>
and use promo code **PRINT** to receive a **20% discount** when purchasing.

* 9 7 8 1 6 8 4 3 3 0 3 4 8 *